AMY COLE
HAS IT ALL
FIGURED
OUT

Elizabeth McGivern

PERNICKETY PUBLISHING

ISBN 978-1-9996403-5-4

Cover Design: Maire-Clare Doran

For Ciara

Prologue

There's something unsettling about being at a funeral in the sunshine. It's like the universe didn't get the memo that the whole world should be grieving.

How is the world still spinning when a light as warm and bright as this has been extinguished?

I can feel Ben's hand at my waist but it doesn't bring me any comfort. I'm numb to everything but the familiar feeling of my heart breaking. As I get older the pain of heartbreak isn't as sharp and overwhelming as it was when I was a teenager, now it's like a deep wound that never truly heals.

I hold the single white rose in my hand, unwilling to part with it. If I do it will mean I have to let them go too and I don't want to do that yet.

I want one more day

I beg fruitlessly into the cosmos for one more conversation or glimpse of their face. That way I could really listen to the way their voice sounds, or their facial expressions when they speak about something with so much passion.

I took it for granted. I took all our time for granted. I thought I'd have more time. There's never enough time.

The hot tears rolled down my cheeks and I don't bother to wipe them away. The graveside is still so crowded with people wanting to pay their respects and I want to scream at them all to go away. I want to have the monopoly on grief and I don't care that I'm being selfish or overdramatic I just want to be alone with them.

They're gone. This is just a body in the dirt.

Today will be noisy and irritating but I'm also scared of the quiet that tomorrow will bring.

How can I face going into work and not see them anymore? Is there even going to be an office anymore? Questions for another day…

"Amy?" Ben asks, "Are you going to let go of your flower?"

I mutely drop the rose into the ground and return to stand beside him.

"Are you ready to go?" he says, tentatively.

"No."

We stand together, in silence, and stare at the hole until my back aches and the baby rolls in my stomach making me queasy.

This time, he doesn't ask, he leads me back to the car to rest my feet and cry in private.

"I don't know what I'm going to do, Ben. I just don't. I need Elle; I don't know what I'm going to do without her."

Six weeks earlier

Chapter 1

"I've decided I'm not going to die," announced Elle, through my bathroom door.

"Oh, well that's handy," I replied, "I don't know why you've convinced me to do this, it's completely unnecessary."

"Female grooming shouldn't be thrown out the window just because you're up the duff," she replied, matter-of-factly.

I rolled my eyes, in the safety of my bathroom, as I read the instructions to the home-waxing kit for the fourth time.

Why have I let her talk me into this?

"How are you getting on in there, Sasquatch?" she said, "Why don't you just go to my beautician's?"

"The place that almost blinded me? Pass, besides the thought of having my lady parts on display in front of strangers scares the bejesus out of me."

"You get it out for the doctor all the time. They're all professionals."

"One: I don't 'get it out all the time' for my doctor and two: he's really cute and I want things to look their best for the delivery."

"I feel like he will be concentrating on other things at that point, like your baby? I'm pretty sure, in that line of work, once you've seen one muff you've seen them all."

I opened the bathroom door to find her lying on my bed on the laptop, absentmindedly scrolling through the internet.

"Might I remind you, that this was your idea? You're the one that said it was rude of me to show up to the hospital with a 'pooch like a rainforest'; *and* for the record: he would remember a vagina like mine. It's epic."

I closed the door once more and checked the temperature of the wax. It seemed to be ready so I positioned myself on the floor, in front of a large mirror I'd placed to help me navigate the spread of the stick – my thirty-week bump was making it impossible to see my feet clearly, never mind try to find my bikini line.

I always blew up in pregnancy, but this time was ridiculous. I was tested for gestational diabetes (it was negative) and I was constantly asked if I could have miscalculated my dates (I hadn't). I accepted that I just made big babies; however, western medicine didn't like my verdict on the matter.

I struggled to find an angle on the floor that would allow me to get the wax in the places I needed without the bump pressing down on my bladder, or even covering the area completely.

I groaned in frustration and threw the stick into the bath. I lay down, flat on the floor, and gave up

"Are you ok in there?" Elle called.

"No, my baby is trying to ruin my chances with the cute doctor and now I'll always be known as the pregnant lump with the hoo-hah like a grizzly bear."

"I'm coming in, you bloody drama queen."

Elle squeezed through the door and found me looking completely pathetic on my bath mat.

"For the love of God, shift your arse and let me get this done."

"No!" I cried, "There's no way I'm letting you see down there."

"For one thing, Amy, you're not my type and secondly, it's not like I give a rat's arse what your bits look like. Just lie back and it'll be done in a jiffy."

I lay on the floor, like a turtle stuck on its shell, and accepted my fate.

You're just going to be an adult and let her sort out the waxing. Grow up, Amy.

My stern talking to did little to make me feel more comfortable but she was already positioning herself, armed with the little stick covered in wax so there was no backing out now.

"Alright, princess, there's the first bit of wax in place. Brace yourself!"

Brace yourself? How is that comforting?

With one swift motion she tugged on the strip and sent the sensation of searing pain all over my body. I shut my legs together and tried to sit up but as I was an egg on legs I just rolled back to the lying position. I could feel more wax being applied and another strip of the cloth placed on top.

"*Stop!*" I screamed, "Elle Wilde if you pull that fucking cloth I will end your life."

Her head came up from behind my bump, wax stick in hand and a confused look on her face.

"What have I done? I'm doing a great job."

"You are the devil and I'm not letting you touch another hair on my body."

"Haven't you ever had a wax before?" she asked.

"Yes, but whatever you're doing is bloody torture!"

"You know what? I've actually read somewhere that because of all your extra fluid and hormones and shit, that your skin becomes more sensitive when you're pregnant so this is bound to feel a bit more painful. That's why I didn't wax when I had the twins."

"Are you fucking kidding me?" I screamed, scrambling to my feet, "This was *your* idea, *you're* the one who convinced me of this stupid bloody plan."

"Well, I dunno," she replied, sheepishly, "I must have forgotten, you know I have other things on my mind – like cancer."

"Don't you dare play the cancer card with me; it already got you out of that meeting with the bakery because the guy 'has a weird left nostril'. You know you're only allowed to use it three times a week for non-emergency purposes."

"Fine, fine. Look, come back here I have to finish this."

I opened the bathroom door and backed into the bedroom, making sure to face her the entire time in case she tried to ambush me.

"Not a chance, you're not touching me again."

"You can't go out like that! You've got one bit waxed, another still with the cloth stuck on and the rest looking like a ferret. Get over here, Amy," she said as she walked towards me, still wielding the wax stick.

At that moment, Ben came into the bedroom to collect me for the doctor appointment.

"What's going on?" he said.

"Elle is trying to attack me," I replied, standing behind him in order to make it more difficult for Elle to get her waxy hands on me.

"I am not trying to attack her; I'm trying to fix that bearded clam of hers!" She lunged towards me but Ben managed to wrestle the stick out of her hands.

"What the hell is this? It's hot," he said, shaking the excess drips from his hand.

"It's wax, you moron. I'm trying to get your wife's junk looking good ahead of the doctor appointment."

"Amy? Seriously? We've talked about your inappropriate crush on the doctor. There's only so much I'm willing to chalk up to pregnancy hormones. You are not waxing for this man, besides it's a bloody ultrasound he won't be going anywhere near *there*, until the delivery," he stated, sternly.

"I know!" I said, "I didn't want to but that maniac was forcing me."

Elle threw her arms up in exasperation as she retreated back to the bathroom to wash her hands.

"Alright patch, I give up."

"Amy," said Ben, "get your coat; we're going to be late again."

I wasn't convinced that Elle wasn't going to try one last sneak attack so I stayed hiding behind Ben as we went downstairs for my coat and out the door, leaving her to wash up in the house.

It wasn't until we reached the car park at the hospital that I realised that in my rush to leave the house I was wearing no pants underneath my dress and the cloth was still tugging at hairs.

Fuck. I'm going to have to try and rip this off myself.

I shifted in my seat uncomfortably hoping that some sort of friction would do the deed for me. It wasn't working and it was making Ben concerned.

"Are you ok?" he asked, with a look of panic on his face.

"Eh, yeah, I'm fine."

Ok, just get through this appointment with my dignity and then I'll rip it off when I get home. Simple. I am never listening to Elle ever again.

I waddled up to the maternity department and sat in the overheated waiting room with the other expectant parents. The only seats left were beside a woman with the neatest-looking bump I'd ever seen. Even in early pregnancy I don't think I ever looked that tiny. I just woke up one morning and this gargantuan belly was there.

Her name was Catherine and I guessed she was here for her first scan. She rubbed her stomach protectively and she looked serene as she waited, whereas I was beginning to sweat profusely at the panic of my knicker-less state.

"How far along are you?" she asked.

"This is my thirty-week scan," I replied, waiting for her to look shocked and ask if it was twins. To her credit she simply smiled.

"I started to get really uncomfortable with this one at that stage, thank goodness I've only three weeks left," she explained.

"Piss *off*!" I exclaimed, shocking the rest of the people in the room to silence, "I'm so sorry, it's just that you're so… tiny," I added, trying to sound more apologetic than jealous.

"You think?" she replied, "I feel massive."

Don't punch a pregnant woman, don't punch a pregnant woman, don't punch a pregnant woman.

She was called into her appointment next and I returned to the magazine while trying to find a position in which the wax strip wouldn't tug.

"Why do you keep squirming?" said Ben.

"Because I have giant baby sitting on my bladder and it's a bit fucking uncomfortable, ok?"

Ben, sufficiently chastised, returned to the game on his phone while I decided that I would just have to go to the bathroom and pull the strip off myself.

Just get this over and done with; you're sweating like a pig.

As I stood up to go to the bathroom, I felt the cloth slip down my sweating legs and drop on the floor, complete with the next section of my hairy bikini line.

I tried to find a way to discreetly pick it up without bringing it to the attention of the entire room but the man next to me had already got up to buy something from the vending machine, stood on the cloth and gotten it attached to the bottom of his shoe.

"Ben," I hissed, "Ben!"

He eventually looked up at me to realise that I had the look of wild panic in my eyes.

"What's wrong? Is it the baby? Sit down," he urged.

"No, stop and listen a minute," I whispered, "You've got to get that wax strip off that man's shoe."

"I've got to do what now?"

I repeated my request and pointed to the man in question's shoe.

"Not a chance in hell," he replied, "Just pretend we don't see it."

9

I considered going along with this plan but it was scuppered by his partner who came up to join him at the machine and noticed the cloth.

"What is that?" she asked.

"Ben, do something!" I pleaded.

He automatically stood up and shouted, "That's mine."

He walked towards the couple and bent down to the man's shoe to dislodge the hairy paper.

"It's...it's eh my... comfort blanket," he said, feebly.

"A comfort blanket?" asked the woman, incredulously.

"Yes, I get a bit anxious at the hospital so I bring this along to comfort me."

He started to rub the strip along his face in order to convince the couple of his lie but they both decided it was safer to just turn around and ignore the strange man rubbing a used wax strip across his cheek.

What the hell is he doing?

Ben sheepishly returned to his seat, still holding his 'blanket' and glared at me.

The nurse entered the room and called out my name to be seen.

"Are you coming?" I asked, "You can bring your blanket with you if you're nervous."

I tried to stifle a laugh but Ben was yet to see any humour in his predicament.

"Sometimes I really wonder what I did in a previous life to deserve you, Amy."

"I don't know, Sweety, you're just lucky, I guess."

Chapter 2

It was the day of Elle's surgery and I had been pacing my living room for an eternity, waiting to hear from River.

I wanted to go along but Elle forbid it, she said the last thing she wanted to do was wake up and have my teary face looking back at her.

I offered to have the girls but, again, this offer was rejected as Keith was being uncharacteristically helpful since he found out the news of his ex-wife's diagnosis.

Anytime my phone went off I would jump and try to read the messages with shaking hands. It was Ben, again.

Ben: Any word yet?

I threw the phone away without replying. It was the fourth one he'd sent since this morning and my reply had been the same for the previous three.

I had spent most nights trawling through the internet finding out everything I could about her procedure and the treatment plan. She was undergoing a lumpectomy followed by a course of radiotherapy treatment. Her doctor was confident of this course of action and, more importantly, so was Elle.

After the initial shock of her diagnosis she got to work getting her head around it all. Not the facts and figures or even the semantics of what the operation was, she just wanted to be in a place of positivity and being mentally ready for what was to come.

By the time I was leaving her house, the night before, she seemed in great spirits and was ready to show cancer who was boss.

"Don't worry, princess," she said, "I'm going in for this boobectompy and then it's all going to be fine. I'll be back in the office by next week annoying the hell out of you."

This idea was already shot down but I did promise to spend, at least, an hour with her a day talking about non-cancer related topics because she didn't want me to 'depress the shit out of her'.

I knew all of this could have been an act and her putting on a brave face for mine and everyone else's sake but I didn't think it was. I genuinely believed her when she said she wasn't worried and this was just a 'blip' on the road but still I paced the floor and waited for the phone call.

I was on the school run when my phone rang and River's name flashed up on the screen.

"Well?" I said, as soon as I picked up.

"She's out," he replied, "She's awake and a bit groggy but they said after a couple of hours I can bring her on home to rest properly."

"What? Are you serious? Shouldn't she be there for a while instead?" I asked, shocked that she had been sliced open and kicked out all in one day.

"No, no, it's perfectly normal."

I wasn't convinced but I wasn't about to drive to the hospital and demand that they change their whole procedure to accommodate an irate, pregnant woman who wasn't a blood relative or had any medical knowledge.

"We'll be back this evening, I don't think she'll be fit for visitors until tomorrow though," he continued.

"That's wise, I'll be there tonight."

"That's the exact opposite of what I just said."

"I don't count as a visitor, River, I'm practically her mother so shut your damn face and bring my daughter home in one piece."

Several mothers stopped their conversation and stared at the despicable woman, cursing in the playground.

"Oh, piss off, Susan I'm talking on the phone."

I wasn't sure any of them were called 'Susan' but I just thought I'd make a point.

"I'll see you later, River," I added.

I kept eye contact with the less-than-impressed mum brigade as I hung up the phone, daring them to say anything else about my call.

Both boys came walking out to the gate with their usual level of enthusiasm and demanding to be fed. The pregnancy was working in their favour because I was also constantly hungry so they usually got treated to a pit-stop at the local garage for crisps on the way home.

"Now, what do we tell Daddy we had for our snack?" I asked.

"Fruit," they replied in unison.

"Good, now tell me about your day."

"I got Star of the Day," said Adam.

"I punched a boy in the throat," said Arthur.

Crap.

"Let's circle back to the throat punching, Arthur. First, let's hear about the Star of the Day," I said, ignoring the dread in my stomach about having to chat with Arthur about lashing out in the playground.

By the time we got home I had worked up enough courage to find out what happened.

"It wasn't my fault," he said.

"It never is," I replied, "You can't go around punching people, it's a nasty thing to do and makes me wonder if I'm raising a bully."

"He punched me first!" protested Arthur, "He was going around pulling up all the girls' skirts and I told him to stop it but he punched me in the tummy and told me to 'piss off'."

"Don't say that phrase," I scolded. I was secretly happy that I wasn't the mother of the resident sociopath but actually mothering a decent child who had been trying to help others.

"Why not? You say bold words all the time like -"

"Let me stop you there," I interrupted, "What you did – trying to stop that other child from pulling up skirts was the right thing to do but you just went about it the wrong way. "Violence isn't the answer, it never is. How did you feel when he punched you in the stomach?"

"Sick."

"Well then, you know how unpleasant being hit is, so don't do it back. You use your words and tell a grown up what they were doing," I explained, not entirely buying my own advice.

"Ok, Mummy," he said, with a downcast face.

"I love you, just don't be so quick with the violence the next time you see something wrong, please?"

"Ok," he replied.

"Go play with your brother before tea-time."

He ran upstairs and it didn't take long for me to hear the roughhousing going on before I knew that my sage wisdom had fallen on deaf ears.

Bloody kids.

Parenting was a minefield and I was never sure I was giving the right advice but I figured that I should probably stick with the zero-tolerance to violence approach when it comes to school. Best to toe the line with this particular issue, in case he gets thrown out and I would have to consider home-schooling him.

This was a fate worse than death for me. Not because home-schooling is bad for kids but I was genuinely concerned that my children would end up overtaking my learning capabilities and they would finally have proof that I don't have a damn clue what I'm doing.

By the time Ben came home from work I had all but forgotten the punching incident but it didn't take long for Adam to spill the beans.

"Arthur was fighting in school and I got Star of the Day," he said.

What a little suck up.

Arthur was made to recall the tale, once more, and I waited to hear Ben's response on the matter. I knew it would be pretty similar to mine but I figured that I should let him have his say none-the-less.

"Did a teacher see you punch him?" asked Ben.

"No, I don't think so," he replied.

"Good. Next time, you should trip him over – that way if anyone sees you, you can just pretend he fell by himself. Do you want me to teach you how your fist should go? That way you won't hurt your thumb?"

"BEN!" I shouted.

"What? I've just found out my son is even more of a legend than I previously thought. He's practically a vigilante, helping his classmates from the wrath of... what's his name?"

"Stanley," replied Arthur.

"Stanley doesn't really sound that scary as the villain of the piece," Ben mused, "Let's go with: 'Psycho Stanley'."

Christ, he's not remotely helping.

The rest of dinner was spent with the three of them making up scenarios of what Arthur could do the next time he spotted injustice in the playground.

I left them to play superheroes while I put on my coat and headed to Elle's house in order to see how she was doing with my own eyes. I didn't like depending on River's text updates, they were never detailed enough and I worried that he was being too positive so I wouldn't be worried.

He answered the door with a smile and told me to go up to the bedroom to find Elle. She was propped up with pillows all around her, watching television. Her eyes were glazed and I knew she wasn't really seeing what was on the screen. The door creaked and broke her concentration.

"Alright, princess," she said, drowsily, "I'm off my tits. I suppose that's got a different meaning now doesn't it?"

"Not really," I said, "More like you've 'got a bit off your tits' but that doesn't really roll off the tongue as well."

I tried not to let tears fill my eyes but the relief of seeing her home and making a joke was exactly what I wanted to hear.

I finally started to believe that Elle was going to be ok.

Chapter 3

Our business, which still had no name – despite Elle continuously pushing for *Badass Business Inc.* – had moved location to Elle's bedroom.

She insisted on being kept in the loop on everything that was going on, although I knew most of it wasn't going in. During one particularly unproductive meeting I caught her staring into space, looking glum.

"What's up, buttercup?" I asked.

"I don't have a Will."

"Remember the days when you would just come out with inappropriate sex questions? I miss those days."

"I'm being serious," she continued, "what if this treatment doesn't work and I die really quickly leaving the girls with no clue about their future? Shouldn't I make one? You know, just in case?"

I hated the thought of even having this conversation but I promised to help her in any way I could while she was sick and if this is what she wanted to organise then I had to just suck it up and help.

"Yes, you should," I replied, eventually, "but not because you're going to die, because you have children and you really should have it all organised already."

"You have one?" she asked.

"Yes, we've had one for years. I insisted as soon as Adam was born because on the happiest day of my life, I started to be petrified of dying and leaving this little person behind."

"You are so dramatic."

I didn't have the first clue about what you needed to do for a Will, Ben had taken care of it after I continued to cry at him whilst holding our new-born son and wailing that we were going to die, tragically, and leave Adam as an orphan.

I tried to make it sound like I knew what I was talking about and added in some legal jargon to seal the deal but once I finished my speech, I turned to find her staring at me as if I had two heads.

"You are talking out of your arse, aren't you?" she said.

"Absolutely, yes."

We both laughed and decided that we should just make a list of things that she wanted for the girls and leave the actual grown-up parts for River to sort out.

"I suppose they'd go to their dad fulltime then," she mused, "I hate the thought of River being all alone."

"I'm sure he won't just disappear out of their lives, besides this is for light-years in the future; the girls will be grown up and he'll probably be dead."

"Well, that's a cheery thought."

Our 'Last Will and Testament' talk got derailed at the prospect of us both being rich widows after both our husbands died under mysterious circumstances and our children had flown the nest. We decided that we would travel the world and refuse to grow old or stay around the children long enough that they'd lock us up in a nursing home and steal the last of our money.

At one point I could feel myself getting annoyed at my kids for daring to send me away into some shady old 'folks' home until I realised that they were still small children and I was insane.

"Where's River?" I asked.

"Hopefully out getting himself a life insurance policy, so we can afford our mansion in Miami when we're eighty."

"Great, a couple of million should do us rightly."

At that moment we heard the front door open and close, followed by the sound of something heavy hitting the ground.

We both got out of the bed and went to investigate what was going on.

"River?" shouted Elle, from the top of the stairs.

"Hey, yeah it's me. Sorry, I didn't mean to disturb the *Badass Business Inc.* meeting."

"It's not called that," I shouted, "What's all the noise about?"

"I found one of those discount supermarkets and did the shopping there," he explained, "I've never been before! The middle aisle is full of all this really cool stuff."

"Did you get bananas for my smoothie?" asked Elle.

"Ah, damn, sorry! I knew I forgot something but I got something better! Come down and see."

Elle and I shared a knowing look and decided to go downstairs to find out what the hunter-gatherer had returned with. When we got to the bottom of the stairs we were greeted by River, who looked extremely pleased with himself and one of his legs resting on a large cardboard box.

"What do you think?" he asked.

"What is it?"

"It's a kayak!" he replied, obviously delighted with his find.

"What am I meant to do with a kayak? I wanted bananas."

"I'll go and get bananas in a minute but I couldn't just walk past this and not get it. I mean, who wouldn't want a kayak? Surprise kayaks are the best."

Because people normally expect kayaks?

River jumped over the box and gave his wife a passionate kiss, after which he flashed a smile at me and announced that he was off out again in search of bananas.

"I know he's ridiculous," said Elle, with a smile, "but he's my kind of ridiculous."

I told her to go back to bed while I made us tea and we could start plotting out our diaries to arrange work and childcare for the next few weeks of her daily treatment. River insisted that he was going to be the one to take her there without argument, so I settled in my role as child minder for the days that the girls weren't with Keith. I didn't mind having her daughters around more often; they kept my boys entertained while I got to put my feet up and try to stay awake. Lugging the giant bump around was exhausting, especially when I could never find a comfy position to lie in bed for longer than fifteen minutes at a time.

I began to think about my own mortality, when Elle went upstairs. What on earth would I do if something happened to me? Or Ben? Or both of us? The thought of our children being raised by Ben's mother sent shivers up my spine. I would obviously prefer to have them with my own parents but doesn't everyone? They seemed like the obvious choice; I mean, I made it out relatively unscathed and my mother did seem to prefer my children to me.

Maybe that's because she gets to hand them back when they're being obnoxious?

I felt that this was a dangerous topic to dwell on; I was having trouble not crying at the best of times, because of my bloody pregnancy hormones, so thinking about a genuinely sad thing was not going to help matters.

By the time River came back – with enough bananas to make a Carmon Miranda headpiece – I took my leave and went home to my family just to give them all a hug. Unfortunately, by the time I got home I had discovered they had managed to make their own slime and it was now being stamped into my carpet. At this moment I was feeling ever so slightly homicidal.

"Ben?" I asked.

"Hmmm?" he replied, as he scrubbed the congealed slime further into the carpet.

"Is the life insurance up-to-date?"

"Yes, why?"

"Just in case you can't get that stuff out of the carpet, I want to make sure the kids will be cared for should I murder you."

"I'm not sure it covers murder, so best be on the safe side and keep me around – at least until the baby comes and you can see your feet again."

"Fair point."

Dinner had been a beige affair, which meant that the kids didn't complain about every mouthful, but I spent the rest of the evening feeling guilty and looking up articles on 'how to sneak vegetables into your family' which I knew I would never actually do.

Just as I was about to say 'good-night' to the kids, I noticed Arthur looking morose as he stared at his uniform.

I sat on the edge of his bed – which was hideously difficult to get down to when you're a damn whale – in order to figure out what was going on. He shrugged as way of reply, which set off my concerned parent alarm.

Oh damn, there's actually something wrong.

"What's up, dude?" I asked, in the worst attempt at a relaxed tone in history.

Dude? Who the hell says 'dude'? Get it together, Cole.

"I just don't want to go to school tomorrow, that's all," he said.

"That's all? Ok, that seems like a pretty big thing though; you love school."

He didn't, this was a lie that my parents drilled into me and therefore I did the same with my own children, in the hope that they'd one day believe it and not cause a fuss every single morning.

"It's Stanley," he said, "He's just so annoying."

"Has there been another incident you haven't told us about?"

"Not really."

What the hell does that mean? Is my son being bullied relentlessly and I haven't even noticed?

"He just says stuff," he continued, "Most of the time I can ignore him, but he's really annoying."

I'm going to have to sort this little twerp out, I hate seeing Arthur like this and kids can be so fragile when it comes to teasing about even the smallest of things.

"Arthur," I said, "Sometimes people can find it funny to make remarks about your appearance or your clothes and other meaningless things but it's just to get a reaction. You know you're such a brilliant person and he's trying to get a rise out of you. Try not to let him, but if it's getting to a point where you don't even want to go to school then I'll come and have a word with the teacher, tomorrow, to see if we can all sit down and talk it out."

"Oh, he's not saying things about me – it's you."

Say what now?

"He's been calling you mean things and that you should stop eating the buns from *Joseph's* and try selling them. Stuff like that."

I'm being fat-shamed by a seven-year-old. Kids are the actual worst.

"Well, maybe the next time he says something like that you should kindly tell the little turd to take a running ju-"

"*Amy*!" interrupted Ben.

"I think what your mum means is that we are going to arrange to meet Stanley's parents and see if we can put an end to this. We can't have you worrying about going in because of this boy."

"Ok, Dad."

I kissed Arthur and let him go to sleep. He already seemed a bit more relieved at the prospect of school, knowing that help was on the way.

"Amy?"

"Yes?" I replied, as innocently as I could.

"Please don't threaten small children, remember what happened at that ice-cream place, last summer?"

"No," I lied.

"You threatened to break that little girl's leg if she took the last of the sprinkles."

"She was hogging the toppings!"

"She was five!"

"She was — "

"No," he said, firmly, "We are not having this argument again; you don't have a leg to stand on, especially when I had to convince her father not to phone the police to report threatening behaviour over sprinkles."

I went to bed in a huff, examining my stretching body in the mirror. I felt sad knowing that, even in the wonderment of pregnancy I was still expected to look a certain way. Yes, I knew he was a child and I shouldn't let it bother me but it was frustrating.

It felt like the second I hit puberty I was on a diet. I had to look a certain way, see a certain number on the scale in order for a boy to notice me and therefore finally give me worth. What a sad way to live a life. That's why I felt relief when I had two boys – I reasoned that puberty might be kinder on their self-esteem but the more I looked around me, the more I knew that was utter nonsense. They had it bad too, just in a different way.

I was still mulling it over in my head when Ben eventually came to bed.

"Why can't everyone be kind?" I said, "Can't we all live on some isolated commune where everyone is nice to each other?"

"I think you're describing a cult and historically they don't usually work out too well for all involved."

"Fine, have it your way; we'll remain part of society and constantly worry that some little jerk is going to ruin our child's life."

"You're getting a bit melodramatic, Amy."

"That's what us fatties do."

"I'm not indulging this. Take your own advice: 'he's trying to get a rise out of you, don't let him'.

"What do I know? I wanted to join a cult."

"Good-night, Amy."

"Piss off, Ben."

Chapter 4

The thing about routine is: it doesn't take long for people to get into a new one. I thought the weeks of treatment was going to be chaotic and stressful but it had very little effect on the business and general day-to-day goings on. I'm not sure if that meant that I was already used to mayhem but I decided not to overthink it and just carry on.

One big change was my daily visits from Joseph. Up until now, he had preferred to remain downstairs and keep our offices out of his rounds. I wasn't sure if it was because he knew I would like the company, or if I was coming down less and less in order to get the work of two people done. Either way, I breathed a sigh of relief when I saw the door open and he came in – usually carrying a hot drink and a tray bake.

Maybe he's a feeder? No wonder my son is getting bullied for having a whale as a mother.

"My Amy, you're working too hard. You need to keep your strength up with food."

Definite feeder.

"I have fruit with me," I said.

"Isn't that the same apple from yesterday? And the day before?"

"Just hand me the bun, old man."

He laughed and settled himself into Elle's chair while I tucked into the buttercream treat. He let out a sigh as he looked around the room.

"It's very quiet when Elle isn't here," he said, "Sometimes it's nice, but I've got used to hearing her curse around the place and her loud laugh."

"She'll be back soon, only a few days left of treatment and she's itching to come back to work – I think River is doing her head in."

"Ah, good, good."

He sighed again, spinning back and forth on his chair. I had the distinct impression he wanted to talk about something but wasn't sure how to bring it up.

"Is everything ok, Joseph?"

"Ah, yes; just an old man thinking about his life."

"You're hardly old – you're not even sixty. 'Old' doesn't come into effect until you're at least one hundred."

He laughed to himself and continued: "It's Isabella. She wants me to retire. She thinks it's time for Michael and Maria to take over here so we can do all the things we said we would before we're too old to do them."

"Like what?"

"She wants to go visit our families in Colombia for a while – whatever is left of them. I don't really keep in touch with those we left behind, but she does and I want to make her happy."

"Why don't you just take an extended holiday then? You don't have to do one or the other."

"Perhaps," he replied, "I just don't know how we got here so fast. Talk of retirement? I still feel like the same young man who came to this country and set up my first business. It was a car wash and it was hard work. Isabella was pregnant with Maria and I worked around the clock to make sure I could give them both everything they deserved."

I was annoyed at myself that I hadn't known this about Joseph; I always assumed he'd been in the food business, in some capacity, but I never bothered to ask. In all the time I'd known him I realised that he was the one collecting everyone else's stories whilst giving none of his own away.

"Tell me more about it," I said, genuinely interested in how he got from there to here.

The car wash didn't last long – his real passion was creating authentic Colombian food. Unfortunately for him, the Irish were not ready for his delicacies in the 1980's so he followed the crowd and settled into making the food people wanted to eat.

"I was never passionate about it though," he explained, "I wanted to bring a taste of my home here so Isabella wouldn't miss it so much. I would move the earth for that woman."

"How long have you been married?"

"It will be thirty-five years next month but it doesn't feel like it could possibly be that long. She hasn't aged a day. Colombian women are the most beautiful in the world."

"That's your answer then."

"What is?"

"You book a trip to Colombia for your anniversary, rediscover your passion for authentic cooking then come back refreshed and inspired to do something with the menu downstairs. It's not the eighties anymore; if anything people will probably go crazy for something new."

His face brightened as he ran through the plan in his head.

"I think you're right, Amy."

"I suggest you go and book it before you change your mind."

He got up from the chair and left the office without a backwards glance and I felt happy that I was able to give him some direction for a change. Lord knows I owed him enough for everything he'd done for Elle and me.

I wondered if Ben spoke about me with such reverence in his office. I couldn't imagine him talking to Leon from accounts about how magical my stretch marks looked as they glistened in the sun.

That bastard, I can't believe he talks about my stretch marks to Leon from accounts.

I pulled my mobile out from my bag and started to furiously type a message before stopping myself from pressing 'send'.

You know he didn't really do that, that whole scenario was all in your head?

I knew this was right but I also knew that I didn't care.

Amy: If you think it's ok to talk about my body with Leon from accounts then you're dead wrong. My body has safely birthed two boys and is in the process of cooking a third so if I'm carrying a little extra padding it's for the good of the baby, you complete knob!!!!

I felt validated in my rage and proud that I had the nerve to hit back against the patriarchy.

That will show him. Show him that you're a complete and utter nut. I give up, I'm going in the back to play re-runs of old movies – you're on your own.

It didn't take long for the three dots to appear, meaning that Ben was attempting a reply.

Ben: There's no one called 'Leon'

Amy: The name isn't important; you just shouldn't be talking about my appearance in a negative way to anyone.

Ben: Have I missed something? Did I annoy you in your dream again? I thought we agreed you wouldn't get cross at me because of what 'dream Ben' does?

I began to lose steam in my self-righteousness and realised that; perhaps, I shouldn't have arguments with my husband based on fictional scenarios I made up five minutes previously.

Amy: It's lasagne for tea

Ben: That's nice. You're pretty. See you later xo

One of the best things about Ben? He never held a grudge and was so used to these random outbursts from me he had probably already forgotten that it happened. This summation of his character suddenly made me emotional so I went back to my phone once more.

Amy: I love you so much. I think you're brilliant and I'm lucky you're mine.

Ben: That's nice. You're pretty. See you later xo

Amy: Did you just copy and paste that message? I'm pouring my heart out and you send me a mirror message because you can't be bothered to reply with something authentic? You really are an utter bastard sometimes.

This time, it took him longer to reply. I was about to send another essay about how I should have married my previous boyfriend, from school, instead of settling for him when his reply came through.

Ben: Do you want me to bring some garlic bread home?

I was torn. On the one hand, I had decided that I hated this man for reasons I could no longer remember. On the other hand, all I could think about was garlic bread.

Amy: Yes – but I still hate you though

Solid burn.

Ben: I know. 'Pregnant Amy' always makes things interesting.

I was going to come back with a scathing retort but my stomach started to grumble and I had the urge to go downstairs and ask Michael to make me fresh garlic bread.

I refused to believe that the whole episode was due to pregnancy hormones, I was not some crazy person not in control of their own emotions but it would explain why I was crying, again, after I was told that Michael didn't have any time to make me my request.

There may be some truth to Ben's theory...

My mood was only made worse by the entrance of my mother, Eloise, who had a face like thunder.

"Amy," she announced, "I'm leaving your father."

What?

Chapter 5

This wasn't the first time my mother had threatened to leave my father. It wasn't even the twentieth – but it was the first time she'd announced it to a coffee shop full of strangers on their lunch break.

I ushered her over to a seat and made her some chamomile tea in the hope she would calm down and stop looking up divorce lawyers on her phone.

"What's happened?" I asked.

"Your father is a pervert."

Well, this is new.

"I'm not sure I want to hear where this is going, Mum."

"Well you're going to!"

Of course I am.

"I had just come home from the book club and there he was, in the middle of the day, fumbling with his bits in the living room with some floozy," she said as she burst into tears.

I couldn't believe it. My dad couldn't possibly be having an affair. He was the first man I've ever trusted and he'd never let me down. I know Mum could be hard work but she loved him, she supported him, she's an intelligent, passionate and beautiful woman so how bloody dare he?

"I can't believe it, Mum, I'm so sorry," I said, hugging her tightly and letting her get all her frustration out.

"I know you love him more than me, but I just can't believe it. How could he do that? In the middle of the day? Deirdre was with me! The poor woman didn't know where to look."

31

The door to the café opened and there stood my dad, pale and embarrassed. I wasn't sure how to even begin to speak to him; I was having trouble even looking at him.

"I think you should go," I said, keeping my voice as even as I could.

"I think we should all calm down and have a chat somewhere private," he replied.

"Like where, James?" said Mum, "Like our front room? We can't though, can we? You defiled it with your fancy woman. "I've been run out of my own home by this man and his mistress."

I often wondered at the double-standards of men and affairs were one of them. Why was there no label for the man? The woman was the mistress while the man was what? A mister? An idiot? I figured that now wasn't the best time to get lost in this train of thought and should probably try and get my parents out of here before someone started filming them for a viral video and put it online.

I tried to manoeuvre them towards the back of the shop and to the stairs leading to my office but Mum was having none of it.

"No, Amy, I won't be hidden away I'm not his nasty little secret; *she* is."

A woman sitting next to the commotion, eating a cream bun, looked completely gobsmacked and mouthed 'me?'

"No, not you," said Eloise, her tone becoming more exasperated by the minute, "I was pointing at his phone."

Now I'm completely lost.

"Dad, do you have this woman on the line? That's messed up."

"What woman? I don't have a nasty little secret or some fancy woman. This is completely mortifying! Eloise, can we please talk about this privately."

"Absolutely not," she replied, "You clearly have an exhibitionist side that I've continued to ignore. First you were posing naked for all those strangers and now you're having it off in the middle of the day, in our front room.

"Well, here's your chance. Let's have all our business out in the open just like you had your bits on for the world to see."

James' face was practically puce by the time Eloise had finished speaking and he knew he was beat.

"Fine, have it your way," he said, throwing his arms up in defeat.

They were both scowling at each other from across the table and I knew the remainder of the lunch crowd were only pretending to eat their food as they waited to find out about Dad's exploits. After three long minutes of awkward silence I decided to take up my role as mediator and try to find out what was going on.

"How could you do that to Mum?" I asked.

"I hardly think this is the end of the world, Amy, and I don't particularly feel like talking about this with my daughter."

He kept his gaze firmly on the table in front of him as he spoke and I was appalled at his whole attitude towards infidelity. Did I know this man at all?

"How long has it been going on?" I continued.

"What kind of question is that? How should I know?"

"Dad, this isn't like you took the last teabag here, you've betrayed Mum's trust and destroyed your relationship. Your attitude about this is frankly astounding."

"Well I think you're both blowing this way out of proportion. We are animals, we do as animals do and that's that. Ask Ben, he knows what I'm talking about."

"Ben? He wouldn't dare, he wouldn't dream of cheating on me and splitting up this family."

"Amy, what are you talking about?" asked Dad.

"What am I talking about? What are *you* talking about? I'm talking about Mum walking in and catching you having it off with some woman on the sofa."

His mouth fell open in shock but no noise came out.

"Seriously, Eloise? You're telling people I'm having an affair?"

"Amy isn't people and that's exactly what you were doing."

"No it wasn't and stop saying that," he hissed.

"Can we all just take a breath and someone tell me exactly what happened. Word for word so there's no miscommunications. Mum, talk me through what happened," I said, keeping my voice as even as possible and not trying not to lose my temper at either of them.

This mediation role was proving harder than I thought, especially when they were both gunning for an Oscar in their perspective performances as 'wounded spouse'.

"You want me to relive it?" she said, hand clutched to her heart as if to even think about the whole episode again would be unthinkable.

"Yes, Mum, I want to know the full picture."

"Fine," she began, "It was a pleasant morning at the book club. Deirdre and I were having a lively discussion about the merits of the latest work by Andrew Cornell on the walk home. I find his work completely derivative while she finds his earlier stuff ground-breaking. Sometimes I wonder how we're even friends at all. To describe his earlier work as -"

"I'm going to stop you there," I interrupted, "Just skip to the part where you decide to leave your husband."

"I was setting the scene, Amy, honestly this is why you could never be an artist, you've no soul or sense of painting a picture with your words."

I know she's the injured party but I'm inclined to side with Dad by this stage.

I bit my tongue and gave my best understanding smile as her glare darted between Dad and me.

"As I was saying: we were having a lively discussion and by the time we reached our home – the home that I've kept for all these years and provided love, sanctuary and comfort to all those who came across my threshold – and what did I find other than my husband fondling his thing in one hand and that woman in another."

She burst into tears, so I decided to take over from her death stare at my father and waited to hear his defence.

Defence? Like there could be any.

"There was no woman!" he said, louder than he intended. He cleared his voice and began again: "For the last time, I was not 'fondling another woman' I was... for goodness sake...I was... you know?"

I continued to stare at him blankly.

"I was showing myself some...appreciation."

Oh God. Please stop talking.

"You were showing your stuff to another woman on the internet. The whole world probably has a photo of your down below, now."

I will give anything if they stop talking.

"I was doing no such thing!" he replied, indignantly.

"I saw the woman on the screen when you were trying to preserve your modestly in front of Deirdre."

"I wasn't talking to anyone! I was watching a video on my phone and it was a bit...racy."

I wonder if a butter knife would cut off my ears?

"Now, I'm very sorry that you and Deirdre had to see that, but I was not fondling another woman or cheating on you, and I certainly wasn't sending pictures to strangers on the internet. I was doing something completely natural and I will not be ashamed of it."

His voice didn't carry the conviction his words wanted and his face was still bright red but I was relieved at the silence.

"Amy? Are you going to say anything in my defence?" he asked.

Orphans have it lucky.

"Erm...well, that's put a slightly different slant on the situation," I said as I stared at my hands, hoping that both of them would stop looking at me.

"I don't see why?" said Mum, "He still got his jollies from someone other than his wife, and therefore he cheated."

"I think that's a bit dramatic, Mum."

As soon as the words came out of my mouth, I knew I shouldn't have said it.

"I knew you would take his side, you always take his side against your 'silly' mother," she raged, "Next you'll be telling me I'm being too stuck up and we should all be interfering with ourselves."

"Well, I wouldn't exactly call it that," I replied, "I'm sorry, Mum, I know it was a big shock to see Dad like that – especially with Deirdre – but I really feel you need to take a deep breath and realise that this isn't that big of a deal. Dad is right, it's natural."

"Natural? Natural? Right then, I'll just pop down to that sex shop on the high street and get one of those giant neon penises on my way home. We'll just see how natural it is."

She slammed her hands on the table and pushed her chair back.

"I thought better of you both."

She stormed out of the shop with my dad in hot pursuit, while I tried to smile normally at the remaining customers. All I really wanted was the ground to swallow me up.

I don't know how long I was sat there before I felt Elle's hand on my shoulder.

"What's up, princess? What have I missed?"

"My mum is off to buy a giant, neon penis, to annoy my dad."

"Really? I should phone her and tell her my recommendations; I don't want her to get ripped off."

Just when I thought today couldn't get worse.

Chapter 6

It took three days for my mum to answer my calls after the porno incident and even then, the conversation wasn't based on honesty. I sent her a message saying that Arthur had a temperature (he didn't) and I was worried about him (I wasn't).

There's nothing my mum liked more than feeling like she's an expert at parenting so, sometimes, when I needed to earn some brownie points I played the 'I'm a useless mother, I need help' card, so she can feel superior and therefore invaluable to me.

I'm not saying it's a healthy or sane plan of action but it always worked when I was getting the silent treatment. After she had given me her usual 'no-fail' remedies – basically ibuprofen and fluids – she went back to her usual self.

"You'll be happy to know I've let your father off the hook for cheating on me with that woman from the internet," she said.

"I don't mean to nit-pick here but it really wasn't cheating."

"I'm not getting into the finer details of the exact definition of infidelity with you, Amy. It's over with and his phone has been confiscated for a month."

Basically, she's grounded her husband.

"Did you go to that shop?" I asked, trying to disguise the laughter in my voice.

"Yes, I did."

Ask a silly question; get a therapy-inducing answer.

"Elle sent me some recommendations, actually," she continued.

Bloody Elle!

"I'm not saying I'm going to use the thing – to be honest, it looks like it would do some internal damage, but I like your father to know that I have options too. I could trade him in at any time."

"I feel like that's not exactly a healthy way to resolve this issue, Mum."

"Oh, don't start your therapy nonsense with me. I've been married a lot longer than you and I will do as I please."

"Have it your way," I replied in defeat, "I'm calling because Elle has organised a baby shower for me, this weekend. I was hoping you would come."

'Hoping' was a stretch but it was better to invite her and put up with her there instead of spending the rest of my pregnancy apologising for not including her.

"A baby shower? What kind of garbage is that? We're Irish; we don't do that sort of thing."

Ideally, I would actually agree with this but I wanted to give Elle something relatively easy to organise away from the stress of the office. In theory, all I wanted was some cake and sandwiches in my living room but I knew Elle would be trying to put a bigger affair together.

Whatever keeps her happy.

"It's just a tea party, Mum, you don't have to come."

"Of course I have to come, I'm the grandmother!"

I can't win.

"Ok, well I'll tell Elle to send you the details and I'll look forward to seeing you there."

"No, you won't."

"No, I won't what?"

"You won't enjoy seeing me there. You're always so grumpy these days. In my day we weren't slaves to our hormones. We were expected to carry ourselves through pregnancy like everything was normal and not show how bloody horrible it is at all times."

Nope, not going to take the bait.

"Love you, Mum, see you at the party."

I hung up the phone and took three cleansing breaths before having to deal with the next thing on my to-do list: rein in Elle.

With therapy coming to an end, and other than occasional bouts of tiredness and talk of Wills, Elle had handled the whole experience beautifully. She was positive that this was just a little bump in her highway and was eager to get back to work and into full swing. I wanted her to take more time off – not because I didn't miss her or I wasn't in dire need of help – because I wanted her to take a minute to make sure she was processing it all properly and not just trying to be stoic for everyone else's sake.

"I'm fine," she said.

It's all she ever said in reply to my constant badgering.

"Today is the final treatment and I want you to come with me. You get to ring a bell and everyone cheers, it will be fun. Well, as much fun as one can have getting radiotherapy."

I readily agreed to coming along and was thrilled that it was finally going to be over. I knew the doctors were confident that they'd removed all the cancerous cells during the surgery and the radiotherapy was just a precaution but I still wanted all of it to be over with. I felt constantly terrified that there was going to be some other disaster and they would find more cells or she would need more surgery or treatment. All I wanted was to get her far away from that hospital and doctors as fast as I possibly could.

The drive wasn't long and I was 'treated' to Elle singing Celine Dion's back catalogue. Until you've heard *'Baby think twice'* sang on top volume by an emotional South African then you haven't lived.

I was only allowed to turn down the volume when we were parked at the hospital.

"My ears are ringing," I said, louder than usual.

"Mine too; it's great, isn't it? Like we've just been to a concert or something like that."

"Hmmm, yes, something like that."

The hospital was enormous, but Elle navigated herself through the corridors like a pro. I suppose she would know the route by heart after her daily visits for the last few weeks. It came to no surprise that she knew several random members of staff we met along the hallway on a first name basis, as well as countless patients waiting for their buzzers to go off so they knew it was their turn.

"Always making friends," I remarked.

"Of course, just because we're in this grim place doesn't mean I can't meet new people."

I smiled to myself and loved that the whole experience hadn't dulled her vivaciousness. I couldn't bear the thought of not being around her zest for life. It was an attitude that vibrated from her continuously and was one of the things that I envied her for.

It didn't take long for her buzzer to sound but I was told to sit where I was.

"I don't even let River come with me," said Elle, "I need to do this part on my own. Don't worry, I won't be long."

She disappeared around the corner with a nurse and I went back to staring blankly at my magazine, not really taking in any of the information. I gave up pretending to read once I realised I had reread the same paragraph four times.

Instead, I opted to people watch and see if I could come across any interesting characters. I realised that I was staring at one man in particular. There was something so familiar about his face that I couldn't quite place, like we'd met in a dream. He was picking up magazines and chatting with people sitting next to the coffee table.

Why can't I place him?

He looked like he worked here but he didn't have a uniform and I racked my brain trying to place his face. He looked up and caught my eye but I couldn't look away. He had the same look of curiosity on his face but it was soon replaced by a warm, genuine smile.

"Amy?" he said, walking towards my seat, "Am I glad to see you."

I blushed at his recognition and was mortified that I couldn't do the same.

"I can see your wee brain working overtime trying to place me; it's ok I don't expect you to remember me. My name is Malcolm.

Malcolm ... I met a Malcolm once ... why can't I ... the lake

"Malcolm!" I cried as I jumped from my seat and threw my arms around his neck, in the most spontaneous bout of affection I've ever showed anyone in my life.

"I take it that means you do remember me?" he said, laughing.

"How could I not? You saved my life."

All the memories of that horrible day came flooding through my mind, once again. They didn't hurt as much anymore but they still stung my heart. I may not recognise the woman that threw herself in the lake at her lowest point, but she was still part of my story.

"I promise I'm much better now," I explained, trying not to let my emotions get the better of me, "I wanted to see you so many times, to thank you, but after that day I never did see you at the lake with your dog."

"Really? I was the same, I hoped I would run into you and see that you were happy and healthy but I can see you're doing well."

He addressed my giant bump but thankfully didn't cross the line by actually rubbing it.

"I'm good, I'm really good," I said.

"Well, not too good if you're here?" his expression darkened and I worried that he was reliving his own trauma of losing his wife to cancer and their son in the process.

41

"It's my friend's last day of radiotherapy, I'm here to witness the bell-ringing and be a chauffeur."

"Well, that's good news. I'm glad she's finishing her journey."

"Do you work here?"

"I volunteer on my day off. I don't do much. Keep the place tidy and spirits high."

"That must be hard."

"Not really," he said with a shrug, "I've time to kill and people to distract. Seemed like the obvious thing to do after Aurelia died – although I don't go telling people about all that, I can't see that particular story being of help to anyone."

"It helped me."

He stared at me for a few seconds, his expression unreadable.

What the hell did you say that for? He's going to think you're still a nut.

"I mean, meeting you on that day and listening to someone – someone who validated my grief – it helped," I said as I shuffled my feet and avoided his eye contact.

"You literally saved my life by pulling me out of the lake and then when we spoke about everything we'd both been through, I felt heard for the first time. I felt that maybe I wasn't crazy or dramatic but that I'd been through something shitty and others would understand that. From the second you pulled me onto the bank of the water I started on a whole new path which basically led me here," I continued.

Tears pooled in my eyes as I rubbed my bump. Emotion was choking at my throat but I knew I had to keep going. I had practised this speech for a long time in the hope that one day I would run into him and thank him for the gift of a second chance that he gave me on that day.

"I know a simple 'thank you' doesn't cover it but it's all I have right now."

He said nothing at first and I wasn't sure if I should just continue to speak or let the silence grow between us.

Eventually he cleared his throat and turned in his seat to face me.

"Do you think that sometimes the universe has it all figured out already?" he asked.

"I have been having a very bad week, a bad couple of weeks if I'm honest. I've been questioning my worth in the world without my wife and child and I honestly felt like I was being led down a dark path. I'm not saying I was considering suicide or anything, I just mean it was getting harder and harder to get out of bed in the morning and push forward.

"I've spent a long time convincing myself that if I just kept pushing forward then I would be ok and I would eventually feel like me again. It's been getting harder to do that.

"I almost didn't come here today, I was lying in bed and I couldn't think of one convincing reason to come to this place, but I realised I had run out of dog food and would need to leave the house anyway. It's funny how something so small can change your whole day.

"You've no idea how much I needed to hear that, to see that, somehow, I made a difference in this great big world. It has filled my heart up. It really has."

"Thank you for giving me my life back, Malcolm," I said.

"See you around, Amy."

He gave me a wave as I watched him walk down the corridor and vanish from my life once again.

I was stuck in a daze of self-reflection when I realised Elle was standing in front of me, trying to get my attention.

"Earth to Amy?" she said.

I snapped out of it instantly and stood up to give her a big hug; which, at the rate my bump was growing, was proving more difficult by the day.

"Come on, Humpty Dumpty let's ring that mother-fucking bell," she said.

I took pictures and beamed with pride as Elle rang the bell to signal the end of her treatment. I tried not to cry as the people in the waiting room cheered and applauded her achievement.

We strolled, arm in arm, through the corridors and back to the car, feeling like a weight had been lifted from our shoulders at long last.

"Now, if you hadn't have been so stupid and gotten yourself knocked up we could be out on the piss right now," said Elle.

"Oh yes, because that's exactly what you need – a hangover on your first day without treatment - and stop saying he was an accident, he'll get a complex."

"He?"

"I've accepted that I am the maker of man – like one of those Spartan women."

"Of course you are, princess."

I'm a damn queen.

We sang and talked incessantly on the drive back to her house until we had to stop because Elle 'was giving herself a headache with her own voice'. Perhaps, now she would know how the rest of the world felt listening to her every day.

River had prepared a little party in their kitchen, complete with enough hummus to feed fifty people. He asked me to stay but I wanted them to enjoy the evening as a family. The four of them looked happy and relaxed so I made my excuses and left them to it.

Just as I was getting into my car, I heard the front door open.

"You didn't think you could get away that easy did you?" said Elle.

"What do you mean?"

"Well now that this therapy shit is done with, we have other things to discuss."

"Such as?"

"The baby shower! It's going to be epic."

Oh crap.

"You realise I only gave you that project to keep you from work stress and out of the office?"

"I know, but I didn't get to be your maid-of-honour so now I have to be godmother-of-honour to make up for it."

"That's not a thing."

"Yes, it fucking is," she replied, indignantly.

"Ok, godmother-of-honour, do enlighten me."

"All in good time, you just be ready for the night of your life and perhaps check that you don't have a latex allergy."

"I really hope you're joking."

"You'll find out soon enough, see you soon."

I don't think she's joking.

Chapter 7

I tried to mentally count up how much time I wasted staring at my wardrobe. It's like when people open an empty fridge but return fifteen minutes later in the hope that food will have magically generated in there. Every single day I spend an unknown amount of time staring into the abyss, willing it to give me something wearable.

Since the pregnancy my choices were becoming even more stunted because, for some reason, maternity wear in my local shops meant: large floral print.

If I wanted to look like a giant tulip, I would buy the stuff, but I didn't.

Ben said he admired my pig-headed refusal to accept that I no longer fit into my work trousers. I found that if I put an elastic band around the button and attached it to the fastener on the other side, I could sit the bump quite comfortably on top of the waist band and hide it all with an oversized t-shirt.

Maternity jeans were a different matter altogether. They were something made by angels and sent down from heaven. I resented having to put them away after I lost my baby weight after Arthur. They were so comfy that I basically lived in them every single day for a month until Ben had to stage an intervention, by stealing them while I was in the shower and refusing to give them back to me.

I didn't speak to him for four days and every time I overeat, whilst wearing normal jeans and the button digs into me, I still think about that heavenly garment and scowl in his general direction.

To his credit, he bought me three new pairs for this pregnancy but I was told by Elle that I had to get dressed up and not show up to my party in a pair 'of those fucking hideous jeans'.

I wonder did everyone get that particular, strict dress code?

It had taken a couple of days but I managed to convince Elle that I didn't want a mad party and we could plan something raucous and 'epic' once the baby came along. I knew she was disappointed but if I hadn't said anything then I would more likely have been spirited away to some tequila-fuelled bender as I sipped water and looked after my mother.

No bloody thank you.

We were meeting at her house and having a small tea party complete with a dozen baby shower games she'd found online. I was still staring at my hopeless wardrobe when I heard the doorbell go.

The sound of Elle was echoing through the house before the door even closed and I heard her run up the stairs and burst into my room.

"You're staring at that fucking wardrobe again, aren't you?"

"Maybe."

"Just buy new clothes, you cheap bastard."

"I'm not buying those floral -"

"Stop! I beg you to stop; I can't hear about your crusade against floral maternity wear again, I just can't."

"Fine," I huffed, "What are you doing here?"

"I come bearing gifts!"

She was carrying a large shopping bag and tipped out the contents. There were several tops, skirts with elasticated waists and two maxi dresses strewn across my floor.

"And not one fucking floral print in sight," she announced, "Look, I basically know you better than you know yourself at this stage and I knew you'd be over an hour late if you were

trying to get some inspiration from that wardrobe of yours.
It's just various shades of black clothing."

"There's some grey in their too."

"Cheery!"

She held up the first dress she could get her hands on and
forced me into the bathroom to get changed.

"Shove it on and don't fall into the bath, or anything else
Amy-like, while you're in there. We have a schedule to keep
to."

I had to admit that the dress was very pretty. It was a teal
green, my favourite colour, and had a pattern on it which
reminded me of peacock feathers.

I admired my reflection in the mirror and vowed to
introduce some form of colour into my wardrobe when I had
this baby.

You look flipping fabulous.

It's rare that I would give myself a compliment and mean it,
but today was one of those days. I came out of the bathroom
to do my catwalk and announced: "Who knew that I could
make pregnancy look so fabulous if I would just wear clothes
that fit me."

I came out to find Elle jumping up and down, trying her
hardest to pull a skin-tight dress over her cleavage.

"What the bloody hell are you doing?" I asked, "What is
that?"

"It's a dress, obviously."

"It's never going to fit over your chest."

"Yes it fucking is. Just help me pull."

"Is it plastic? It's so shiny."

"It's latex."

Ah, makes sense now.

The more she wriggled, the harder it was for me to keep a
grip of her. We were getting nowhere fast.

"Do you have an alternative dress?" I asked.

"I don't need an alternative; I'm wearing this damn dress.
Call Ben."

"Because you need an audience for this particular humiliation?"

"If you both pull, it will work."

I called Ben whose face soon went deathly white when he came in to find his wife trying to stuff her friend into an oversized sausage casing.

"I don't want to be here," he said.

"Tough luck, Benny, get to the other side of Amy. I'm going to jump and you're both going to pull at the same time. We are going to get me into this damn dress."

"It's a dress?" he asked.

"Just pull the fucking dress, Ben," she shouted.

With us both in position, she counted to three and we yanked as hard as we could, as she squirmed.

"What if I get rid of the bra?" she asked.

"That's it, I'm out of here," said Ben as he put his hands up to surrender and left the bedroom.

Traitor.

"Keep the bra, we will get you into this and you will look fabulous."

I knew all this was about more than just a ridiculous, latex dress. She wanted to feel sexy and celebrate her body and if that meant greasing her up with butter and pouring her into the damn thing, then that's what we'd do.

"I have an idea," I said.

"I'm not wearing anything from your black widow collection."

"Funny, just shut up and trust me."

"Like I have a choice."

I left her standing awkwardly beside my bed. She looked like she was ready to fall over at one stage, through lack of oxygen from her latex monstrosity, but I didn't want to try and convince her to wear something more sensible. She had her heart set on this thing and it was my job to help.

I rummaged through drawers in the bathroom in order to find something that would help grease her into the remainder of the garment, when I came across a long-forgotten bottle of lube that I had impulsively bought to spice up my sex life. I think we used it once, I don't remember why we stopped, but at this moment I was glad that there was enough in the bottle that would do the trick.

I came out of the bathroom looking triumphant with my find.

"Well, well, well, Amy Cole, you dark horse. I didn't peg you as the sort for arse play."

"There's so much wrong with that sentence that it makes my brain hurt, but I'm not wasting time lecturing you on sex shaming."

"Wow, Nelly, there's no judgment here I just thought there wasn't a chance of Ben getting any backdoor action due to that giant stick already up your arse."

"Who says it was my bum we were playing with?"

"Well there you have it. You're a freak in the sheets, I fucking knew it."

"Can we not do this right now? I have a party of people waiting for me and we need to get you looking like a cocktail sausage as soon as possible."

I generously poured the lube onto my hands and started to rub it over her stomach and trying not to get it all over her bra – although the chest was the actual problem.

"If we get enough speed over the stomach part then maybe the momentum will get it over the boobs," I offered. I knew I was speaking complete and utter rubbish but she seemed to be going along with the plan either way.

"It's got a strong smell, doesn't it?" she said.

I picked up the bottle and read the word 'tingle' on it and then it all came flashing back to me. The night Ben and I decided, after a bottle of wine, to use this. It was the same night that we realised that it had an extremely high concentrate of eucalyptus in it which basically made Ben think his penis was on fire. He spent the rest of the evening soaking his bits in a bowl of cool water while I had a cold compress over my eyes to stop the burning sensation.

That night we used the recommended amount, today, I'd used half the bottle and it was currently slathered all over my best friend's body.

I could feel my eyes starting to stream and I knew the sneezing wouldn't be far behind. I looked up at Elle and noticed that her eyes were becoming redder by the second.

"Amy, what the fuck is this stuff?" she asked with poorly disguised panic in her voice.

"The thing is: it's a bit pungent so let's calmly move into the bathroom and wash it off."

"Because having the word 'calm' in a sentence is always nothing to worry about. Fuck, my eyes are streaming."

I took her by the hand and tried to blindly navigate us both into the bathroom to try and wash the lube off. Mercifully my eyes weren't as bad as Elle's so I helped by throwing more and more water at her.

"Just get into the shower," I said, "Trying to do it this way is ridiculous."

"I will have to be literally cut out of this dress, there's no way I'm getting into the shower. The water is taking it south of the border and I'm not wearing any bloody knickers."

She was squirming uncomfortably as she stood by the sink.

"It's really fucking stinging. Do something, Amy; it feels like my labia is getting a chemical peel."

I ran out of the room, not entirely sure what I was looking for. I grabbed my hair dryer and plugged into the wall, blasting cold air up her skirt.

"You know what? That actually feels marvellous," she said.

Ben called from the bedroom to see if either of us needed medical attention but Elle kindly explained that everything was fine, his wife was simply 'giving her a blow job'. I knew there were times that Ben seriously called into question the exact nature of the relationship between Elle and I, so this would do little to help.

"Lucky you," he called, before closing the door again and leaving us in the en suite to finish the cleaning process.

"You can stop now, that devil juice seems to have been washed away," she said, "What were you thinking? There's fucking baby oil over there that would have done the trick."

"Well then throw it on and get your chest out of my face."

She poured it over her and, with the help of me, hoisted the remainder of the dress over her chest. She was barely contained into the outfit when she turned to the mirror and said to herself:

"You are a fucking badass, cancer survivor that can rock the fuck out of pink cellophane and make it look unreal."

I couldn't help but laugh at her pep talk but she didn't take her eyes off the mirror.

"You've got this, now go show everyone how to fucking party."

She turned from the mirror and dragged me out of the bathroom to finish getting ready. I watched her apply her make-up to reveal a dark, dramatic look on her eyes and nude lips.

"You're getting awfully dressed up for a tea party," I noted.

"You didn't actually think I was going to listen to you and do a poxy tea party, did you?"

"You said you liked my tea parties! You loved your hen do."

"I did, I did. I just think that this time we should do something a little bit different."

"Why when you say you want to do something different, I get the ominous feeling that something terrible is about to happen?"

"Well, because you worry too much – and probably because of past experience with every endeavour we undertake."

"Should I be worried?"

"You could, but it wouldn't change anything so it's really just a waste of your time. Now, let's fix that make-up of yours because the bus is going to be here in any minute."

"Bus?"

"Of course! We can't have a party without a party bus, can we?"

Of course we can't.

Chapter 8

When Elle had finished her work on my make-up we went downstairs to find my mother and Ben's mother, Althea, standing in my living room.

"I thought you liked me?" I whispered to Elle.

"Behave!" she replied, "Now, ladies, thank you for taking the time out of your very busy schedule to help celebrate the imminent birth of your new grandchild."

"Why are you dressed like a condom?" asked Eloise.

"I like your energy Eloise, but let's just leave my outfit out of this. The bus will be here any second and will be taking us to our secret destination."

"Amy do you know why she won't tell us where we are going?" asked Althea.

"I have nothing to do with this I'm afraid; I'm here as a victim – just like you guys."

The mothers made awkward small talk while Elle filled their glasses with wine and mine with orange juice. Ben had mysteriously done a bunk with the children before I had come down the stairs – probably because he realised I would be trying to convince him to take me with him.

There was an ominous sound of loud music making its way up the street and I groaned when I realised that Elle was smiling broadly, signalling our ride was here.

"I don't think a bus was necessary for four people," I said.

"Would you just stop being so pessimistic, we are the last to be picked up. Everyone else is already on the bus."

Everyone else?

Apart from Elle, I basically had no other friends. Well, at least ones I didn't feel like socialising with on any sort of regular basis.

I locked up the house and watched as Elle clambered aboard the bright pink and black bus. It had blacked out windows and awful dance music blaring from the oversized speakers in the doors. I heard a large cheer when she got on the bus and I started to panic.

I was last on the bus and was faced with ten other women all smiling and drinking as they sat in random places on the vehicle. There were two stripper poles – one at the front and one at the back of the bus – and Elle was already making a beeline for one before the doors had closed.

The lights were dim so it was making it even more difficult for me to realise who was making up the party. There were several women I used to work with in the PR firm – thankfully none of whom were Rita – the regular performer from *Joseph's* who played to the brunch crowds at the weekend (we'd spoken twice, I think) a couple of our favourite clients (which I was genuinely pleased about seeing) and one woman who looked familiar but I couldn't quite place her.

The mothers had settled on seats at the front of the bus and kept to themselves as I struggled to find a seat close to them.

"Amy, get your arse back here, you need the practise!" cried Elle, "There's a seat beside Mags."

Who on earth is Mags?

I squeezed through the excited gaggle of women and tried not to knock their drinks over with my bump, until I finally planted my bum on the seat beside 'Mags'.

"Let's get this party started!" shouted Elle, "Onwards, driver!"

The bus took off with a shudder but I seemed to be the only one that noticed. The disco lights soon started to spin around the body of the bus and after my ears adjusted to the noise of the music I actually decided that this wasn't such a bad idea after all.

"It's good to see you, Amy," said Mags.

"I'm sorry I'm going to seem completely rude here but I'll blame it on baby brain. I know your face from somewhere but I just can't figure out where."

"I got a haircut and a bit of a transplant," she said, "And you didn't really know me as 'Mags' I keep asking Elle to call me by my full name but she refuses. She said a new start deserved a new name."

"Oh, ok ..."

She started to laugh and continued: "That sounded more dramatic than I intended. I meant a personality transplant. It's me: Margaret, Margaret Clunting."

My mouth fell open. This woman had raged a war against Elle and me, as well as trying to get *Joseph's* shut down for a made-up health violation, and now she was sitting here, smiling at me as if everything was ok. I know we had decided to bury the hatchet and move on with our lives but I never thought I would see the day that Elle would be inviting her out to socialise or have a nickname for her. Well, a nickname that didn't include a curse word.

"You look a bit shocked," she said.

"I guess I am. I just didn't realise that you and Elle were on friendly terms. I didn't realise you were on any terms at all."

"It was a surprise for me too," she explained, "Elle reached out when she had her cancer diagnosis and I think she was trying to get some good karma or something – not that I deserved it. She apologised for her part in all that business and I did the same. Not just because she did, but because I really wanted to. To be honest, I don't think I would ever have done the brave thing and reached out to her but I'm really glad she did."

She went on to explain that she was no longer a chairperson for 'Smug Club' but was involved in making changes within the group as a whole. She was also trying to take a more relaxed approach to her parenting beliefs but I wasn't buying it. I rubbed my bump protectively, worried that she would start shouting some toxic nonsense at me because I was sitting too close to the stripper pole and therefore I would damage my child's self-esteem from the outset. As the journey progressed she relaxed and talked about her kids. She even started to share that her marriage had seen improvements since she took a step back and evaluated her attitude to all the mums she'd 'wronged' (her words, mine would have been harsher when describing her treatment of us 'undesirables').

"I like your hair," I said, honestly. She looked a million miles away from the matronly battle-axe we fought. It was much shorter and blonde now.

"Thanks," she said, "I wanted a fresh start and I read this Coco Chanel quote somewhere that said something like: 'When a woman cuts her hair, she's ready to change her life'. It's probably made up, but it resonated with me.

"I don't expect you to believe me, Amy, but I have changed."

"I feel inclined to believe you, actually," I said, "Elle usually has pretty woeful judgement when it comes to people but you do seem ... different. More open. I think that's how I'd describe you; and I like the name Mags."

"I do too, but don't tell Elle that."

Her smile was genuine and I was glad that I could make her feel less self-conscious about being here.

I heard a thud and without looking I knew it meant that Elle had fallen on her ass off the pole again. We had been on the bus for a half hour and she'd capsized, at least, a dozen times.

"If you don't quit that, you'll rip that damn dress," I warned.

"You're right, and I wouldn't want to miss our stop."

"Is there any chance you're going to tell me where we are going?"

"Not a snowball's chance in hell, dearest Amy."

I couldn't work out where we were headed but I honestly didn't care. The seats were comfy enough and I was enjoying my conversation with Mags. She was actually quite funny, once you got past the fact she used to be a mummy-shaming maniac.

Elle was keeping us entertained and some people were playing a type of volleyball game using an inflatable baby.

You can bet I will be having some weird dream about using my unborn child as a tennis ball, tonight.

By the time the karaoke started up at the front of the bus my jaws were sore from laughing. Althea's rendition of *Wuthering Heights* by Kate Bush brought tears to my eyes. It was swiftly followed by Elle singing *Mustang Sally*. I don't think it counts as singing when she spent the majority of the song literally shouting the words down the microphone like a type of crazed lecturer.

I sat and looked around the party, feeling happy that I was still popular enough to fill a bus full of women to celebrate with.

Of course, they could all have been here because Elle threatened them with physical violence or they were just as desperate as I was to get out of the house. I didn't care what their reasons were, I decided to be kind to myself for a change and believe that I was a good person and people wanted to be here because they liked me. Showing myself that little dose of kindness lifted my spirits even higher; high enough that I decided I didn't need the usual bottle of wine in my system to attempt karaoke.

I waded through the drunken revellers and demanded the microphone from Elle. For a moment she looked panicked, my track record with speech-making was not very good, but once I assured her I was there to sing she happily handed the microphone over.

I told her to pick something for me and, for reasons unknown, she decided on some pretty hard-core death metal which resulted in me bellowing down the mic for several minutes.

Why would this even be on a karaoke machine?

Once it was finished, I was treated to a lack lustre round of applause before my mother snatched the microphone off me and told me to 'sit down'.

"Stay where you are, princess," ordered Elle, "We're here!"

The whole party peered out the window in order to see where we had ended up. From the outside it was a dingy-looking club with broken neon lights and blacked out windows.

"Looks like a classy establishment," I noted.

"Always the cynic, just wait and see," replied Elle.

We all piled out of the bus and remained in a close huddle, as if we would feel safer in a crowd.

"Come on, girls, follow me," she directed.

We were like lemmings as we all followed the walking johnny and went into the club. My feet instantly stuck to the carpet and the place stunk of stale drink. We were greeted by a scantily-clad woman, who embraced Elle warmly.

"We're here for a pole dancing lesson," she announced.

For the love of God.

"But of course, nothing says 'baby shower' like an evening in a sex club," I replied.

"Look, I could have gone down the usual route with an actual licensed class but my friend, Sylvia, owed me a favour and she's agreed to give us a few tips. Afterwards we'll all do a performance and the winner gets a special price.

"Yeah, hepatitis," I grumbled.

Sylvia split us all into smaller groups and several other dancers came out to lead them. I was with Elle and Mags and breathed a sigh of relief that I didn't have to be in a group with the mothers. Sylvia was in charge of our particular threesome and I let my eyes wander in order to search for a comfortable seat.

"Ok, ladies," said Sylvia, "What would you like to learn?"

"The lot, babes, don't go easy on us," replied and over-enthusiastic Elle.

Sylvia looked at me and my bump, cautiously, as I smiled.

Keep looking, lady; I'm not going near a pole.

"Ok, well we can start with a few easy moves and then you guys can really put your own spin on things. We're not going to have time to do anything technically difficult so let's make this more about self-expression."

When she finished, she signalled for some music to come and as soon as it began to blare out of the speakers she nimbly jumped onto the stage and started a routine. For someone who said it wasn't going to be 'technically difficult' she was sure doing a whole lot of moves that I wouldn't be able to master in my life – bump or no bump.

The routine was beautiful though. I had imagined that it would be seedy and involve a lot of gyrating up against the pole, but it was more of a prop and an extension of the dance rather than a metaphorical penis to dangle off.

When she was finished, she invited Elle up to the stage to show her moves.

"You're in for a treat, I've been practising the whole way here on the bus," she said.

"Oh…great! Show me," replied Sylvia, sounding rather wary of her eagerness.

Elle's dance wasn't as subtle as Sylvia's. She might as well have been riding a mechanical bull and every time she tried to jump onto the pole and wrap her legs around it she would inevitably hit her knee so there was always some expletive shouted from our group.

I think at one stage I heard her shout the phrase: "You fucking, arsehole, wombat."

I'm not sure what wombats had done to her in her life, but I made a mental note to ask her about it later.

Mags' efforts were a more gentile affair and she wasn't half bad. She did a few half-hearted spins and smiled but she declined Sylvia's offer to be shown any more complex moves.

"I'd really like to get off the stage now, please," she said, nervously looking at Elle in case she was going to be forced to stay on longer.

"Ok, it's time for the lady of the hour's turn," announced Sylvia, with her hand outstretched to help me onto the stage.

"Oh, no, no, no," I replied, "It's bad for the baby and I'm a health and safety nightmare at the best of times."

Elle was already pulling out my stool from under me and pushing me towards Sylvia with all of her strength.

"No one is expecting you to climb up the damn thing, just get up there and shake your arse to the music for a bit. Go on, Cole, you're pregnant, not dead."

I knew when I was beat, so after a big breath I hoisted myself onto the platform and waited for the music to begin. There was a spotlight pointed right at me and I could barely see my audience – which made me much less self-conscious. The music kicked in and I tried to pretend that I was at home, in my kitchen, the place where all my impromptu dancing occurs. I could hear them cheering as I started to sway to the music and soon I didn't feel nervous anymore.

This is my party and I can shake if I want to – just don't get carried away or you may pee.

The more the music went on, the more my confidence grew. I reached out for the pole and decided to be braver. A spin was enough for the crowd to go wild and I didn't end up on my arse, which was always a bonus.

My turn had come to an end and I was escorted safely off the stage. I spent the rest of the time watching the other groups. The mothers had flatly refused to do anything and spent their time harassing the bartender into keeping their glasses full at all times.

We were treated to a few more performances by the professionals and it was mesmerising to see how it should really be done. By the end, we'd forgotten all about our group performance plans and were just happy having the show. Just as we were getting ready to leave, Sylvia approached me privately and asked to have a quick word.

"Amy, have you considered earning a bit of extra money before the baby comes?" she asked.

"Not really, I'm pretty much as busy as I can manage."

"It's just that I have a bit of a side hustle going on, separate from here, and I know there are clients that would really love to get to know you."

"Oh really? Do they need marketing advice?"

"Not exactly - it's more of a fetish thing."

"I'm going to stop you there, Sylvia; I have zero interest in that sort of thing."

"It's nothing sexual and you wouldn't be meeting them in person or anything, it's all done via webcam and it can be pretty fun.

"I know for a fact that pregnant women willing to rub stretchmark oil on their bare bump for an audience can earn a pretty penny."

"How much? No, wait, don't answer that – I'm not interested."

"If that's too much nudity for you, you could also put some videos together of you eating? You don't even have to say you're pregnant – with your puffy face you could get away with it, there are tonnes of people out there with a fat fetish."

"Please stop talking, Sylvia," I said as sweetly as I could.

"Well, if you ever change your mind, Elle has my number and I could get you all set up. Oh, there are also a few guys on my list that are looking for a large lady to sit on them repeatedly, you could do that."

"Good-bye, Sylvia."

I had never been so grateful to leave a place in my life. When I told Elle all about her proposition, she was outraged.

"What a cheeky bitch," said Elle.

"It's ok, I handled it myself."

"What? No, I mean why didn't she ask me? I could have done loads of kinky stuff on camera for those guys when I was stuck in the house. They could have watched me crochet in my undies."

"You are a strange, strange, woman."

"Only figuring that out now? Come on, there's bound to be people out there that would love to see some girl on girl crochet action. Throw in the fat fetish ones and we'd be millionaires in no time."

"I'm going to sit somewhere else."

The bus ride back home was a much more raucous affair now that people were all eager to display their newly found skills. I hoped that they all had private health insurance because I really felt that one or two would need someone to take a look at their coccyx after witnessing, at least, four of them fall flat to the ground whilst attempting an over-ambitious move.

I knew I should go down and make sure the mothers were doing ok but I was enjoying my evening and I really didn't want it to be spoiled by having a conversation with either of them. They looked like they were thick as thieves and had barely stopped talking since we'd got on the bus.

I told myself that I would be rudely interrupting them if I went down so I kept a safe distance. As we sped down the motorway, the energy and the dancing died down. We all settled into our seats and changed from party animals to exhausted adults wishing they were off the loud bus. The change of energy was not missed by Elle, who refused to go quietly into the night.

"C'mon, you lot," she shouted, "Let's play a game."

She dug through her bag and pulled out tiny yogurt pots that I normally reserved for the kids.

What on earth?

"Now," she began, "I looked online for some fun, baby shower games but they were all a load of bollox so instead I thought we could do this one that I remembered from one of those sex toy parties. It was great!

"We split into two teams, one person lies on the ground with the yogurt pot between their legs and the others have to suck the contents out without using their hands. The team that demolishes the most pots in the thirty seconds wins."

Most of the party laughed but I downright refused to take part. I explained that I could fall or someone could fall on top of me at the traffic and hurt the baby. This excuse was viable and accepted by Elle, for once, so I was given the job of adjudicator as they split into teams. The mothers were more eager to participate than I thought, but then I remembered they were both ridiculously competitive so they needed to prove that one of them was the 'cool, fun grandparent'. Neither was, of course, but whatever kept them happy and away from me was fine.

"Can I just point out that we are on a moving vehicle and I think this is a terrible idea," I offered.

"It's duly noted, shit craic," called Elle, from her position on the bus.

I counted them down and held my phone out to keep an eye on the timer so I had something to look at, rather than watch my friends and family pretend to go down on each other in some sort of lesbian orgy.

There was chaos from the get-go. People unsteady on their feet, competitors falling over as soon as they put their hands behind their back, the poor women who offered to lie on the ground were head-butted in their foof numerous times, as well as having dribbles of yogurt spilled all over them and accusations of cheating from both sides. It was the longest thirty seconds in history.

By the time it was over I was hoarse from shouting and I refused to declare a winning team because I genuinely didn't know who belonged to whom. Elle decreed that the game was a roaring success but as I looked at her more closely I realised she had a very defined ring around her mouth.

"Elle, I can't take you seriously when you have yogurt all over your face, wipe it off," I shouted over the ensuing arguments.

"I don't have any on my face, dry as a bone."

"Then what's going on with your mouth?"

She ran up to the driver's seat, ignoring his protests for her to 'stay behind the line', and examined her face.

"Fuck me!" she wailed, "It's like a fucking suction mark. I look like I've a bloody tash."

"You do, actually."

"Amy! What the fuck am I going to do? Come over here and help me."

I had no idea what she thought I would be able to come up with, but I decided to act the part anyway. At first, I wiped her mouth harder with my sleeve but all that did was make it look redder.

"Hang on a second, I have make-up."

I returned with my powder and started to pat the aggravated area, and had some success, but it was still very definitive. Her face fell as she looked at my handy work in the mirror.

"Amy, all you've done is get rid of the bottom part, I still have a bright red moustache and now I look like fucking Hitler."

"I was thinking more Charlie Chaplin."

"You're not helping."

By the time the bus reached our drop-off point, several of my well-meaning friends had used their make-up and know-how to help disguise the redness. However, all she was left with was some lovely eye shadow (in the hope that it would distract people from looking down) but the dictator tash was still very much present.

"I was going to suggest that we head into town and get some cocktails but I don't really want to be accused of being a neo-Nazi or a war criminal," bemoaned Elle.

"That's fine, I couldn't think of anything I'd rather do less than waddle into town and watch all you lot get even more hammered."

"Did I ruin your night?" she asked.

"Of course not, I've had a surprisingly fun time and I may even get a new fetish career out of it. Can I ask you something personal?"

"That sounds ominous."

"Why do you think wombats are arseholes?"

"Oh. Look, they know what they did. Let's just leave it at that."

Chapter 9

"I was thinking that we should do one of those fundraiser things," said Elle, one rainy Tuesday afternoon when she was supposed to be filling out expense reports.

"You will think of anything, rather than do the admin of this place," I replied, not looking up from my computer.

"It's not that, it just seems to be the 'done' thing. Get cancer, say 'thank you' to the ones that got rid of the bastard."

"Ok, we can have a coffee morning, downstairs, will that do?"

"It's a bit boring. I was thinking of like a 'family funday'."

"No."

"Why?"

"That involves a lot more expense and effort and you will inevitably get that dodgy git, Damo, involved and the bouncy castles will blow up. Coffee morning or no deal."

"Fine."

She returned to her reports for a whole thirty seconds before she got up from her seat and started to pace around the room, sighing heavily.

"Elle? Can you just spit it out?"

"What do you mean?"

"There's obviously something on your mind and you can't keep your bum in a seat long enough to do any work so just spit it out, we'll sort it out and I can get these reports finished."

She came and sat at the edge of my desk, her eyes looking wary and the faint red ring of a yogurt pot still showing on her lips.

"It's River," she said, "I think he's gone off me."

"Don't be daft," I said, poking her off my desk with the edge of my pen, "That man is loopy about you."

"No, really, there's definitely something going on. He barely wants to kiss me anymore. I think he's stopped fancying me since I was diagnosed."

"Maybe he doesn't want to kiss you because you look like a German dictator."

"I'm being serious, Amy."

"I'm sorry, are you going to start telling me about '*Mein Kamph*'?"

"If you're not going to take this seriously then I'll just talk to Joseph about it. He can give me a male's perspective."

Hoping to save Joseph from that fate, I promised to behave and listen to her tale of woe. River had been as attentive and supportive as always but in the last week, when she felt that things could finally get back to normal, he had started to become cooler and more distant. When he wasn't constantly on his phone with work, he was upstairs on the computer and acting secretively.

"I can't go through another husband doing the dirt on me, I just can't," she said, "Maybe you were right all along, it was completely stupid to marry someone I'd only known five minutes. What am I going to tell the girls? They love him."

"Ok, ok, slow down. You're making a whole lot of assumptions here. You're putting two and two together and getting 'whore'. Maybe there's something going on at work? What did he say when you asked him?"

"I didn't."

"Well that seems pretty ridiculous. You're imagining the worst-case scenario and you haven't even spoken to him yet. He could have bloody heartburn and is in a bad mood about it."

"You think?"

"No, I've no idea, but the first thing to do is to actually talk to him and ask him what's going on."

"What if it is what I think?"

"Then we'll do what we always do: figure it out together and maybe visit a few of his stores with a petrol bomb."

I sent her home under the strict instructions that she was to sit down and have an honest conversation with River. I told her to take the evening to get to the bottom of what was bothering him and stop driving herself crazy about the 'what if' scenario.

I hoped it wasn't true, I liked River. I had been won over by his warm nature and his ease with Hannah and Louise. They had a dependable father figure in their lives and Elle's eyes would still light up when he entered the room. I know they were definitely still in the honeymoon phase, but I wagered that not many men would take on two kids that weren't his own and a cancer diagnosis, within a few months of meeting someone.

I tried to put the possibility of him being a turd out of my mind and get on with my to-do list, remembering to add 'organise coffee morning for cancer charity' at the bottom.

That's all we need. Shush up, Amy, good karma.

I heard a faint tap at the door and Joseph came in, carrying tea.

"I thought you could use a pick me up," he said.

"You're an angel."

I floated the coffee morning idea by him and he was, as always, very accommodating and suggested we get it organised within the next two weeks.

"I have news of my own," he said, smiling.

"The smile on you! Tell me."

"I have booked Isabella and me a trip to Colombia at the end of the month. Three weeks for her to visit family and for me to rediscover my passion for cooking."

"That sounds amazing! Is she excited?"

"Yes, she's already packing. Silly woman, she will have us heading to the airport two days before so we can be early. Three weeks isn't that long, so tell that baby of yours to stay put until I'm home."

"I will; if he's anything like the other two he'll be well overdue. I make rather large, lazy babies."

"Good, good, now you get a list together of what's needed for the charity thing and leave it with me. It will give me something to work on away from Michael; I swear that boy is getting more stupid. My daughter could have married a surgeon and instead she -"

"Chose someone passionate about cooking with good business acumen, sound familiar?"

"Pfft, he's nothing like me."

He batted the idea out of the air with his hand and retreated back downstairs, but I knew as much as he complained about his poor son-in-law he would be lost without him. That's the thing about family, they can drive you mad at every given opportunity but you wouldn't be without them. I wasn't sure if it was thinking about Joseph or my hormones that was making me feel particularly sentimental but I decided to give my mother a call and check in.

She picked up eventually, in her usual brusque manner.

"Who's that?"

"It's me, you know it's me, my name comes up on your mobile."

"I could know more than one Amy."

"Do you?"

"No, but you didn't know that. So, to what do I owe the pleasure? Need a babysitter?"

"No, I just thought I would give you a call and see how you were?"

"What's wrong?"

"There's nothing wrong, I just wanted to speak to you."

"Amy, you've never wanted to 'just' speak to me about anything; now tell me what's wrong? Are you pregnant?"

"What? You already know I'm pregnant, you were at my baby shower."

"I mean more pregnant."

"How can someone be more pregnant?"

"I remember reading somewhere that a woman had twins and they were by two different fathers."

"So?"

"Is that's what happened to you? It would explain why you're so big."

"First of all, I'm a perfectly normal size -"

"For someone having twins, yes."

"Christ, Mum, I was phoning because I was feeling sentimental and fancied a chat with you and now not only are you fat shaming me, while I'm heavily pregnant, you're also asking me if I've cheated on my husband and this person has fathered an imaginary baby?"

"So, you really were just phoning for a chat?"

"Yes, Mum."

"Well I don't have time for all this chat, some of us have things to be doing."

"Good-bye, Mum."

I hung up the phone and decided never to be sentimental ever again. The woman was a nightmare and all this experience served to do was to get my blood pressure up.

On my way out of the office and heading home, Michael handed me a bag of leftovers from their lunch rush so I was off the hook for making dinner. To be honest, that was most nights these days. I felt constantly tired and my bump was killing my back. Ben did his best with cooking but I couldn't face another night of fish finger sandwiches.

When I got home from the school run and parked myself on the sofa, with my feet up, Arthur took the opportunity to disturb me because I obviously looked far too comfy.

"Mum?" he asked, tentatively.

I decided not to continue to pretend to be asleep and actually talk to my son; just on the off chance the discussion was going to be about something other than football.

"Something happened at football today," he continued.

Fucking, football.

"Stanley kept fouling me on purpose. He really hurt my leg and he said if I told anyone I'd be a gay wimp or a gimp for short."

I decided that the most pressing part of this sentence wasn't to correct the definition of 'gimp' but to address the fact that some little shit was making my son feel lousy.

"I'm glad you told me, son. Tomorrow I'm going to talk to the teacher and arrange a meeting with us and Stanley's parents."

"No, don't! That will make things worse. He'll tell everyone I'm a gimp. Besides, you already said you'd do that and you didn't."

Well, now I feel like shit.

"Stop saying that word and no he won't. The right thing to do is to have a discussion and get to the bottom of this."

"I'm only telling you so you wouldn't be mad when I punch him tomorrow."

"You're not stooping to his level, do you hear me?"

"I have to, it's all organised."

"What is?"

"Our fight; it's tomorrow at lunch and I'm not scared of him I just wanted to let you know first – in case the teacher finds out and phones you."

I had never been in an actual physical fight in my life so I was impressed with his bravery on the matter, but I was not prepared to take my husband's viewpoint on this. I don't care what he thinks the 'manly' thing to do was; my child was not starting his wrestling career in primary school.

"It's not happening, Arthur, I mean it. We are going to sort this out once and for all."

He sulked out of the room and I tried to close my eyes again but I couldn't get the thought of some little hooligan picking on my son. I was thankfully never bullied in school, or at least not to the point where I actually noticed. Girls would mostly talk behind each other's back, as opposed to letting things boil over into a fist fight. Not that that was the case all of the time. There wasn't a more talked about day in school than the day Sinead Waters challenged Samantha O'Riordan to a fight after school. Apparently Samantha had copped off with the boy that Sinead liked and therefore deserved a beating.

The whole thing resulted in about five minutes of name calling from a safe distance then Sinead threw the first punch. I half expected some hair pulling and slapping but what we didn't know was that Samantha did Karate at the weekend so she flattened Sinead within seconds. It was all very spectacular to 14-year-olds. We talked about it for months afterwards. By the end of the year the incident had blown up into an epic battle that lasted a whole period in people's retelling.

Needless to say, I didn't want people's memories of my son to be that of someone who was going around battering people. I knew Ben wasn't going to be much help with this; in fact, he'd probably spend the evening showing the kids some wrestling moves.

Instead, I looked up videos on mediation online so I could be prepared for the meeting when the time came. I figured that if I was prepared I would be less likely to resort to screaming at this child's parents and blaming them for their horrible son.

Why was parenting so difficult? I should have got cats instead.

My research was interrupted by a text message from Elle which read:

Elle: I cornered him and he said we would talk when he was home from work. He sounded really weird, Amy.

That doesn't sound good.

Amy: Don't panic, I'm sure it's going to be completely fine

I hope that lie comes across better in text than it would in person.

Elle: You're a terrible liar. I'll give you a ring later but if it's a disaster I may need an alibi instead.

Amy: Deal

I put down my phone and tried to drown out the noise in my head. Why was it that when you finally think that things can move along nicely and calmly, for a change, the universe shits all over it? I wasn't a bad person; I picked up litter and gave my husband blow jobs on his birthday so why couldn't I just catch a break? I wondered what things would be like if I managed to go a whole month without drama; heck at this rate I'd take a week.

I kept breathing deeply in the hope that I could slow the noise down but it wasn't going to work. I was too worried about Arthur and Elle and now the baby had decided to stretch so much it was pushing my bladder like an accordion.

On my way to the bathroom I saw Arthur and Adam in their bedroom practising punching.

"Hit my hand harder, Arthur, or else you'll not knock him out," urged Adam, "Put your whole weight behind it."

How does he even know how to punch? Have I been sleep walking through my kids' childhood and I'm actually raising cage fighters?

"Daddy told you that you have to put your thumb on the outside of your fist," he continued.

I'm going to kill my husband.

74

Chapter 10

After I read Ben the riot act for trying to incite violence in the school yard, I finally convinced him that contacting the teacher to arrange a meeting between the parents was the best course of action for everyone.

It took nine days and forty emails to get a time that suited everyone but we were finally sitting in the classroom, on those uncomfortably tiny chairs, awaiting Stanley's parents.

"I'm really glad we're doing this," said Arthur's teacher, Mrs Arbuckle.

"I'm not," I said, "I mean; I just wish there wasn't a need for it at all."

"Oh, of course, of course, but I'm just grateful that you're being so proactive."

I felt like I should get a medal for doing a good parenting job, for a change, or at least try and slip it in cryptically on social media so I could get praise from strangers.

Note to self: more self-esteem work needed.

I noticed that Stanley's parents were late, unlike Ben and I – who I made leave a half hour earlier than necessary. I wanted to make sure we weren't even a second late, so we would start off as the 'bad' parents who didn't care enough to be on time.

Ha! Take that 'Psycho Stanley', Arthur's parents care more than yours.

We all looked towards the door when we heard the unmistakable sound of loud arguing, closely followed by an agitated man and a red-faced woman.

Arguing parents, 2-0 to the Coles.

"Welcome, Mr and Mrs Tanner, it's good to see you again," said Mrs Arbuckle.

"Well it ain't so great for us, Mrs, we've got work to be getting on with instead of this nonsense, If their boy has got a problem, take it up with Stan in the playground, like a man," replied Mr Tanner.

Ben shot me a look as if to say 'I told you so. You should respect the law of the playground'. I decided to ignore him and kept my eyes firmly on Mr Tanner.

"I don't believe in toxic masculinity or sorting out problems with violence," I interjected, "These are children and an intervention is important when my son is getting a hard time at school."

I caught him roll his eyes, as he took his seat. Thankfully, Mrs Tanner looked much more reasonable and kept shooting me an apologetic smile.

"They are both interesting viewpoints on this situation, so let's keep the communication going and see what we can come up with," suggested Mrs Arbuckle.

The back and forth wasn't very productive. Mr Tanner was convinced his son had just been roughhousing and my 'soft' child hadn't taken it very well.

"Maybe he should stick with playing with the girls if he's going to run home to mummy after a bit of messing around. What's the world coming to?" he said, nudging his wife enthusiastically.

"Do you actually hear yourself?" I replied.

"Oh, here we go. You're one of those. Well at least we know where the son gets it from."

"One of what exactly? A human who has an actual understanding of how people should be treated?"

"You're probably a feminist too."

"I want equal rights for women? Yeah, I think most people are; unless you're a troglodyte."

"I'm no feminist. Women should be women, men should be men."

"What does that even mean?"

"Perhaps we should take a little break," interjected Mrs Arbuckle, "Let's get a glass of water and cool our heads then we can make a plan."

So far, Ben and Mrs Tanner hadn't spoken so I pleaded with him to step in or I was going to murder this man.

"How, in this day and age can someone still think and act like that? No wonder his son is a menace," I whispered, rubbing my temples and trying to find the strength to carry on dealing with this conversation.

"You sit this next round out," said Ben, "I'll take over, get this sorted and get us the hell out of here."

When we returned to the table, to face the walking-talking-arsehole, I wasn't surprised to find that Mrs Tanner was still remaining silent.

Poor woman, she probably can't get a word in edgeways with that nightmare.

"I think we should put our personal feelings aside and just stick to what we are here to talk about," said Ben.

"I'm glad she finally let you off the lead long enough to talk some sense," chuckled Mr Tanner, "Why don't you ladies talk about knitting while the men sort this out?"

I'm not even sure he's joking.

"The way I see it is: my boy was messing around and exercising his right to become the alpha male of this particular pack. I don't see a problem with this. I mean don't feel bad, mate, not all sons can live up to their potential, someone has got to be the runt."

Breathe, Amy, breathe.

"Well, the way I see it is: your son has absorbed your ridiculous notions and viewpoints of the world and has decided that instead of making friends and discovering who he is, he's making my son's life a bit more difficult. I bet he's thinking: 'my old man gets by with being a complete wanker, this must be how normal people should operate.'"

"Now, wait just a minute — "

"No, I think I've heard enough from you. It's obvious why Stanley is acting the way he is, if you're his role model. I'm not going to tell you how to parent, but I'm sure as hell not going to listen to you spout poison about my son.

"Mrs Arbuckle, something needs done about Ben and Stanley. We will work with you in what you think will work best, but I will not subject my wife to a second longer with this man."

I've never fancied Ben more.

Ben stood up and reached down his hand to pull me up off the tiny chair. I couldn't help beaming at him and we walked out of the room, triumphant.

"You do realise we probably should have waited to find out what the plan of action is meant to be?" I said, as we reached the car.

"I know, but it felt like a mic drop moment and I just had to go with it. I'll send an email later to apologise for our departure and find out what we are going to do.

"That felt bloody fantastic though."

As I recalled the tale to Elle, later that evening, I had already managed to embellish it to the point that Ben had to be restrained by Mrs Arbuckle to stop him from flooring Stanley's dad.

"No way," she said, "I didn't know Benny had it in him."

She had called over to put together suggestions for the charity coffee morning and had refused, point blank, to tell me what was going on with River until she was there in person.

So far, she had avoided answering my direct questions about her marriage four times so I gave up and decided to regale her with my afternoon instead. Once there was a lull in the conversation I decided not to do my usual thing of trying to fill it with any type of inane chit-chat but waited to see if she would tell me what was going on in her own time.

This patience thing is proving more difficult than I anticipated. How long do people stay quiet for?

"So, I spoke with River," she began.

Finally.

"And he isn't going off me or running off with someone else because he's got bored," she said.

Despite this all seeming like good news, her eyes remained downcast and there was no hint of relief in her tone.

"The thing is: his chain is doing well. Really well, in fact."

"So, he's been stressed in work?"

"Yeah, I guess, but there's more."

"Just spit it out, Elle, I'm dying over here."

"He has been approached by an old university friend who thinks he can help the chain really take off and expand but it's a big commitment. He's really excited about it but he wanted to wait until I was finished treatment before he broached the subject."

"Well that's nice of him, I guess. Why do I get the feeling I'm missing something, because this doesn't really seem like bad news."

"The friend is based in Toronto, he wants to take the brand there and roll it out all over Canada."

And that's the sound of the penny dropping.

"You're... you're leaving?" I asked.

"I don't know, we haven't made any firm decisions yet, there's a lot to consider with Keith and the girls and our business, of course."

"Right, well I guess that's that then."

"Hold on a second," she replied, "Don't start freaking out and cutting me out of your life this very second. We might not even be going, we haven't decided on anything for definite. I needed time to digest things and I was hoping to get some sage advice from my best friend."

"Well, you came to the wrong person then."

"Are you going to be a petulant child about this? We need to have a conversation."

"What's to talk about? You're a newly-wed, you're hardly going to want to be spending months at a time away from each other and this sounds like a great opportunity so you're obviously going."

"Obviously? Is that right?"

"Well, you're hardly going to stay because of me; I didn't even make the list of reasons to stay."

"Oh, come off it, you're being silly now. You know I was just listing the big things to consider off the top of my head."

"Exactly, the big things: family and business. There was no mention of friends you'd be leaving behind."

"You are my family, you daft bitch."

I didn't know what to say in response to that. My cheeks were red and my heart was thumping wildly. It was sore from even the thought of her leaving but I knew deep down she was going to go, so I'd better just get used to it; sooner rather than later.

"Are you going to say anything?" she asked.

"What's there to say? You've got decisions to make, don't let me keep you."

She looked as though she was about to argue back but thought better of it. She closed her mouth, picked up her handbag and left the kitchen, knocking into Ben at the door as she did.

"*Wow*, Nelly, what's the rush?" he joked.

"Sorry, Benny, lot's to do – bags to pack and lives to ruin, that's me."

"Oh, ok."

It was all the reply he could manage as he watched her walk out the door, slamming it behind her.

"What was all that about?" he asked.

"Elle's moving to Canada with that no-good hippy, husband of hers."

"I thought we liked River now?"

"Not anymore," I said, sulkily.

"Do you want to talk about it?"

"No. I'm going to bed."

"It's 7 p.m. The kids aren't even in bed yet."

"And your point?"

"Good night."

He retreated into the living room, closing the door behind him to prevent his miserable wretch of a wife following him.

Trudging up the stairs I began my usual mental admonishment over my handling of Elle's news. I was so annoyed at myself for not even being a little bit calm. She needed my help and I was less than useful.

That's the thing though: she always needs your help. You're always the one picking up after her and now she's leaving. This is how you're repaid for having friends in your life. They leave.

I knew it was a toxic train of thought that had little or no place in reality but I indulged it nonetheless. I was having a pity party and I was the guest of honour.

I picked up my phone and started looking at pictures of the two of us, like she was already gone or if I was going through a bad breakup.

Ok, you're going to have to snap out of this. She's not gone yet and you can still be a decent person. Just text her now and say you're sorry. This is fixable.

"Oh, for once, just do shut up," I said into the darkness of the bedroom.

I put down the phone and forced myself to sleep. I would deal with this when I was good and ready; but today was not that day.

Chapter 11

It was an icy atmosphere in the office, the following day. One good thing about us both giving each other the silent treatment was that it was the most productive we'd been in weeks.

When Joseph came up to have a chat we both pounced on him like hungry lionesses desperate for conversation.

"This is a nice welcome," he said, nervously, "I just wanted to make sure we were going ahead with the coffee morning."

"Yes, thank you, that would be great," I said.

"Well, I'm not so sure," replied Elle, "I'm flying out to Toronto with River and the girls the day before."

"What? Were you planning on telling me?"

"Of course, I was. I've been waiting for you to get your head out of your arse and speak to me."

"Well, you'll be waiting a long time."

Wait, that didn't sound right.

"The girls are off for midterm and River needs to meet with this friend of his so they can work on the logistics of how the expansion would happen. We can't make a decision until we know exactly what the plan is."

"That makes sense," offered Joseph.

"Butt out, Joseph."

"Hey!" he protested.

"I'm sorry, I'm so sorry, I didn't mean that."

"No scones for you, today," he replied, picking up the plate as he left.

"Nice one, princess, now we're stuck with just boring tea."

Elizabeth McGivern

"You're the one ruining my life and I don't even get a scone to ease the annoyance."

We both returned to our desks and refused to look at each other. I knew she was typing aggressively on her keyboard to get me to look up and give out for making unnecessary noise, but I put in some earphones instead. I decided to put on a meditation but their voice was so bloody boring, all it did was make me more enraged.

A rubber landed on my keyboard, making me jump.

"What was that for?" I asked.

"Your phone has been ringing and I'm not your secretary."

"Might as well get used to doing things by myself anyway," I huffed.

I'd missed a call from the school and there was a voicemail waiting for me. It was the office to let me know my presence was needed right away as Arthur had been in a fight.

But of course he has.

I let out a growl of frustration into the office which piqued Elle's curiosity.

"What's up with you?"

"I have to go to the school; Arthur's been in a fight.

"I'll go with you."

"No."

"Shut up, you stubborn mule. I'm coming with you."

We drove in silence to the school. Well, not complete silence, Elle insisted on continuously whistling – a noise she knew I hated – just to annoy me.

She parked, illegally, outside the main building, where I could see Arthur and another boy sitting sit-by-side outside the office.

I knocked the window to get the school secretary's attention and was waved through the door.

"What's going on?" I asked.

Arthur and his partner in crime both refused to look up and answer me so I figured I would have to wait and hear from

Mrs Arbuckle. It didn't take long for the familiar click-clack of her heels to be heard coming down the hallway.

"Mrs Cole," she said, solemnly, "What a palaver."

She recalled how the children had been out in the yard for their break when she happened to look out the classroom window and spot a group of boys and girls all gathered around in a circle. She went out to see what the commotion was and found Arthur and Stanley about to 'engage in a fist fight'.

"So, there wasn't actually a fight?" I asked.

"Only because I intervened in time. We have very strict rules about fighting and zero tolerance against violence of any kind. It results in an automatic suspension."

"Suspension? For what? There was no violence, you said it yourself."

"But there was about to be."

"According to you; you can't punish them for your perception of a situation. The violence didn't occur and if you start suspending children for arguing with each other then you'll have a pretty empty classroom."

I really don't know where I'm going with this. Wrap it up, Cole.

"I have already tried to sit down with this child's family and it was a disaster. I can only parent my own child and vouch for his good nature. If there was an argument it was probably down to Arthur sticking up for himself. If you want to arrange another meeting with his parents and him in attendance, then I can do so, but I won't allow my son to miss out on his education because a cave man has been allowed to raise a child. Come on, Arthur, we are going home. We will see you in class tomorrow."

I walked towards the door with my head held high and planted my face straight into the glass.

"I'm sorry, Mrs Cole, that door automatically locks. You need to push the green release button to get it open."

Fuck my actual life.

Arthur did a good job of hiding his laughter and happily jumped into the backseat of Elle's car.

"Alright, Rocky?" she said.

"Hey, Elle."

"Don't make jokes, we are not to make jokes about this," I said, "Can you just leave me home? I need to sit down with my son and find out why he's determined to give me dangerously high blood pressure."

"No problem, m'lady," she replied, tipping her imaginary cap in my direction.

There was no whistling to fill the silence this time and it made the journey feel twice as long as it usually does. When we pulled up to the house I deliberated about asking Elle in to chat but I couldn't bring myself to. By the time I got Arthur up the steps at the front door she had already taken it upon herself to get out of the car and was already making her way into the house behind us.

"Get out of your uniform and don't leave it on the floor, you are in big trouble," I warned.

He went upstairs without protest and left Elle and I in the living room.

"I'm sorry for my reaction," I said, sheepishly.

"I know. Look, it's a lot to take in but I'm not just going to run off to the other side of the world and drop you. Whatever we decide, you will be a big factor for the 'stay in Ireland' list."

We hugged, briefly, and waited for Arthur to return.

"What am I going to do about this Stanley situation?" I asked, "I really don't know what I can do. Arthur i trying to stick up for himself against this kid but now that I know what kind of role model Stanley has as a father I can't bring myself to be mad at him either."

"Yeah, this is a tough one. Stanley is obviously a little shit but why would he care about his behaviour if his dad tells him he's being a 'man' by going on the way he does? He thinks he's doing the right thing, just like Arthur does."

"I can't just let them fight it out. That's never going to be my answer for anything."

"I hate to say it, but you're going to have to meet those pair again, Sit down with them and the kids to hear all sides of the story. Chances are you'll probably bore the kids straight."

"I live in hope."

Arthur had earned himself a tablet-time ban but he did put up a good fight against his punishment. Unfortunately for him, it didn't work. Elle and I decided to go ahead with the coffee morning without her, as it was the only date that suited Joseph before he left for Colombia.

"All these jet-setting friends of mine, while I sit here getting bigger by the day," I moaned to Elle.

"Don't worry, we'll organise a girls' weekend when you finally pop."

"If you haven't run off to Canada by then."

"I will swear to you, here and now, that I will be here when that baby decides to make his debut. Canada can fucking wait."

My heart warmed at her words, and I realised that it was the thought of this baby coming into the world and there would be no Elle to greet him which was worrying me most. Obviously, she wouldn't be in the delivery room – a stipulation that Ben had made me swear to – but I figured she'd be the first onto the ward.

"I really need you," I said, "I know I'm being selfish and I know I can't keep you here indefinitely, if River needs you to go, but what if something goes wrong or I go crazy again?"

"Firstly, nothing is going to go wrong. I've had a word with the bump and he promises to behave. Secondly, are we sure you aren't still crazy? I mean, you put on a very good impression of someone who has definitely lost their mind."

She finished her tea and left to do some holiday shopping while the girls were still in school, and I began to look up parenting articles in the hope that someone would have the exact advice I needed to sort out our Stanley problem.

Except, it wasn't a Stanley problem; the kid was a product of his environment. I couldn't *not* think that; especially after meeting his odious father, but I also couldn't turn a blind eye when he seemed determined to use my son as a punching bag.

I called Arthur into the living room to get more details on today's run in. He explained that he had been playing football, when Stanley tripped him up and told him 'gays aren't allowed to play football'.

"I just had enough of it, Mum, everyone hates him and they were all telling me to punch him to finally shut him up. I was just about to when Mrs Arbuckle showed up," he said.

"Violence is never, ever the answer," I replied, "We will get this sorted but in the meantime, no matter how much he winds you up, you're not to engage with him. Don't even look in his direction."

"Then everyone is going to think I'm soft," he stressed.

"I don't care what everyone else thinks, everyone else didn't almost get suspended today. You father and I will have another go with Stanley's mum and dad. We will sort this; now go clean your room."

I have absolutely no idea how I'm going to sort this.

He reluctantly did as he was told but stomped his feet on every stair on his journey up to his bedroom to emphasise his displeasure at his treatment.

At dinner, later that evening, Ben was as perplexed as I was over the situation. He didn't relish the fact that we would have to go back into school and try to come up with some type of solution but he agreed it was the only way forward.

"Maybe I could just approach Mrs Tanner? She seemed more willing to cooperate," I suggested.

"I suppose, but we need both of them to reinforce that this isn't ok."

"You're right."

"So, this is what being right feels like? It's new, I like it."

"Don't push it, Cole."

Chapter 12

It was the day of the coffee morning and there was enough bunting hanging from the ceiling that would keep even the fussiest of brides – who dreamt of the ultimate shabby chic barn wedding – happy.

"Do you think you've enough bunting there?" asked Michael.

"I've some left over to strangle critics; does that answer your question?"

He retreated into the kitchen and I smiled at my handy work. With Elle in Canada it was left to me to make the place look the part and I refused to use any fairy lights. That woman had an obsession with them so for my first solo project I thought we could do without them. As I stood back to take a picture and send to her, I stopped myself.

Best wait until I know she's definitely in Canada before I send it to her or she's likely to throw a strop on the plane and land back here to string up the lights.

I'd sent the e-vite out to clients and everyone I could stand in my social network friend list (which, turns out, wasn't that many people). The café was filling up nicely and everyone was in good spirits.

See? Cake solves everything. Maybe cake can cure cancer? Don't say that out loud, please, for the love of God, don't say that out loud.

Joseph was busy hovering around people and making sure their cups and plates were full. He looked flushed but he didn't stop for a second until Maria called him to one side.

"Drink some water, papa," she scolded.

It was nice to know that someone could tell him to slow down and he'd listen. The conversation was flowing nicely but I felt that there was some background music needed to really relax everyone. I rummaged through the ancient stack of CD's that were under the counter and reminded myself to pester Joseph about getting a more advanced music system – preferably one that didn't include dusty and scratched CDs.

I settled on a compilation one that didn't make me want to hurl it out the window and did my best hostess impression by going around all the tables and making small talk with people. I figured that the more talking I did the more people would hand over their cash in order to get me to stop pestering them. There was an added bonus that the more I spoke to people the less time I had to actually stuff my face with all the cake.

Win, win.

By pure luck, my parents were unable to attend so I automatically felt happier. There was no one here to judge my efforts – or they were too polite to say anything – but I felt confident that things were going well.

Mags had brought a nice group of friends with her, some of whom I recognised from 'Smug Club', and they were all very well behaved. It was still unsettling to actually consider her the same woman who helped set Elle and me onto the path we were now on. Pushed on by the hostility and hate that she threw our way, we were both determined to make *Joseph's* the haven that it is today. Of course, it helped that Joseph happened to be the most accommodating businessman I'd ever met. We helped him, and in return he gave our ideas a home and a place to let our dreams as entrepreneurs become a reality. I was glad he was getting a holiday; I was beginning to suspect that Isabella was getting sick of the two demanding women in his café taking up his time.

I missed Elle; she was always the one to bring people out of their shells and get the fun flowing, even at a boring coffee morning. I dreaded to think about having to carry on the business without her. Would I hire someone else? Would I try and do it by myself because I couldn't face the idea of someone else taking her place? Would I shut up shop?

All these were questions I wasn't prepared to answer right now, or ever. People who claim that denial is an unhealthy place to be clearly weren't doing it right. They just needed more cake to keep them on a sugar high whilst simultaneously letting their responsibilities and important decisions to build up in another room.

Solid psychology. Speaking of which: I need cake.

I made my way through the tables and the chatting guests to sneakily get myself a large slab of chocolate fudge cake when I felt someone's hand on my shoulder.

Damn it, caught.

I turned to find Joseph, looking deathly pale and staring at me with panic in his eyes. His legs buckled beneath him and he collapsed to the ground, taking me with him. He grabbed onto my hand, tightly as I screamed for someone to help. There was commotion in the background with people shouting for someone to call an ambulance and screams for Maria and Michael to come and help.

"Amy," he whispered.

"It's ok, don't worry, Maria is coming now and an ambulance is on the way. Can you tell me what's wrong? Did you slip? Are you faint? Is it your heart?"

I decided against asking more questions, he didn't look like he could answer any of them anyway. His eyes were losing focus so I decided to get up and yell for Maria myself. As I went to get off my knees he grabbed my hand tighter.

"Amy, I'm scared."

Chapter 13

There's something unsettling about being at a funeral in the sunshine. It's like the universe didn't get the memo that the whole world should be grieving.

How is the world still spinning when a light as warm and bright as his has been extinguished?

I could feel Ben's hand at my waist but it didn't bring me any comfort. I was numb to everything but the familiar feeling of my heart breaking. As I got older the pain of heartbreak wasn't as sharp and overwhelming as it was when I was a teenager, now it was like a deep wound that never truly healed.

I held the single white rose in my hand, unwilling to part with it yet. If I did, it would mean I'd have to let him go too and I didn't want to do that yet.

I want one more day. I begged, fruitlessly into the cosmos, for one more conversation or glimpse of his face. That way I could really listen to the way his voice sounded, or his facial expression when he spoke about cooking with so much passion.

I took it for granted. I took all our time for granted. I thought I'd have more time. There's never enough time.

The hot tears rolled down my cheeks and I didn't bother to wipe them away. The graveside was still so crowded of people wanting to pay their respects and I wanted to scream at them all to go away. I wanted to have the monopoly on grief and I didn't care that I was being selfish or overdramatic I just wanted to be alone with him.

He's gone. This is just a body in the dirt.

Today was noisy and irritating but I was also scared of the quiet that tomorrow will bring.

How can I face going into work and not see him anymore? How can I set foot in the place without his smile to greet us? Questions for another day...

"Amy?" Ben asked, "Are you going to let go of your flower?"

I mutely dropped the rose into the hole and returned to stand beside him.

"Are you ready to go?" he asked, tentatively.

"No."

We stood together, in silence, and stared at the ground until my back ached and the baby rolled in my stomach, making me queasy.

Ben led me back to the car to rest my feet and cry in private.

"I don't know what I'm going to do, Ben. I just don't. I need Elle; I don't know what I'm going to do without her.

"I can't lose her too. How am I going to cope if she leaves for Canada?"

"Settle, love, she'll be back as soon as she can and nothing has been decided on the move yet. Today isn't the day to worry about that," he soothed.

A massive heart attack took Joseph from this earth. He lost consciousness, lying on the floor of the café he loved so much, and never opened his eyes again. By the time Isabella arrived at the hospital, he had already gone. I couldn't bear to think of what she was going through. The thought of not making it in time to say 'good-bye' to Ben would crush me, never mind the actual pain of losing him so suddenly.

Ben told Elle the news; I couldn't bring myself to say the words out loud. She couldn't get a flight home until today and was devastated that she was missing the funeral. Michael had interjected on her behalf, to postpone it for a day but Isabella was resolute. No doubt she held us partly responsible for running her husband into the ground with our events.

My parents had the children; I didn't want them to come to the funeral. I didn't want to have to explain about his passing and fill their heads with nonsense about heaven, I just wanted to get my head around it all first then broach the conversation of death and losing someone you love. I knew I was stalling but I didn't care.

Let them have another day of peace before some of their innocence is taken away.

I hadn't really spoken with Elle since it happened. She had been busy pestering airlines to try and get a sooner flight and I was barely speaking at all. Ben kept forcing me to eat and drink throughout the day, despite my protests. He pulled out the 'think of the baby' card when I was being stubborn which meant I would always relent and take something from him.

It wasn't on purpose, I couldn't stomach anything. Food stuck in my throat and liquids sloshed around in my empty tummy. It had been a whirlwind of activity from the second Joseph collapsed. I tried to be helpful with the funeral arrangements or offering words of comfort but Isabella only wanted family around her – I accepted her wishes and stayed out of her way. Despite being Colombian, she insisted on a traditional Irish Wake House for Joseph.

Two days of people calling to pray by his coffin while I helped to make hundreds of cups of tea and coffee for the mourners that came to pay their respects. I kept myself in the kitchen trying to keep on top of the mountain of cups that needed washed. It helped keep me focused on something I could control and meant I didn't have to endure a lot of small talk. Sometimes Michael and Maria would come to hide out beside me in order to get a break from it all.

"I don't know why she wanted this," said Michael, "I know he wasn't particularly religious but he wasn't Irish either."

"Mama is Catholic, she wants to respect the traditions of the country her and papa lived in most of their lives. In her heart

93

she will always be Colombian but this is where we grew together as a family," replied Maria.

He kissed her head and spoke to her quietly, she smiled at whatever he said and they both went back to drying the cups.

"I didn't even know we had this many cups," said Maria.

"I took some from the café, I figured there would be a lot of people coming and going over the next few days."

"You know you don't have to chain yourself to the sink? Your back must be broke," she added.

"I rest in between sets," I lied, "It's better to do something useful than sitting in the room and annoying your mother."

"You don't annoy my mother. Stop thinking that, seriously; she doesn't blame you or Elle. She knows papa was a workhorse and would never even think of retiring. This isn't your fault, so don't even go down that road."

She gave me a squeeze and went back out to talk to the neighbours who had just arrived.

"It's going to be strange going back to the café without him," said Michael.

"When are you going to reopen?"

"I don't know. The weekend, maybe? I'm trying to convince Maria to take her mother on that trip to Colombia that her dad was meant to go on. I think it would be good for both of them to be around family for a bit. I can run things at the café and I can always hire some help if it's needed."

"You'd hire someone so soon?"

"I can't do it by myself; I'll need another full-time person in."

I knew he was right, but I hated the thought of someone sitting in Joseph's spot at the counter when he wasn't even cold in the ground.

"It doesn't need to be decided today," he continued, sensing my uneasiness, "Today is about saying 'good-bye' to our family."

I wish Elle was here.

When the crowds died down and it was only a few remaining close friends left with immediate family, I decided to go home. It was time to face Joseph's grieving widow and hope that she didn't hate me.

"Amy," she said, taking me into her arms, "You are a good girl and you made Joseph very happy."

I tried to swallow down the tears because I didn't feel like I had the right to cry in front of her. She was his wife, she was the mother of his children, she didn't get to say 'good-bye'.

"I wished he'd retired a long time ago," Isabella continued, "but we both know he would never have agreed to that.

"You did a good thing with that café, he became passionate and excited about it again, and that's because of you and Elle. Never forget that. You be sad, we will all be sad, but not forever, he wouldn't want that."

She kissed my cheek and led me to the front door. I didn't have the words to express how thankful I was to their family for everything they had done over the last few years. I don't think I would ever find the words.

"We'll see you soon," she said.

The door closed behind me and I managed to make it to the car before breaking down.

I let my head rest on the wheel while body-shaking sobs escaped from me. I had no idea how I was going to pull it together to drive. Ben and the kids would already be in bed and my phone had died earlier so I couldn't even phone a taxi. I switched on the engine to try and get some heat flowing into the car but I could barely see the dials to work them.

A rap at the window made me scream and jump so high out of my seat I almost hit the hand-break off. I turned to see Elle staring at me, with a half-smile on her face. I leapt out of the car and into her arms, knocking the wind out of her.

"I'm sorry, I'm so sorry I wasn't there," she said.

I didn't reply. I didn't have the energy to say anything of comfort; we both stood on the side of the road, under a flickering streetlight and held each other, tightly.

I didn't know where to start to even tell her about the last few days, everything had happened so quickly and I was still in a state of shock. One minute he was standing beside me and the next he was gone forever. What little sleep I was getting had been plagued by the last few seconds of his life. The look of panic in his eyes as he fell onto the ground, the panic to find Maria, all of it was on repeat in my head.

I hated the thought of having to go through the details with her, but I knew she'd want to know as much as possible. It was already a comfort that she was home and we were there to support each other once more, but I really wasn't sure how we were going to be able to continue as we were.

"I can't fucking believe this," she said, staring into the distance, "I really wish I smoked at a time like this.

"I was screaming at poor airline reps to try and get an earlier flight but everything was booked solid. In the end I had to get four separate ones and just leave River and the girls out there. They'll be home on another flight in a few days, no point in dragging them back to watch me fall apart."

"Is that the plan? To fall apart? I'm ok with that."

"I'll schedule a breakdown for the next few days but then we've got to get our shit together, do you hear?"

I managed to nod, unconvincingly, in agreement.

"Now, let's get into this car and get you home. I think you've got bigger in those few days."

"Probably, but it's mostly just sandwiches and cake from the Wake House, not actual baby."

"I'm glad I missed the Wake bit, I still think it's fucking weird," she said, with a shudder.

"You bloody foreigners, coming into this country and trying to ruin our traditions."

"That's me."

I didn't attempt any more light banter on the drive to my house; I felt comfortable in the silence after days of constant noise with people coming in and out.

Elle handed me over to Ben, like a fragile package and took my car home with her. She refused to stay with us, claiming that she needed her own bed to try and get some real rest before dealing with the coming days.

Ben led me upstairs and gently undressed me. I felt like a new born – but with the capability of keeping my own head up – it was nice. I realised if I kept things simple and just took things one step at a time I didn't get engulfed with the uncertainty of facing decisions of the future.

All I had to do was brush my teeth, not decide on if we would be able to face the café again.

Then I just had to wash my face, not plan out eventualities of the business if Elle left for Canada.

Finally, I just needed to lay my head on the pillow, not try to decide how I was going to cope with a third child or worry that I would be hit with a fresh wave of postnatal depression.

Sleep would come eventually; all I had to do was listen to my breath.

Count the breaths, Amy, not the problems.

Chapter 14

The next few days were a blur. Some days I would waken up and manage five whole seconds without remembering the dull ache of grief but I still pushed myself out of bed and into my life. Even on those days I wasn't a pleasure to be around. I would snap and bark orders at the kids then spend the next few hours feeling guilty about what I'd done so by the time I was picking them up from school I was already an emotional mess.

I spent more and more time thinking about more outlandish and mundane scenarios in which Ben and the kids would die, or what they would do if I died. Most evenings, Ben would come home from work and find me stressing about not being able to pick the right flowers for his casket.

"Although I appreciate the emotion and detail you're putting into this daydream, please stop killing me off and turn off the sad music, I don't think that's helping anyone," he said.

"I was choosing which one to play when they're taking you out of the church."

He stared at me for a few seconds, trying to gauge if it was safe to laugh – it wasn't. He played it safe and decided to contribute to his funeral arrangements.

"I don't want to have a church thing," he said, "It's not like we're religious and we only did the church wedding to keep our mums happy."

"What do you want then?" I asked.

"I was thinking a cremation, then you can attach me to a fire work and send me off into space."

"Space? What kind of firework would make it to space? Knowing our luck it would be one from Elle's dodgy friend, Damo, that will explode before it leaves the ground and we'd all be wearing you. It's a firm 'no' to cremation."

"Who said you're outliving me? Your immune system is shocking; you'll be long gone before me."

This, of course, set me off again and before Ben had the chance to try and backtrack on his joke I took myself up the stairs to sob in private. I hadn't heard much from Elle, a few text messages and work emails. I hadn't known her work ethic to be so strong, but I knew she would do anything for a distraction. She had forwarded the office calls to her phone and neither of us could face going back to the café yet.

Maria and Isabella decided to go on the trip to Colombia and be with family. Michael offered to stay behind and get things back to 'normal'. We all knew things would never be normal again, especially as he had to hold interviews for help with Joseph gone.

It was a pleasant day, so Elle had come over with her computer and we were both working in my garden.

"I think we should go back tomorrow," she said.

"I was wondering how long it would take you to say this. You lasted much longer than I thought."

"I just didn't want to stress you out or put you through some PTSD shit that would make your labour start early."

"No, you're right. I've been a wimp and it's been really shitty that we haven't been there to support Michael."

"It's not like we've disappeared, we've been phoning and texting. Now that I say it out loud it really does make us sound like complete shits."

"Tomorrow. We go back and face reality tomorrow."

"It will be fine; we can get through it together."

I felt better knowing that we were going back for the first time with each other. I hated the feeling that our haven was now a place to dread. I knew I would be haunted, stepping through the door. I'd see his ghost sitting on the stool, reading his paper and 'tutting'. I'd wait to hear him walk up the stairs, to see his head pop through the door with his smile and his usual 'Ah, my Amy'. My heart would twist and ache at every sight and sound that reminded me of him, but it would be worse if it didn't. I didn't want a single thing about him to be erased from my memory or from that place.

We worked on through the afternoon while our kids played around us. Normally this would drive me crazy but I welcomed the distraction. The third trimester was being a bitch and throwing a few bouts of insomnia in the mix, which wasn't helping anyone at this rate. I looked up when I heard the sound of the front door 'slam' at the other end of the house. I looked at the time and realised it wasn't nearly time for Ben to be home from work so I went to investigate but was faced with my beaming husband holding a box.

I gave him a quizzical look as I tried to figure out what was going on. Ben wasn't one for surprises and when he did they were usually down to weeks of my heavy hinting. I hadn't been able to have a normal conversation with anyone for weeks so I knew that whatever he'd done was of his own volition.

"What's in the box, Benny?" asked Elle, "It's not a head is it?"

"What? Why would there be a head?"

"Like in that movie? Never mind, fucking philistine," she replied, rolling her eyes.

"Ok…. anyway, Amy, I know things are tough at the minute and I haven't been around a lot with work, but I just wanted to show you I'm thinking about you all the time. I decided that when I can't be here to comfort you I could provide you with a little stand-in."

Please don't tell me he was this stupid.

"Say 'hi' to the newest member of the Cole family," he announced, pulling out a wriggling puppy from the box.

100

Yep, he was that stupid

I kept my face unreadable as the children all rushed towards him to try and get a better look at the dog.

"No, no, no," he shouted, "Mummy gets the first hold because it's for her. Mummy, say 'hello' to the new Cole."

"I'm still cooking 'the new Cole', Ben, and will be doing so for the next few weeks."

"I know, the timing isn't great but I read somewhere that emotional support dogs are great for people in crisis."

"They're specially trained animals, Ben, not puppies who are going to turn the house upside by chewing everything and peeing everywhere; and yes, it will be up to me to train and clean up after it because – as you've already said – you won't be here!"

"Just give him a cuddle, you'll love him," he continued, handing me the thing.

"What even is it? I mean, I know it's a dog but what kind of mutt is it?"

"It's a pug and you can name him whatever you like."

"Gee, thanks."

I had to admit: it was kind of cute, but the fact that it was busy chewing my fingers and yapping made me realise that I was completely correct on how this new dog ownership was going to go.

"What are you going to name him, Mummy?" asked Arthur.

I thought for a moment and continued to study his pudgy little face.

"His name is 'Colin'," I announced.

"Colin?" asked Adam, "That's a weird name for a dog."

"It's a weird dog for a name, but there you have it. His name is 'Colin' and that's that."

I handed the puppy over to the kids and went inside to wash my hands and prevent myself from strangling my husband.

I didn't want a dog; I've never wanted a dog. I have been, and always will be, a cat person but we decided against getting one because Adam was allergic. The usual dog conversation came up, at least, once a year from the kids but it's always a firm 'no' from me. I knew his heart was in the right place but it was very close to being ripped from his chest.

Elle followed me into the kitchen, trying to hide her amusement.

"Don't bother laughing or I'll be packing him off to live with you," I said.

"Which one? Colin or Ben?"

"Perhaps both at this rate."

"He is a cute thing," she mused, watching the kids coo over the dog.

"Which one? Colin or Ben?" I asked.

She laughed and switched on the kettle to make me peppermint tea, in a vain attempt to calm me down.

"One thing I am looking forward to is a decent cup of coffee," she said, "This making-my-own shit has been doing my head in. I'm used to the finer things now, complete with little tiny biscuits on the saucer."

"Hey! I have biscuits somewhere."

"Yeah, the depressing, plain ones."

"They help my heartburn."

"I rest my case."

Ben came running into the kitchen holding a pee-ing puppy.

"What do I do with it?" he asked, panicked.

"Put him outside or at least on some paper, why would you bring the pee in here?"

"I panicked! Dry that up please, before someone slips on it?"

And so it begins.

Elle seized the opportunity to grab her children and head home before I murdered my husband. She promised to call in the morning and we would head into the café together. Even making the plan to go was filling me with dread but I knew we had to face it soon or I would never go back.

After I waved them off, I went to hunt down my family – who were all besotted with the tiny, wrinkly thing in the garden. I decided to take a look through the other bags Ben had brought home, in the hope that he'd at least got something nice for dinner to help butter me up – he hadn't.

He had bought nappies though, which I thought was very organised and thoughtful of him. It made my heart swell a little in appreciation for my daft but lovely man. I was smiling to myself when he came up behind me and put his arms around my waist.

"You're smiling, I knew you'd love him," he said.

"I'm not smiling at that thing; I'm smiling at the nappies."

"Oh those? Yeah, I thought I was going overboard but then I thought it will be handy when you're out and about and he's in your bag. He's too small to be walking yet."

"Yet? Ben the baby won't be walking for like a year and it's not a bag, it's a baby sling; you can't have forgotten everything about a new born, have you?"

"What are you talking about? The nappies aren't for the baby, they're for the dog."

I wonder if being a single mum is as difficult as they say?

"Why on earth would I be putting a dog in nappies?"

I instantly regretted asking this question as soon as the words were out of my mouth.

"Well, now you're going back to the office you can't be leaving him here on his own all day. The walk there might be a short one for you but his little legs won't make it just yet; so I figured you could be like one of those posh women who carry him around in a handbag."

"The word you're looking for is 'idiot'; you mean: 'those idiots who carry a dog around in their handbag'. No, Ben, I can't see that happening and besides can you not take paternity leave to mind the 'newest Cole' member?"

"I'm planning on using that for the baby."

"Oh, so you have remembered I'm heavily pregnant? That's good; I was just making sure that hadn't escaped your notice, because that's the only reason I can come up with to explain why you would add to the stress around here."

"Like I could forget!"

"What the hell is that supposed to mean?"

"Nothing, it doesn't mean anything."

He looked down at his feet and tried to avoid my piercing gaze but he was never very good at avoiding eye contact.

"Ben, would you care to explain what you mean by that?"

"It just means that pregnancy is tough, this one especially, but you're not the only one going through it. I'm trying my best but you're not exactly making things easy."

You've got to be fucking kidding me right now.

"Oh, I'm sorry, I hadn't realised that this pregnancy was taking its toll on you. What's been going on? Has it been the constant nausea? The vomiting that left you so dehydrated you had to be hospitalised? Carrying around a bump so large that you have nightmares that you're giving birth to a velociraptor? The insomnia? The near-constant heartburn? The swollen hands and feet? The fact that none of your clothes fit anymore? The unpredictable typhoon of emotions at any given second? Please, enlighten me about your particular predicament."

I wasn't sure if he was just digesting the information or he was genuinely considering a reply to my speech but he was saved from more of the same by the boys coming into the kitchen with the dog.

"Can you two stop fighting, you're upsetting Collosus," said Adam.

"That's not his name," I replied, firmly.

"Dad said — "

"Your father has said and done enough, now give me Colin and go do your homework."

Adam reluctantly handed me the dog and I walked up the stairs towards my bedroom in order to put some sort of distance between me and that fight. Colin and I sat on the bed and I studied the brown swirls on his sandy coat.

"You are a bit of cute thing," I said, quietly, "but I'm not admitting that to anyone. If you want to pee, then do it on Ben's pillow. Then we can be friends."

Chapter 15

I had a rubbish night's sleep. It wasn't all completely down to the baby using my bladder as a squeeze toy, my body thinking it was day time or the whining puppy downstairs; I just didn't want it to be time to go to *Joseph's*.

Would it still be called that? Yes, stop being silly.

Ben woke up, fresh as a daisy, and found me mopping up various puddles Colin had managed to do in the three minutes he was out of his crate. The puppy training pads were left dry, of course, and he had decided that it would be a fun game to try and catch the mop, making it impossible for me to get anything done. By the end I was just rolling him around in his own urine.

"I give up!" I shouted, "Dr Dolittle, get over here and clean up after your emotional support puppy. I'm going to have a shower."

We hadn't really spoken since my outburst in the kitchen. To be honest, I was beyond caring how he was feeling right now. My self-righteousness was beginning to wane but I wasn't ready to admit that, perhaps, things were tough on him too. Every time he tried to make up and reach for my hand, I would walk out of his reach or give him the dog. A part of me kept bugging me to stop this nonsense and be friends. I kept telling myself that life was too short and to look at Isabella, she would give anything to have one last day with Joseph but the other part of me said: "fuck it!"

The more tired I was, the more inclined I was to listen to the latter.

Elle could sense the atmosphere as soon as she arrived at the door. I hated when that happened, I preferred if people just assumed we were perfect all the time instead of at each other's throats – mostly because I thought people would take his side.

"Well, this is nice," she said, making herself a cup of tea.

"What?" asked Ben.

"It's nice to know you guys are human and capable of acting like other married couples."

"What's that meant to mean?" I said, instantly getting my back up.

"Calm down, princess, you're allowed to be pissy at each other without it being the end of the world. All I meant was it can be exhausting sometimes to always compare my relationship to perfection. You guys are always so 'good'; so it's nice to peak behind the curtain and find that there's imperfection lurking.

"Just kiss and make up already, whatever it was it can't be that bad."

Ben looked towards me, hopefully, but I refused to let my guard down.

"He bought a dog, Elle," I said, "I'm heavily pregnant and he bought a dog and now he wants some sort of medal because pregnancy isn't a damn picnic for him; but what does that matter as long as I'm here to wipe up the piss from the floor?"

"Yes, well you also hired a woman to wee on him not so long ago so I guess this makes you even."

I couldn't stop the laughter. It was unexpected and hearty. The feeling of relief from this one thing was amazing. My whole body started to relax as the laughter shook my entire body and I looked at Ben for the first time, this morning.

"Can we be friends?" he asked.

"Yes, we can be friends but you can't ever use the water sports incident to get yourself out of trouble ever again, you're to mention nothing about your hardship during pregnancy and you're walking the dog every single day."

My terms were agreed to and peace was once again restored in the Cole household. Ben even agreed to take all the kids to school to earn him a bit more grace, but on his way out the door he managed to spoil my increasingly good mood by reminding me the dog needed to come with us.

"Are you being serious?" asked Elle.

"Apparently," I replied, "I suppose he's right, I don't want to leave the thing here on his own all morning."

"I can really hear the affection in your voice," she laughed.

"Hand me his nappies."

"Now, you've got to be fucking kidding me."

"It's for when he's in my handbag, I don't want him to poop on my stuff."

"Or just let him walk on a lead like a normal dog?"

"He's too small, look it's just until he's trained and only when he's in my bag. Just help?"

"No way, I'm taking no part of this. I feel like I should phone PETA or something."

I took a long cleansing breath and decided to not get into a full-blown argument over this issue. I picked up the packet of nappies and realised that Ben had bought pull-ups for toilet training.

How on earth did he think these were ever going to fit?
Right, time for plan B.

I decided to hunt under my kitchen sink to find a suitable replacement bag. With all my good intentions to save the earth I had managed to collect a few hundred bags-for-life, which were then put under my sink, never to be used again.

I got the smallest tote bag I owned and shoved a blanket into the bottom of it.

"Now, don't pee on this," I said in my best, calm-sounding voice, as I lifted him in and set him on the blanket.

"Are you both ready?" asked Elle.

"I think so. I'd better take some puppy pads for the office."

"Christ, what's it going to be like when you're trying to get out of the house with the baby? One bag for him and another for the dog? You're going to be like a damn Sherpa anytime you need to go to the shop."

"I can't think that far ahead."

"It's not that far away, Amy."

"We are dealing with fifteen minutes at a time, for the foreseeable future, ok?"

She shot me a military salute and ushered Colin and I out the door. I opted to walk because I wanted to delay getting to the café for as long as possible. This was easy, because my ankles were swollen and I had begun waddling fulltime.

"By the time we get there, it will be time to get the kids," remarked Elle.

I ignored her and concentrated on keeping my balance instead. Colin was making that increasingly more difficult, however, because the more he wriggled around the bag, the more it put me off my stride. Despite this, we were there sooner than I would have liked. I used to breathe a sigh of relief at the sight of the purple paint on the door but today it was nothing but dread.

"Come on, you big wimp. We can do this together."

I let Elle push open the door and go in front of me. The familiar smell of coffee and warm, fresh bread hit my face and I felt sick to my stomach. I wondered if I could get away with saying that the dog was unsettled by the noise and it was safer to take him home.

"It's so good to see you both," said Michael.

He appeared, as if out of nowhere, and squashed us both into his arms.

"Watch the dog," I replied, pushing myself out of the hug sandwich.

"The what?" asked Michael.

"Amy decided that she needed a grief dog," said Elle.

"That's not exactly what happened."

"Ok, well that's interesting," he offered, "While you're here, let me introduce you to Barbara."

Oh, no.

I looked up to see a slim, blonde woman walk towards us, smiling. I wanted the ground to swallow me whole, I wasn't ready for this – any of this.

"Hi," she said, "It's really nice to meet you both."

Who the fuck even is this and how dare she just walk into here and act like she knows us?

"Hey Barbara," said Elle, "Welcome to the mad house, can I call you Babs? Or Barbie – ah, please will you let me call you Barbie?"

Barbara laughed nervously and agreed to the name change. I assumed she agreed out of fear more than actually wanting to be known as 'Barbie'.

"I'm going upstairs," I said, pushing through the three of them and walking towards the stairs. As I walked up to the office, I heard Elle apologise for my greeting and offer to sit with Barbara and get to know her a bit more.

The office was freezing. No doubt the heating upstairs had been switched off for weeks and it would take all day to get rid of the coolness from the room. I let Colin out of the bag and was delighted to find that he'd not done anything in the bag. My delight was short lived when he decided to relieve himself in the middle of the office floor before I was able to get any of the pads down.

I really don't like dogs.

Elle came upstairs shortly after and went straight to her desk.

"So, are you planning on being an ignorant bitch to Barbie forever? Just so I know if I'm allowed to be her friend or not?"

"I don't know what are you talking about, we are here to work and that's all."

"Right, so we are just going to ignore the fact that you are pretending that everything is fine and you're taking your grief out on some poor woman who is here to help Michael in his time of need so he doesn't also keel over and die of a heart attack from stress?"

"Not funny, Elle."

"Ok, too far, but let's not start the day with another one of your vendettas against another woman."

"What does that mean?"

"Margaret? Then there was that diet club woman? Do you hate women?"

I knew she was joking but I wasn't in form for her sarcasm and attempts to make me smile. For once, I wanted her to just act the same way I was. Why couldn't she admit that this was hard? This whole day was hard enough without having to pretend that Barbara was just some new member of staff and wasn't taking the place of our friend.

"Can we not play this game? Just let me get on with work and get out of here."

She didn't reply, instead she switched on her computer and got to work as well. Michael came up to check in on us, and bring hot drinks. We listened to him tell us about how things had been going in our absence. At first, he spoke about the practicalities and the authentic Colombian dishes that Isabella had requested to be added to the menu. They were still on their travels but were sending recipes in, daily, for him to try. He offered to send us some of his favourites up so we could have a taste and make a toast to our friend.

I tried not to feel sad at the thought of trying the food without hearing the stories of how Joseph came to fall in love with them on his trip. I hated everything about this conversation but it wasn't stopping. Barbara had started working in the café a week ago and was 'heaven-sent', according to Michael.

"She's lovely and friendly, you'll both really like her," he said, enthusiastically, "I know it's been difficult for you to come back here, it was for me too but we have to keep moving forward. The last thing Joseph would have wanted was for all our work to just stop and fall apart.

"Your office will be here for as long as you want to it to be."

I couldn't hold it together anymore; I started to cry and couldn't stop. I looked at Elle and she also had tears in her eyes but was keeping it together a lot better than I was.

"You're right, Michael," she said, "We are going to keep pushing forward, all of us."

I nodded but couldn't find the words yet. In that moment I was thankful for Colin being in the room, he was able to distract both Michael and Elle for long enough so the conversation about the future and our friend was stalled. I just wanted to bury my head in the sand and deal with this in twenty years or so.

"He's a pretty cute dog," Michael remarked, "His wee teeth are sharp."

"Yes, he's losing favour with the kids already because he keeps nipping them. Do you want a dog?" I asked, as I used my sleeve as a tissue.

"Eh, no thanks."

He eventually went downstairs to get the lunch ready and I went back to answering emails while Elle paced up and down, trying to come up with a press release for our newest client's opening. It was a fish mongers that specialised in exotic fish called: '*Sofishticates*'.

I had absolutely no idea what we were going to do for them but Elle was a sucker for any business that had a pun in the title. It didn't take long for Colin to turn her pacing into a game and attacked her feet, it took even less time for Elle to stop working and play back.

There was another tap at the door and Barbara came in with several plates on a tray.

"Hi, Michael said it would be ok to bring this up to you?"

"Ah, Barbie, you're an angel. We definitely need some food, it will get the old grey cells moving; won't it Amy?"

112

I grunted in response and refused to look up from my screen. Too much was changing around here and I refused to just go along with it, no matter what people thought Joseph wanted. I would grieve my own way and that was apparently to be a stubborn bitch.

Not sure that's the healthiest option there, Amy.

"Awh, what a cute dog," said Barbara, "What's his name?"

I didn't answer and let Elle continue to hold the conversation with the intruder. The smell of the ajiaco and arepa was making my mouth water and I couldn't hide behind the screen anymore. I tried to manoeuvre behind the desk towards the tray without Elle or Barbara seeing me. Thankfully the dog had chosen that particular moment to put on a cute display of falling over so I could slide over on my chair, undetected.

I had never smelled soup as beautiful as this and the waft of the bread was making my tummy rumble an embarrassing amount. The noise made them both turn around to hear where the growling was coming from and caught me with the spoon midway to my mouth.

"Just checking to see if it had cooled down," I said, as way of explanation.

"Sure, you were," replied Elle with a wink.

"Enjoy, ladies, I'll come back up for the plates in a little while," said Barbara.

"You don't need to," I called after her, "It's not like we're completely helpless and need someone looking in on us. In fact, we don't need you at all; we're trying to work here."

She smiled, kindly, and closed the door behind her.

"Well, that was normal," said Elle, sitting Colin down on the ground to eat her lunch.

"Are you going to wash your hands?"

"Why?"

"You've been on the ground with that dog for ages."

"So? It's a baby, it's not dirty."

"It's an animal."

"Exactly, the germs don't pass from animal to human."

I sat down my spoon and started to rub my temples in frustration. I knew all those occasions that I had decided not to correct her flawed logic and awful sense of general knowledge would need to be addressed, but today was not that day.

"Eat your soup before it gets cold."

The lunch was taken in silence and I knew she was itching to press me further on the whole grief-denial spin I was in but she must have thought better of it and spent the rest of the time thinking of fish puns.

"Do you want me to leave the dog with you?" I asked, hopefully.

"And deny you the pleasure of walking him home in your little bag? I would never do that."

I was about to leave and face the unfamiliar sight of not seeing Joseph wave me 'good-bye' when I turned to her and asked:

"Why are you ok?"

"You think I'm ok? Well, that's a dick move if ever there was one. You don't have the monopoly on grief or the textbook on how to do it correctly, you know? Some people, like you, cling to the status quo to try and kid yourself into thinking that you've some sort of control over the universe. Like if you be a complete bitch to Barbie it will mean you're not being disrespectful to his memory or something but that's your own crap you're projecting. Amy, I thought you would have realised by now that we've fuck all control over what the universe has in store for us but remembering those we love doesn't mean we can't make room for new people in our lives when they're gone.

"You really think Joseph would approve of this bitchy, teenage behaviour?"

"No."

"Exactly, I miss the man that walked me down the aisle and gave us the chance to build a business but it doesn't, for one second, mean I'm going to piss on other people to show how much I'm hurting.

"We have to keep moving forward, Amy, or else we're just dead fish."

"Are you lecturing me and trying to work fish into the conversation as well?"

"I'm multitasking. Look, do what you've got to do but we both know you can't hold a grudge for shit and she's not deserving of this misplaced hostility. Take it out on your husband, like a normal woman."

I picked up Colin and placed him back in his bag, he thanked me for this by biting my hand as I tried to take it out.

Bloody dog.

I waved to Michael and ignored Barbara's 'good-bye' as I made my way home to pick up the car and get the kids. School runs were stressful enough without the added nonsense of a needy puppy. I knew the children would be disappointed that it was just me but they'd have to put up with it.

It was the usual anarchy at the gates and I ended up parking up a stupidly steep hill that I would have to drag the boys up on the way back to the car. I wasn't looking forward to hearing their complaints the entire time but I decided to remind them that the quicker we got to the car, the sooner they would be reunited with the puppy.

As I waited for Arthur to come out of his classroom, his teacher caught my eye. I knew things weren't going to be good when she asked me to step inside and she would ask Adam's teacher to send him round to the classroom so he wouldn't be left wondering where I was.

She explained that there had been another incident between Arthur and Stanley. This time it was more name calling, which had left Arthur upset, however, as she wasn't there to witness it herself she was relying on the children there at the time for their version of events. Arthur was refusing to say anything but 'it doesn't matter' and Stanley was as unrepentant as ever.

"Have Stanley's parents arrived yet?" I asked.

"No, I'll be calling them in to tell them the situation. It's usually his mother here and she's always very apologetic."

"Yes, but that's not getting us anywhere is it? Look, I'm sorry, I don't mean to be taking this out on you but it's very frustrating to know my child is getting regularly picked on by this child and nothing seems to be changing."

Mrs Arbuckle stood up from her seat and went out to the door; seemingly she had spotted Mrs Tanner and was telling her the situation before showing her into the classroom. To my surprise and disappointment, it was Mr Tanner who followed the teacher into the classroom.

"Right," he said, "What's the problem this time? Has her little poppet scratched his knee and is looking to blame it on my son?"

Well, we're off to a good start.

I was exhausted. I sat and listened to Mr Tanner rant to Mrs Arbuckle about how everything was 'political correctness gone mad' and how I was raising a 'soft lad' who just needed to experience the 'life of hard knocks' in order for him to really know what it was like to be bullied.

"I was bullied," he continued, "and it was the best thing that ever happened to me. It taught me that you need to stick up for yourself in this life or people will walk all over you. That's what you should be teaching that boy of yours instead of always rushing in and stopping things before it's even started."

I let every toxic, ignorant word soak into my brain and didn't react. I knew there was no point trying to point out everything wrong with his viewpoint because he thought mine was as ridiculous as I viewed his. We were never going to see eye-to-eye and I would spend the rest of the year being dragged in and out of this classroom having the same conversations. I knew what I had to do and I had to do it now.

I let Mrs Arbuckle talk about setting up yet another mediation session while I stared at Mr Tanner. I kept staring at him, even when he caught my eye; and I didn't look away when he eventually did. I kept my eyes on him as the teacher talked on about the importance of communication and I continued to stare even when she asked me questions about dates that suited. I kept on staring as we led our children out of the classroom and I waited patiently for Mrs Arbuckle to close the door behind us. Only then did I take my eyes off him and cheerily spoke to the kids: "Guys, why don't you run onto the gate while the grown-ups have a chat."

"What's your problem then?" he said, "On your period and want to have a moan?"

Clearly biology wasn't his strongest subject.

"Do you know what I do for a living, Mr Tanner?" I asked.

"No, and I don't care. What's wrong? Not getting enough chat time at the office you want to bend my ear now too?"

"I work for a Colombian drug lord."

Mr Tanner laughed, but I kept my face as straight as I could.

"I'm glad you have a sense of humour about this because I'm done laughing. Now, you see as far as the school is concerned, I have to maintain a zero-tolerance policy against my children expressing violence but as part of my job I have be a bit more… open minded, I guess that's the best way to put it.

"Have you ever heard of the café, *Joseph's*?"

"No." he said, his smug smile still plastered on his sweaty face.

"It's a front for my employer. It was once run by a Mr Joseph Escobar – yes, that Escobar family – however, he passed away suddenly due to a complications with a supplier. Nasty business, anyway, his son, Michael, now runs the place and is hell-bent on making anyone pay who has hurt the family. Grief works in strange ways and Michael's process is basically to introduce everyone that has wronged his loved ones to a Colombian necktie. Ever heard of it?"

Mr Tanner shook his head.

"Well, all I can say about it is: I wouldn't *Google* it with the kids around. Now, would you care to guess who my son's godfather is? That's right: it's Michael. Up until now I've been keeping him out of the loop on this whole situation but I'm starting to really get bored of these conversations with the teacher. There's only so much talking that people can do, you know?"

"You're having me on," he replied "There's no Colombian gang wars going on here, it would be all over the news."

"Ah, that's what they pay me for. I'm great at making problems disappear and I'm also great at protecting my children from a psychotic little asshole who is annoying him, and their caveman father.

"We can leave here today and go our separate ways, letting this play out the way it's going or I can make one phone call to Arthur's godfather and get him to teach you how to correctly parent your son. He's imaginative and emotional; it may be a bad combination for you."

"I don't have to listen to this; you're talking out of your arse."

"Am I? Do you really feel like taking that chance? You could just look me up online and see for yourself? My name is Amy Cole; you'll find plenty of pictures online of me and my Colombian friends all running a 'café'. Or you could do the right thing and make sure Stanley stays the hell away from my child, starting now. Either way, my problem goes away, it's just up to you how that happens."

I took the sunglasses from my pocket, put them on and flashed him a smile as I walked away leaving him in my wake.

Don't mess with a mother, ass-wipe; I eat shit-for-brain morons like you for breakfast.

Chapter 16

"You said what?" shouted Ben.

Against my better judgement I decided to tell Ben exactly what I had done to Mr Tanner in order to fix our Stanley problem.

"What if he phones the police?"

"And says what?"

"That he was threatened by a member of a Colombian drug cartel."

"Don't be ridiculous, he won't tell the police and so what if he does? Do you really think they're going to believe this tiny pregnant woman threatened to murder that giant thumb?"

"Thumb?"

"He looks like a giant, fucking thumb, Ben."

He raised his hands in defeat and backed away from the cursing, pregnant woman in search of the dog. Since I'd come home I had lifted the dog countless times onto the pads or into the garden, prepped with treats to tell him he'd done a good job of relieving himself where he was meant to. Six hours later and no treats had been handed out.

Despite my obvious dislike for him, he clung around me like a tiny, yappy shadow. It was making it impossible for me to walk from one end of the room to the other without tripping over him. He kept managing to position himself right under the bump so even when I tried to keep my eye out for him he would be hiding underneath it and I would need to grab the closest counter to stop me from falling over.

"This damn dog is trying to kill me," I shouted, "That's it; we're going out for dinner. If I stay in this kitchen any longer then we are going to be having a hot dog – the furry kind."

I thought this news would be greeted with more enthusiasm but, apparently, I was ruining my children's lives by taking them away from the game they were in the middle of playing. Ben wasn't exactly helpful by taking their side, but once he clocked the look on my ever-reddening face he decided to parent-up and get them into the car without me having to threaten anyone else with imaginary Colombian gangsters.

We decided to go to the town's one and only themed restaurant. What that theme was remained up for debate. Some people think it's meant to be a 1950's American diner while others think it's an aquarium but that still doesn't explain the giant astronaut statue at the entrance. The boys decided it was the perfect time to start winding each other up, which did little for my stress levels and Ben was immersed in his phone and ignoring the obvious tension in my voice as I tried to get the boys to settle down.

Why do I ever think that my children will behave when we eat out? I completely delude myself into thinking that this time they will act like people and not feral cats.

"Mum!" wailed Arthur, "Adam keeps touching me."

"No I don't," protested Adam.

"Yes, you do. You keep doing it under the table so Mum can't see you and do her horrible, shouty voice."

My what, now?

"Adam, stop touching your brother."

"I'm not touching him," he shouted, "Maybe it's that bloke there."

He started pointing at a man, eating by himself, at the table behind him. I tried to smile at him when his head whipped around to defend himself against the ridiculous accusation.

"Excuse me, I would just like to make it perfectly clear that I am in no way touching your son," he said, his voice becoming louder and more pronounced with every syllable, as if he was attempting to let the entire diner know he was innocent.

"I know," I replied, equally as loud, "They're just kids, messing around."

"Messing around? That's how lives get ruined," he continued.

"Well then you shouldn't have touched my brother," said Adam.

"Adam! Stop, *now*!" I shouted, barely able to contain my panic at how this situation was getting away from me.

Ben continued to eat his food, completely ignoring the situation at hand; as well as not responding to the obvious looks that I was shooting him.

"Ok, let's just stop this and get everyone to calm down," I continued, "Adam, stop touching your brother and accusing the nice man of doing it. Sir, let us pay for your meal and feel free to ignore us for the rest of the time here."

He didn't respond but seemed to accept my offer as he returned to his dinner, while I kicked Ben in the shin in order for him to actually react to something that was happening at the table.

"Hey!" he shouted, "What was that for?"

"I was just checking to see if you were capable of having any type of response instead of just eating your dinner and ignoring the carnage."

"What? I knew you had it under control, besides I think if I intervened I would have made the situation worse. I'd say the wrong thing and probably end up getting decked but I was semi-confident he wasn't going to hit a pregnant woman."

"Semi-confident? How comforting," I said.

The rest of the meal was done so in silence and anytime the children attempted to start messing around with each other they were treated with one of my special 'I will kill you' looks that are normally reserved for Ben.

121

We returned to the house to find that Colin had managed to pee in nine separate locations in the kitchen – none of which were on the training pads.

"How? How are you doing this? You're tiny! Your bladder seriously couldn't hold that much liquid," I asked.

He didn't reply. Instead, he fell onto his back, on the floor, as he slipped in his own urine.

Nice.

I gently lifted him into the sink and ran him under the water while he whined and struggled to get away.

"Amy, why are you running the dog under the tap?" asked Ben.

"I'm washing him."

He came over with a towel and took the struggling puppy off me, with a smile.

"I appreciate the bonding you're trying to experience here but how about I just take care of the bathing – just to take one less thing off your plate."

"I know you're being condescending here but the less I have to do with this bloody dog the better."

I left him to caring for the animal while I decided to sit down on the sofa to try and ignore the growing headache I was experiencing. Another rubbish thing about pregnancy: I got to take none of the good drugs for headaches and flus.

I can't catch a break.

I am a firm believer in western medicine. I do not buy into the fact that you need to just carry on and do without when you feel rubbish. Why on earth would I continue to feel horrible when I didn't need to?

I don't remember falling asleep on the sofa, but it wasn't unusual for me at this stage. I could fall asleep anywhere but bed and not at bedtime. Pregnancy insomnia had kicked in much earlier than in my previous pregnancies, but then again I was sporting a bump much larger than before, so it was proving more difficult to find any position remotely comfortable. This, matched with my nightly craving of cheese on toast at 3 a.m., meant that I was happy to fall asleep anywhere and at any time when I possibly could.

When I woke up, completely disorientated and unsure as to what day it was never mind what time, I found Ben sitting on the floor playing with the puppy.

"Where are the kids?" I asked.

"They've been in bed for ages; I just thought it was better to let you rest."

"Thank you, I really needed that nap. I was hoping it would kick this headache to the curb but it's still pretty brutal. Can you get me a drink?"

My dutiful little manservant reappeared shortly with some orange juice, but as soon as the liquid hit my tongue I spat it out.

"What's wrong?" he asked, panicked, "Is it the baby?"

"Yes, Ben, the baby took control of my mouth and spat it out because there was pulp in it."

"Can he really do that?"

I tried not to let the complete horror of my husband's lack of medical knowledge, even after two successful pregnancies, show on my face. I failed miserably.

"Ok, ok, I know you were being sarcastic; so was I," he said.

I let out a laugh and sat up from the awkward sleeping position I had adopted in my nap.

"Taste the juice; does it taste funny to you?" I asked.

"I don't normally volunteer to taste things after they've been spat out."

"Just taste it, I want to know if my taste buds are changing, like some other weird pregnancy symptom, or it's just a bit off."

He reluctantly took the glass from my hand and sniffed the drink suspiciously. He eventually took a small sip and said: "Tastes fine to me."

"You can have it; it must be something to do with the headache. I'm going to bed; I don't want to hear that dog anymore."

I grumpily left Ben with his new favourite thing and I trudged up to bed in a bad mood. I tried to think of the last time I was even in a good mood. I knew that there were so many people who would love to be in the position I was in now but it didn't make me feel any better.

Now, I just had to add wonky taste buds onto the list of pregnancy ailments along with insomnia, weight gain, unpredictable hormones, tiredness, nausea and dehydration, due to a ridiculous amount of crying, and dog ownership.

Ok, ok I can't blame the baby on the dog but I feel like it's all connected.

The headache woke me a few hours later and I knew there was no point in trying to get back to sleep so I decided to take myself back down to the sofa in order to recreate the successful nap position from earlier. I must have been lying awkwardly because the right side of my face was tingling with pins and needles right into half of my tongue.

It was an odd sensation, not unpleasant but certainly not normal. In fact, nothing felt relatively normal. I tried to stretch my face to see if it would stop the tingling feeling but something wasn't right. I went out to the hallway and studied my face in the mirror hanging beside the door.

My right eye and the right side of my mouth looked lower. I tried to smile but only one side of my mouth responded.

Oh fuck. I'm having a stroke. I've had a stroke? Is this an on-going thing? What do I do? There's an anagram something like 'QUICK' isn't it? Quickly Understand I'm Clinically Killed? That doesn't sound right… oh fuck, what do I do?

"Ben!" I called, the word sounding slurred as I tried not to panic. He came running to the top of the stairs, looking like he wasn't completely awake but terrified at the same time.

"What's wrong? Are you in labour? It's too soon!"

He tried to rush down the stairs but ended up sliding down the majority and landing at my feet.

"Now I don't want to panic you," I began, "but you need to phone an ambulance because I think I'm having a stroke."

Chapter 17

As I tried to get the information out of my mouth, I was drooling and Ben's terrified expression did little to help calm my spiralling mental state.

"You're having a *what*?" he screamed.

"You're not, not panicking."

"You're having a what?" he repeated in an attempt at nonchalance, which sounded more like a drunken person, "I have to get you to the hospital, remember the advice they say: FAST; Face, Arms, Speech, Time."

Ah, that makes much more sense.

Ben decided, in his panicked state, to bang on the door of our next-door neighbour, Mrs White. She was able to sit with the children, while he drove me to hospital instead of waiting for an ambulance. She did an equally poor impression of a non-panicked person, but was significantly better than Ben.

He spent the entire car journey trying not to cry while I looked in the mirror and attempted to move my face. I was just happy that I was taking the whole situation in my stride; I assumed I would have been a lot more concerned but every time I thought about the baby my heart rate increased.

Nope, don't think about that, everything is fine, everything will be fine.

It was all I kept saying to myself, over and over again, as Ben abandoned the car outside of the Accident and Emergency department and marched me through the doors shouting for help. Within seconds there were several nurses gathered around me asking about contractions and dilation. I couldn't make my mouth behave long enough to explain the actual problem before they had me on a trolley and were rushing down a hallway to examine me.

There's not a hope in hell I'm being put through an internal examination just because Ben is too busy sobbing to explain that I'm not in labour. Where the hell is he?

The more they were trying to get me to lie down and settle the more I struggled to sit up and be heard. Eventually I pulled the right side of my mouth up and shouted as loudly as I could:

"I'm not in labour, I'm having a *stroke*."

Funnily enough, this didn't help with the panic around me. There was more rushing and pointless phrases shouted at me, in a futile attempt to keep me calm. I was pushed down a different corridor and managed to spot Ben wandering down a different direction.

"Ben!" I shouted, "Get the hell over here."

The drool from my mouth was becoming unbearable and I just wanted everyone to stand still for three seconds so I could get my bearings. Eventually I was taken behind a curtain while a doctor was rushed into the same place and brought up to speed. Thankfully, she was much better at the calming voice routine than anyone else had been, so far.

She examined me quickly and ordered some tests I couldn't pronounce but turned to me with a smile and said:

"Mrs Cole, I'm confident that you're not having a stroke."

"But look at her face," said Ben.

Thanks, hubby, always the charmer

"I've ordered some blood tests and we can do an MRI to be on the safe side but from examining you I believe you have Bell's palsy."

"Am I going to die?" I asked, deadly serious, although the doctor seemed amused by this question.

"No, you're not going to die. This isn't an uncommon occurrence for pregnant women and can be treated with steroids and physiotherapy."

Ok, let's add: having a stroke that's not a stroke to the list of pregnancy ailments.

"Physiotherapy is completely safe and the use of steroids is highly effective but I'll leave that option up to you because some mothers get a bit nervous about taking medications during gestation."

I took a look at my drooping face in the reflective surface over the counter.

"Give me the drugs," I said.

It took a few hours of hanging around in the hospital to get the precautionary MRI and prescription of steroids before I was allowed to go home. Ben's eyes were puffy from all his crying and I was exhausted and miserable.

"When we get home, I'll get you rested on the sofa and phone in sick. We can do all the research about what this is and get ahead of the game."

What does that even mean? How can you get ahead of this? I'm already deformed.

I couldn't be bothered to verbalise any of this to him, it required holding my mouth up and I wasn't in form for his relentless positivity that he normally does in tough situations. I would find his upbeat attitude more convincing had I not just spent the last few hours comforting him as he cried.

By the time we got home the kids were already at school, and I knew it wouldn't be long before my parents called around. There's nothing they loved better than a good medical condition. The weirder the better. I was lying on the sofa trying to keep my eyes closed, because the headache wasn't going anywhere. The daylight streaming through the windows was making things worse and Ben was not helping matters.

I could hear his fingers furiously tapping on the computer keyboard beside me, followed by gasping and intermittent sobbing.

What now?

"It's ok; everything is going to be fine. Just before I tell you any of this, know that I love you," he began.

Well if that wasn't a sentence to strike the fear of God into a person then I don't know what is.

"Apparently it's from birth," he said.

That doesn't sound right.

"It says here that it's a 'non-progressive but ever-changing condition' and it's 'caused by damage or abnormal development to parts of the brain responsible for controlling muscles and movement'"

I eyed him suspiciously because none of his findings sounded quite like anything that the doctor had described. He started to cry again and continued: "There's brain surgery treatment but don't worry it says here it's minimally invasive."

I've heard that's the optimal kind of surgery one wants on the brain.

I'd had enough of Ben's research and grabbed the laptop off him to read for myself. He had been researching: cerebral palsy.

"It's *Bell's* palsy, Ben, *Bell's*," I said as I thumped the laptop back in his lap and lay back down. After a few minutes he sounded a lot brighter when he finished his new internet search.

"This isn't a big deal at all," he said, smiling.

I scowled at him with my one good eye making him immediately backtrack on the positivity.

"I mean, of course it's a big deal, but it's not brain surgery so that's good, isn't it?"

For the love of all that is holy, please, someone shut this man up.

He was eventually saved by the bell – the doorbell – which heralded the arrival of my parents.

Eloise Galbraith wasn't what you would describe as 'naturally maternal' but there was something comforting about having your mum near you when you're feeling poorly. That was until she started speaking.

"What's wrong with you? You look exactly the same as usual, Ben said you were disfigured or something," said Mum.

"She has temporary paralysis on one side of her face," explained Ben.

"Which side?"

"The one that's fucking drooping!" I exclaimed.

"There's no need to get yourself worked up, I don't have my glasses on. Now that I do, I can see the difference. Yes, you really do look wretched."

Did she think that reaction sounded better?

"My poor baby," said Dad, as he sat down on the sofa next to me, "You're still beautiful, even if you're all pregnancy fat and drooling."

Kill me, now.

"My friend, Kevin, he had a stroke and he still had a very fulfilling life right up until the end... well, anyway that's nothing to worry about you're young and you'll get your figure back after the baby comes," he continued.

Sometimes I feel like my father tends to get lost in his own train of thought. I predicted that by the end of the visit he will have assumed he was here to make me feel better about pregnancy weight and nothing to do with the fact that I could no longer move half of my face.

"I've read lots of things on the internet about strokes and what causes them," he added.

"She hasn't had a stroke," interrupted Ben.

"I think you should get a second opinion before you start saying that for definite. Now, in one of my favourite channels there's a very interesting documentary about how pollen causes strokes in women under forty."

What he calls a 'documentary' other people call 'nonsensical conspiracy theory videos'. I said nothing, in part because it wasn't worth the effort but mostly because I thought if I stayed quiet they would leave quicker. I was wrong.

Mum delighted in moving my mouth up and down and pinching various parts of it to see if I could feel it. Ben eventually stopped her when I faked sleep, in the hope that they would take the hint and go away. Instead I lay back and listened to them talk about me, which was never going to be a good idea.

"She's under too much stress, that's what's caused this," said Mum, "With all that drama Elle brings and Amy's brain being a bit *different*, it was bound to manifest in some way."

I tried not to react at the way she phrased 'different' but one of these days I was determined to sit down with my mother and actually teach her about the complex nature of mental health so she would stop saying shitty, damaging things like that. I could take it, I was her daughter and after thirty-odd years I knew how to rise above it but I shuddered at the thought of her saying it to someone vulnerable.

"She needs to be on bed rest for the remainder of this pregnancy," said Dad, "the Tudor's used to do it all the time."

"The Tudor's? Like Henry VIII and all that?" asked Ben.

"No, like Lorraine Tudor, from up the road. She's had six kids and swears that by spending the last two weeks in bed she was mentally prepared for the baby. I would listen to her, Ben, she never had a stroke."

"She didn't have a stroke," Ben stressed, futilely.

"Come on, James, let them be; we have gardening club anyway and I don't want to be late or Deirdre will steal all the good trowels."

After I heard the door close I felt instantly more relaxed and Ben threw himself down on the sofa beside me, once more.

"I know you were only pretending to be asleep that whole time," he said.

"I'm sorry, but you had things under control. I assume you filled Elle in as to why I wouldn't be in the office today? I feel like we spend more time operating from each other's houses than being in the actual office. Maybe it's time to just close up shop and go mobile, doesn't seem like much point staying there now with..."

I let the sentence trail off without finishing it. We both knew what I meant but I didn't feel like saying it out loud and he didn't need me to, in order to know exactly how I was feeling.

"All you have to do now is rest, Elle is manning the office and will be over later to make you laugh," he said.

"I can't laugh with my banjaxed face; I'll just accidentally spit on people."

"Well then, you'll be the cutest spitter in all the land," he replied, kissing my nose and retreating to the kitchen to make food.

I wasn't entirely sure how I was going to eat without half of it dropping out the side of my mouth and decided that soup would be my safest option until I could figure out a way to comfortably chew, without ending up with more of it on my clothes than in my stomach.

I spent the day in and out of sleep and attempting to relax. By the time the kids came home I had mentally prepared myself for whatever brutally honest thing they would come out with about my appearance, but neither of them really seemed to notice.

Should I be offended or thankful for this?

Elle and her family all called to the house after teatime with flowers and a hamper of goodies for me. I was excited by this, until I realised it was all vegan health food stuff from River's company.

"That's... thoughtful," I said.

"I told you she'd hate it," laughed Elle. "Let's take a look at you then."

She kneeled down beside the sofa and studied my face.

"I thought it was men that start sprouting random hair from their nose when they hit old age?" she asked.

I pushed her back to the floor and onto her bum as she laughed at her own joke.

"You've seen better days, princess, but it's only temporary. Good job I'm the face of the company isn't it?"

I sipped water with a straw but still managed to dribble like a baby, while Elle enjoyed mothering me and catching me up on her plans for the business.

"Now, I've had a chat with Benny and you're starting your maternity leave now," she said, firmly, "It's only a few weeks early and I've already got someone in to help me."

This information shocked me. I was off for one day and I had already been replaced by some skinny, capable business guru.

"Is she skinny?" I asked.

"What the fuck does that matter?"

"It doesn't, I just want to make myself more miserable with knowing that my replacement is younger and prettier than me."

"Ok, one: skinny doesn't equal pretty and two: she can move her face and answer the telephone without drooling – other than that she doesn't have a scratch on you. This is temporary and you need to get better before little Elle Junior arrives."

"You know it's a boy," I smiled.

"You don't know that, I have faith that this is a little queen in the making. An awesome, high-powered business woman; who takes no crap and gets things done. *That* kind of queen, not a fairy tale one."

"At this point, it's hard to believe he's anything but the antichrist."

As the kids played together and River explained all the health benefits of each of the products in his hamper to a bemused Ben, Elle and I talked through names for the bump. I refused to agree to Elle but I did promise not to call him Beelzebub.

"What about 'Lole'?" she suggested.

"Lole Cole? Why do you hate my child?"

"I just think you can't go wrong with rhyming names."

"You're wrong and ridiculous. I was thinking along the lines of Richard or Robert."

"You do realise they'll get called either 'Dick' or 'Bob', don't you? Now who hates this kid?"

"It's impossible, I don't trust my instincts or tastes in anything while I'm pregnant. I shouldn't make any irreversible decisions while I'm creating life. When I was pregnant with Adam I convinced Ben to let me cover the nursery in tiger print. It was everywhere, Elle."

I shuddered at the memory and how I cried and shouted at Ben after the baby was born for going along with that terrible idea. Of course, if he hadn't he would have been cried and shouted at for treating me like an invalid, incapable of making decisions. He couldn't win.

"I don't remember much about being pregnant with those two," Elle recalled, "I remember I couldn't stand the smell of Keith. Just like his natural musk and he would have to constantly shower if he wanted to sit in the same room as me. It really is such a magical time."

We laughed and Elle laughed harder once she looked at how only one half of my mouth was able to move with emotion.

"Your face looks like you got botched Botox."

"You know it's bad karma to laugh at the sick," I said, lisping on my 's' sounds.

My new speech impediment did little to stop her from laughing, but she had significantly improved my mood since she had gotten here so I let it slide.

"Who is my replacement then?" I asked.

"You know her actually," replied Elle, cryptically.

Oh God, Rita? Mrs Clunting? My mother?

"Don't look so worried," she continued, "It's Sylvia."

I had absolutely no idea who this person was, however, that wasn't exactly unusual for me – with or without baby brain.

"Don't look at me like that, you know: Sylvia."

"Saying it again doesn't make me remember her any better," I explained.

"Oh for goodness sake, your memory is getting worse! She was the teacher from the pole dancing club."

"The woman who was trying to recruit me as a sex worker?" I asked.

"The very same."

"And this qualifies her as a suitable replacement for me how, exactly?"

"Like I said earlier: she can move her face and answer queries; and for now that's all I need help with. I have everything else under control and if it doesn't work out I'll find someone else," she said with a shrug.

"What's in for you?"

"What do you mean?"

"Why choose her instead of someone from a temp agency? I know you, Elle, so what's in it for you?"

"Well...she did throw in some free pole lessons to sweeten the deal," she said, sheepishly.

"I knew it. So what happens when she turns our office into a sex dungeon for fetish weirdoes to get their jollies off?"

"You really do just jump to the worst-case scenario don't you? For all you know that fetish stuff is a legitimate side-hustle strategy to earn extra money to put herself through medical school."

"Is it?"

"No, it turns out she just really likes performing for strangers over the internet, but you felt bad for jumping to conclusions nonetheless. I made an executive decision and I've gone with Sylvia so just get the bed rest, pop out that baby and hurry up and get back to work if you're so worried."

"What happens when you go to Canada then? I get stuck with her?"

"We haven't made a decision about that yet."

"Please, take your time, it's not like it will have a massive impact on my life or anything."

"River, girls, it's time to go, aunty Amy needs a nap before she turns into any more of a raving bitch."

135

Before I had the chance to defend myself, the whole family departed out of the room, while I was left with my droopy mouth hanging open in disbelief. Ben came back from shutting the front door with a sympathetic smile on his face.

"I was under the impression that people were actually meant to be nice to the sick but all my closest friends and family have done is insult and irritate me," I said.

"Where does she get off saying that to me? I'm the one that has held this whole business together and kept us growing without so much as a 'thank you' and now she can't wait to get rid of me with some…some… floozy."

"Sweety?" interjected Ben, "You need to calm down with the shouting, you're spitting on me and the children – or at least limit the words with 's' in it.

"Elle is just trying to get help in quickly and this Sylvia person was probably the only one available; and I know that it's an emotional time for you but please don't call employees 'floozy' – that's how law suits happen."

I sulked for the rest of the evening and refused to come up to bed. I reasoned that I would end up waking up and having to come down to the sofa anyway so I was just cutting out the journey at 3 a.m. He didn't push me to reconsider, I guessed he needed the break from the miserable woman he was married to and I couldn't blame him.

I didn't want to be on maternity leave early, I didn't want more time to relax before the baby arrived. The more time I had on my hands the more likely I was to dwell on the grief of losing Joseph and I really couldn't handle that. I would also have to spend exponentially more time with that ridiculous-looking dog also.

Why does everything have to be so complicated? Why can't we all, for once, just plod along nicely without any disasters or drama?

I knew it was pointless to think this way and that it was completely impossible to sterilize yourself from life, but it would be nice. I felt the baby kick and I instinctively rubbed the spot in which he nudged.

"You're a trouble-maker, so you'd better be extra cute to make up for it," I said, "I'm talking symmetrical face, dimples, curly hair – the whole shebang or I'm bringing you back to the hospital with a receipt."

He kicked again and I took that to mean we had a deal. Half my face wouldn't move, my headache was still there, I now had a fetching speech impediment, I couldn't remember the last time I saw my toes, I had a sex worker taking over my job, I lost the man I loved as dearly as a father and my best friend was probably leaving the country for life but at least my son would have dimples.

That makes everything alright, doesn't it? No, I don't think it does.

I was drifting off to sleep with the worries of the world on my shoulders and I didn't know how on earth I was going to get through them all. I wished for some kind of cosmic intervention that would sort out all my troubles but instead I felt pressure in my tummy and as I stood up I felt the warm trickle of my waters come down my leg.

It's too soon, no this can't be happening, it's too soon.

Chapter 18

For the second night in a row, Mrs White was awoken by my husband to come and sit with our children while we made a high-speed journey to the hospital. Ben tried his best not to spend this time in tears but I could tell he was worried.

The baby was early, and I wasn't sure what that would mean. My stomach felt tense but it didn't feel like the pain of contractions. Everything felt unfamiliar. I felt like a stranger in my own body and there was nothing I could do to stop it.

We were greeted at the maternity ward by a smiling midwife called Marcella who took us into a side ward to get checked over.

"It's ok, you're here now and we are going to take a look and see what's going on," she explained, "You did the right thing coming in, you don't need to be upset; we are going to get things sorted."

I didn't realise that there were tears coming until I felt my cheeks with my hand and then realised that I wasn't actually crying.

"I'm not upset," I said, "it's all part of the Bell's palsy. I don't really have much control of the right side of the face so it'll be streaming like that without me even noticing. I can't say the same for my husband though."

We both looked towards Ben who was moments from tears but opted to give a thumb up in our direction and excuse himself for the bathroom.

Marcella gave him a kind smile and explained that she was going to test the liquid to see if it was my waters and see how things looked with the ultrasound.

I wasn't sure why they needed to test the liquid to check if it was the waters, it's not like I was producing tea but instead of asking questions I just got on with things.

"Well, baby looks very contented in there and is a great size," she said.

Yes, yes I make ginormous babies.

"I will be back once I check this liquid and we'll see about getting some steroids into you in case baby is deciding to make an early entrance and will need some help with the lungs."

The cold strike of fear hit my spine and the enormity of the situation began to hit me. I was going to have this baby and things may not be ok. The worst-case scenarios started to come thick and fast and I could feel the panic take hold. Ben reappeared in the room, with puffy eyes, and pretended he was completely fine with the situation. He took one look at my face knew that I was scared.

"What if — " I began.

"No, we aren't playing the 'what if' game. We are going to wait here and talk about something non-baby related and get the answers. We aren't going to panic."

The fake reassurance in his voice was comforting, but neither of us could hold a conversation as we waited; instead we were both lost in our own thoughts of fear.

I don't know how long Marcella was gone, but when she returned she was smiling.

She has a nice smile.

"Now, panic over," she said.

"What do you mean?" asked Ben.

"It wasn't your waters; you're still doing a great job keeping that baby safe and snug for a while longer."

"I don't understand, I felt them go; I'm not making this up," I said, becoming more agitated by the second.

Stop smiling at me, I hate that smile.

"The thing is: it wasn't your waters, it was urine," she said, matter-of-factly.

Holy sweet mother of God, I've wet myself.

"Come again?" said Ben.

"It's nothing to be embarrassed about; it's nothing we haven't seen before. Pregnancy is a beautiful time but not without its discomforts," soothed Marcella.

"Discomforts?" I interrupted, "DISCOMFORTS? So far in this hellish nine months I have vomited my entire body weight and yet put on two stone, I can't sleep because I can't get comfortable, I can't rest because I have two children and a business to run, I can't relax because every time I sit down I get fucking heartburn, I have lost control of the right side of my face to the point where I cry and drool at any given moment and I'm too afraid to take the recommended treatment in case I mess up the baby and now you're telling me that I should expect to wee myself when I stand up?"

I wasn't sure how much of it she understood with my slurred speech but she definitely sensed the tone of the rant and smiled.

"It's our burden and our privilege to bring life into the world. No one said it was going to be easy, if it were, God would have made the men do it."

She left to update my notes and I got myself ready to go home.

"We'll be back in time for breakfast and let Mrs White go home," said Ben, in a foolish attempt to cheer me up.

I didn't bother to reply, I just looked out the window for the rest of the drive home and went straight up to bed to try and sleep. I was tempted to text Elle and tell her about the fake labour but she was probably going to be too busy to reply.

I lay on the bed and decided to keep the curtains closed in the hope that I would be able to get some sleep but I knew it was pointless. I heard Ben and the kids leave for the day

followed by the whine of Colin as he realised he was left
alone in the kitchen.

Damn dog.

The whining continued until, eventually, I felt guilty enough
to go downstairs and let him out of the room.

"Why isn't everyone as enthusiastic about seeing me as you
are?" I asked, "Probably because you haven't figured out I'm
a miserable wretch to be around. Don't worry, you'll find out
soon enough. Come on then."

I waddled down the hall into the living room as he excitedly
galloped beside me, stopping every so often to nibble on my
toes and bark at my feet.

"Foot fetish, eh? No judgements here, pal, just stay away
from the kids' toes or they'll start to hate you."

He was too small to get on the sofa and spent quite a while
trying to jump up to be beside me. He even started to take
running leaps in an attempt to reach his goal. They made it
much worse and he mostly ended up face-planting into the
sofa. I knew I shouldn't, but I lifted him up beside me because
I felt bad and respected his effort.

He clawed his way up on top of my bump and was trying to
chew on the end of my nose.

"You can't get that close to my face, just sit beside me."

He didn't listen, of course, and every time I sat him down
on the cushion next to me he would climb up onto my chest
until I finally gave up. He did a few rotations and finally
settled down on my collarbone, his nose nuzzled in under my
chin and fell asleep. I knew this was a ridiculous thing to
allow but the feeling of his little breath at my neck reminded
me of when the children were new born and they wouldn't
settle anywhere but on top of me.

I read all the books and listened to the well-meaning
advisors about how you shouldn't 'spoil' the baby by letting
them sleep there but I didn't give a damn. They could stay
there for as long as they wanted. I tried not to move too much
so I wouldn't disturb his sleep, but I couldn't reach the remote

or my phone from where I was sitting. I didn't like the thought of being alone with my thoughts so I decided to start speaking to him in the hope he would wake up and move and I wouldn't have to feel guilty.

"I wouldn't get too comfortable there, Colin," I announced, "That spot is reserved for the troublesome child I'm carrying."

His head popped up and he gave my cheek a lick before assuming his sleeping position and closed his eyes once more.

"I see I have another male in my life that refuses to listen and cooperate," I continued, "It's fine, I'm used to it now. I'm used to disappointment all round, actually.

"You wouldn't think of it to look at me but I used to be happy once. I think."

He didn't move this time so instead I just kept talking.

"My voice doesn't normally sound like this, and you picked a good side to lie on or you would be getting drenched right now.

"No, I did use to be happy and I'll be happy again, just as soon as the universe stops its usual cosmic fuckery in every aspect of my life – I'm expecting that to happen any day now. It's been on a bit of a streak for a little while. It's already taken my face, my figure, my friend and it has plans to get rid of my favourite person by sending her to the other side of the world.

"I told you it was on a roll."

The baby rolled and I could see the outline of a limb protrude from my stomach. It had the unique ability to make me smile and want to vomit at the same time.

"I'm looking forward to meeting you, though," I continued, rubbing my hand over the bump, "I'm looking forward to a lot of things actually, like: caffeine and blue cheese dip but also meeting you."

I laughed at my own lame joke and realised that I was actually enjoying my make-shift therapy session with my sleeping dog and bump.

I sat in that position and told them about how I first tumbled into Joseph's café and his life, closely followed by Elle.

"I found my voice in that café," I said, "I never knew I had the strength, the capabilities and the drive to achieve everything I have done over the last few years until I fell through his doors and we became family.

"He was a good man and I'm sorry you won't get to meet him but I promise that I will talk about him and tell you all about him. I don't believe in heaven but if there was one, he would be there.

"I think an afterlife is created by the people left behind who keep talking about those we lost.

"He will forever be in heaven because everyone that loved him will keep talking about what a wonderful person he was. As long as we keep his memory and his legacy alive, then he'll never really be gone.

"That's all I can do for him. It's not a fraction of what he did for Elle and me, but I'll keep trying to be the woman he saw in me, when I couldn't see it in myself."

I was crying as I finished my sentence, real tears not Bell's palsy leakage, and I realised it felt like a huge relief to say all those things about my friend out loud. It was like my own private eulogy that I never got to say at his funeral. After a few minutes, the tears eventually subsided and I began to think about the possibility of life here without Elle.

"I don't like to think about this," I admitted, "It's taken all my strength not to think about it for too long or else I get angry or sad. I suppose now is as good a time as any to just figure out a plan.

"Worst-case scenario: she goes to Canada and our business partnership is dissolved. Is that what I'm worried about though? I can always hire a replacement, someone who can sit still for longer than five minutes at a time and actually gets the work done. No, it wouldn't be the same but let's not lie and say it's because of the business. Get real, Amy.

"I'm scared that if she leaves I will go back to being the scared, anxious, miserable woman I was before I met her. She makes me believe in myself, she makes me fearless, she gives me headaches and drama but also excitement and laughter.

"I love my life with her in it and without her what do I have? I go back to being the mother and the wife, not the fun best friend who has adventures and stories. I don't want to go back to that, not now."

Saying it out loud was scaring me. I didn't like to hear the honesty and the selfishness of my needs. I had a wonderful family, a flourishing career and a new baby on the way. Elle had her own adventure to go on and a decent friend would help her, not guilt her into staying because she was scared of her life being boring.

"Dick move, Amy."

I hated admitting that I was the villain in my own story but I was acting like it. If the situation was reversed I knew she would be excited for me, she would help and probably offer to tag along.

"I have to make this right," I said, sitting up and forgetting the dog was sitting on top of me. I looked on in horror as he tumbled from my chest right down to the floor.

"Colin! I'm so sorry; you're not a bad lad."

I cradled him in my arms and sat him gently down on the training pad, on which he promptly relieved himself.

"See? *See*, Colin? That's it, that's the universe changing the tide, the streak is over. Now, come on and get your bum into your bag and we'll go track down Elle and see if Sylvia has convinced her to put on a webcam sex show yet."

I was going to fix this, I was going to do right by Elle and make sure that everything that we had created would not be lost just because she may, or may not, be leaving. We three (and Michael, if I was feeling generous) had created a safe place for people – as well as Elle and I helping other small businesses reach their potential. Just because I was afraid of losing both of them didn't mean I was suddenly going to stop being the woman I'd worked so hard to become.

They were there to start me on my journey but it was me that sat through the therapy, it was me that ran the business solo and supported Elle, it was me that pulled myself up time after time when all I wanted to do was hide away in my bed. I was stronger and braver than I ever gave myself credit for and just because fear was trying to make me believe it now, doesn't mean I was going to.

Fear is a damn liar.

I was Amy fucking Cole and I was in control of my own destiny, not Elle, not Joseph and not my family.

I've got this.

Chapter 19

I felt a whole new sense of purpose. I felt capable and in control for the first time in months, I walked with energy. There was no more waddling with my head down, instead, I pushed my shoulders back and raised my head up.

You haven't come this far to walk like you've got the weight of the world on your shoulders. You look like a gorgeous, fertility, goddess – droopy face and all – and people should know it.

I tried not to laugh at my own ridiculous pep-talk but it really did help my stride. As I looked around, the world seemed less grey and daunting than it had done yesterday. The weather was still rubbish weather and it was freezing, but thanks to my little hot water bottle bump I was toasty and walking full steam ahead.

It didn't take long for me to become out of breath but I kept that smile plastered on my face and kept walking towards the café, ready to impart my new positive mental attitude to all that I met.

Stomach cramps had been building up throughout the last few hours but I decided to keep ignoring them because that's what someone with a positive outlook on life would do, wouldn't they?

I must have been worrying people because the wider I smiled at strangers as they walked past me, the more nervous they looked. By the time I reached the café my jaws ached and I had a stitch in my side. I leaned up against the nearest table in order to catch my breath and within seconds Barbara was there, looking concerned.

"Amy, what's wrong? Is it the baby?" she asked.

"No, no, I'm just woefully unfit. Can you get me some water?"

"Of course, take a seat."

I pulled out the closest chair and sat down, happily, as I waited for my breathing to slow down. I had wrapped half my face up in a scarf and was sporting sunglasses to avoid stares from people.

No wonder people were looking at you like that, they couldn't even see your smile just some strange woman bopping along who looked like she was trying to hide a dodgy facelift. Maybe they thought you were a celebrity going incognito? Yes, that sounds much better let's go with that.

"How are you feeling, Amy? I hear you were ill – actually I thought you were meant to be on bed rest?" said Barbara.

"I'm fine; it's just a quick visit to see how things are going with my replacement."

"Oh, they're not here. They left for a client meeting over an hour ago, they should be back soon though," she explained.

Fuck

"That's ok; I'm here now I might as well stay a bit. I feel like I owe you an apology too, while I'm YEEOW!"

A sharp pain ripped through my stomach and I gripped the edge of the table.

"Amy?" Barbara rushed to my side, her hand on my back while her eyes searched my face to see if she could figure out what was wrong.

"It's nothing, I just got a *mother fudging fuck*!" I screamed, "Oh, fucking hell I think I'm in labour."

"You *think* you're in labour? Right, ok, let's just keep calm and I'll get your phone to call your husband. What's his name?"

"Ben, he won't answer. Just text him and tell him to meet me at the hospital – if I make it that far."

147

Another pain hit and it was even more intense than the last, followed by the sudden, and familiar, urge to push that came with my previous labours.

"You've got to phone an ambulance, I don't have my car with me and I really don't want to give birth on the café floor," I pleaded.

Colin had escaped the bag and was nipping at my ankles to be picked up. He dashed away when I first started to yell in pain and was currently trying to steal affection from a customer.

"Can you make it to the sofa, it might be a bit more comfortable?" she asked.

"No, just get me to the bathrooms and I'll wait there until the ambulance."

She helped me to my feet just as another contraction took hold.

They're coming so quickly, I'll never make it to the hospital.

I had visions of me slumping to the floor and delivering this child here and now. We heard the bell of the front door chime followed by the familiar sound of Elle's laugh.

"Amy? What are you doing here? Are you ok?" she asked.

I turned to face her and she realised that everything was not ok.

She looked at Barbara and said: "Have you phoned the ambulance yet?"

"No, she needed help to the bathroom first."

"Right, Sylvia get on the phone and get the ambulance here pronto. She's meant to be having a section, it's too dangerous for a natural birth, we need help.

"Princess, you're coming with me, Barbara get some towels or something just in case this baby turns out to be as impatient as his mother."

She led me into the bathroom and closed the door. She threw her coat on the floor and helped take mine off so I could lie on both of them.

"Amy, I'm going to have to check if there's something happening so you'd better get comfortable with me seeing your bits," she explained.

"I can feel another contraction coming, Elle, I really need to push,"

"It's ok spread your legs, we're going to pop off your drawers to see what we are dealing with and the ambulance will be here in no time. You've got this all under control, babe."

I lay my head back on the floor and rested as the pain subsided for a bit.

Keep your energy in between the pain, you're going to need it, it's nearly time to push.

The labour for both my children had been long and drawn out, before having to go for emergency c-sections. It had never crossed my mind that this child would be any different but, then again, nothing about this pregnancy had been expected.

"Can you see anything?" I asked.

"I'm not entirely sure what I'm meant to be looking for, other than trying to look through this national park you're sporting."

"Can we not talk about my waxing please? Do I look dilated? Elle I really need to start pushing, the pain is started again and the pressure is unbearable."

"Women have been doing this for thousands of years so if you're body is telling you to push then give it a whirl."

Give it a whirl? Is she kidding me?

I managed to get into a sitting position and gripped my knees. I dug my chin into my chest and pushed into my bottom as hard as I could. It was working, I could feel the shift of pressure and I started to work with the pain of the contractions.

I can do this.

"Amy?" said Elle, "Amy, you need to stop pushing."

I couldn't stop if I wanted to; my body was following the natural flow of this beautiful experience. Sure, I never expected to give birth on the bathroom floor but there was something really primal and natural about doing it away from the clinical nature of a hospital.

"Amy! Stop pushing, we have to get you standing."

"What are you talking about? I can't stand I'm trying to deliver this baby."

I pushed away her hands as I felt the need for another push and as I did, I felt the sweet release of the completed delivery.

I cried and laughed and felt one hundred different emotions all at the same time.

Why isn't he crying? Why is Elle looking so strange?

"Elle? What's wrong? Hand me the baby."

She bent down and wrapped the quiet parcel in the towel and handed it to me.

"Congratulations, princess, you're the proud mother of rather large turd. I'd guess: two pounds, three ounces? What do you think?"

I screamed and threw the towel across the room watching faeces roll out of the towel.

Elle sat down on the floor beside me and there we remained, in a stunned silence, for a few seconds.

"We tell no one about this," I finally said.

"Suits me, I don't want to be known as the woman who delivered a poo. You have actually given birth before haven't you? You know the difference between labour and bowel movements?"

"Apparently not."

What the actual hell is wrong with me?

"Right, let's get you off the floor and home. I would like a rather large gin and tonic and a very long shower to forget this experience," she said.

"What are we going to tell Barbara and Sylvia? They've already phoned the ambulance."

Elle laughed at my panicked expression and shoved her head out the door to shout for them to cancel the ambulance – as nonchalantly as one would cancel a food order.

"You promise never to tell anyone what happened in this room?" I asked

"I promise," she said, laughing.

Why don't I believe her?

"Aren't you going to hold your baby?" she asked, "You really should do some skin-to-skin time with him."

"Shut up, Elle."

"Are you feeding him yourself? It's better for his development."

"I said: shut up, Elle."

"Have you thought of any names? I think he looks like a 'Keith' to me."

We both started to laugh as I wrapped my hand in toilet roll and gingerly picked up the 'baby' to dispose of it down the toilet.

"Ah they grow up so fast," she continued, "One minute you're pushing them out and the next they're making their own way in life. God speed, little one, enjoy your trip."

I flushed the toilet and washed my hands for longer than I've ever done in my life.

"You're never going to let me live this down, are you?" I asked, already knowing the answer.

"Are you serious? Amy, you just shit into my hands, you're hearing about this until my dying day."

Chapter 20

It was the day we'd been waiting for: Elle's post-op appointment and the official end to her cancer diagnosis.

After her treatment and the biopsy of the removed lump, the doctor was happy that no more treatment would be necessary and she didn't need to come back for a year. The appointment was just a formality, she'd all but expected what they were going to say but it was still a comfort to hear it from them, all the same.

I'd booked us afternoon tea at the fancy seafront hotel a half hour away from home. It was a place that neither of us could afford to set foot in normally and I promised not to think I was going into labour for the whole time as long as Elle didn't curse at the posh waiters.

"Do you feel sneaky?" she asked.

We were sitting in the centre of a large restaurant, looking out over a pristine beach, surrounded by more cutlery on our table that we knew how to deal with.

"About what?"

"I feel like we're cheating on Joseph by having tea somewhere else."

I smiled and patted her hand.

"It was just this one time, it doesn't mean anything and we'll think about him the whole time we are doing it. Better?"

She rolled her eyes and went back to waiting impatiently for our food to arrive. We were the only two people there and it was so quiet we didn't feel comfortable talking much louder than a whisper, but I knew that as soon as Elle started on the prosecco that would change.

I miss wine.

The waiter appeared, pushing out a tray with our tower of sandwiches and tray bakes alongside tea for me and a bottle of fizz for the lush I was with. The offer included one glass of prosecco instead of tea but, of course, Elle had managed to blag the whole bottle with her pure daring and letting them know about her doctor's appointment. She justified her brazenness by saying she 'might as well use the sob-story one last time'.

It worked, of course, it always worked for her.

When Elle wanted something, or could spot the potential of a deal, she would find some way to make it work to her advantage.

It was one of the qualities I most admired. I would have been terrified to even ask for something, other than what was in front of me, whereas she was happy to haggle and cajole her way into extra.

"Are you having fun?" she asked.

"Yes, of course, why are you asking that?"

"Because I can't tell with half your face wrapped up like a mummy and those sunglasses. We are inside; you look much more conspicuous with all that on than if you just took it off and got on with things. You are not Quasimodo."

I had started the physiotherapy for my face and, after much deliberation, I decided to include the steroid treatment also. There were subtle improvements but I was warned that I wouldn't see much more than that until after the baby was born. I was getting used to the random drooling and if I lifted the side of my mouth when I spoke then people understood me much better, but I was still very self-conscious of how I looked.

"Take them off, Amy, there's no one here and if people do come in I'll go over and shove their faces into the tiny cream pie things they're serving here."

153

I thought about it for a few seconds and finally accepted that I was being a bit silly. It was a relief to take them off, I was constantly sweating behind the scarf and when I had them on for too long I would usually have a heat rash across my mouth.

"Why is everything so tiny?" she asked.

"It's all finger food and fancy, it's meant to be small. If you wanted quantity then we should have gone to that all-you-can-eat Chinese."

"We may need to; I'm going to be starving after this."

It was so peaceful as we sat at the table, watching the waves crash. I could understand why people would come to this town to retire; I was ready to sell-up and move here so I could walk on the beach every day and eat teeny tiny cucumber sandwiches in the afternoon. I decided it wouldn't be ideal for Ben and the kids but I would go back and visit them on the weekends.

Well, maybe every other weekend...

I looked across at Elle, who was busy dismantling her sandwiches to examine what was in each of them.

"Can you stop that? This is a classy place and you're dropping food over the cotton tablecloth," I whispered.

"I can't help it; I want to see what's in the things before I bite them. What if there's parsnip in them? I can't stand parsnip, you know that."

"Parsnip? In a sandwich? You honestly believe there is such thing as a parsnip sandwich?"

"I don't fucking know what posh people eat."

I gave her my best annoyed mother glare and she stopped her dissection of the food and started eating. She did continue to sniff everything though and the more prosecco she had, the closer the food would go to her nose. By the end of it she has accidently inhaled quite a bit of fresh cream.

"This is nice," she mused.

"You've got cream on your nose."

"Oh for fuck's sake, people are going to think I have a coke habit at this rate with all this white stuff hanging off me."

"What did we say about cursing?"

"That it's fun and we should do it? Ok, I'm sorry it's a classy joint and I won't be my un-classy self."

"Just until we're out of here; you can return to your obnoxious, chav nature as soon as we're out the door."

"Deal."

As soon as the deal was struck I noticed Elle eating at an increased speed. She'd given up on pouring her drink into the beautiful flute that was provided and opted to just guzzle it straight from the bottle.

There's the classy bird I always knew she was.

I decided to join her in the speed eating so we could get out of the place before we were thrown out for acting like a pair of wild animals and by the time the waiter returned to see if I wanted fresh water for the tea we were already done.

"No need for top-ups, mate, we're out of here," said Elle, "Where's the nearest chippy? No offence but that filled me fuck all."

I dragged her out of the restaurant as I smiled apologetically to the server and pushed her out the door.

"You were so rude!" I said.

"Not at all, I was truthful and it's not like he will take it personally if two women don't get stuffed after finger sandwiches and cream. I'm not ready to go home yet, let's go on an adventure."

She pulled the bottle of the prosecco out from under her coat and drank the last dredges of it before leaving it at the doorstep of the hotel. It was bitterly cold so I was very thankful to be able to wrap half of my face back up in my scarf.

"Aren't you cold?" I asked.

"Not at all, the wind is beautiful and you're wrapped up enough for the both of us. We should go this way, I can smell adventure if we go this way."

155

The only thing Elle could smell was the waft of deep-fried carbohydrates coming from a food truck by the beach. We each got some chips and sat on the bench close to the sand, people watching and trying to eat as quickly as possible before the seagulls dive-bombed us and stole our meal.

"Now, this is my kinda afternoon tea," she said.

"I don't think chips on the beach could really be called that."

"Fuck that, it's beautiful whatever you want to call it. Everything tastes better on the beach: sandwiches, chips, cock. They all get infinitely tastier when there's sand and sea."

Nope, not going to ask her to clarify; I'll take her word for it.

When we finished the chips – which were inhaled at warp speed – we decided it was too cold and windy for a walk along the promenade so we headed into the arcades to lose our money and have some laughs.

It was a lovely afternoon. I didn't feel tired, for a change, and the more I laughed the less self-conscious I felt about my face. The scarf and glasses were put in my bag so I was able to play air hockey better, although the bump did prevent me from making more daring moves to stop her from getting goals. She won – easily – but I did manage to win £3.56 from the penny drop machines. All of which was put back into the machine again and lost.

The house always wins, Amy.

Before we made moves to go home, Elle begged me to go on a swan pedalo.

"Please, Amy," she pleaded, "I'll do all the peddling; all you have to do is steer. I've never been on one because in the summer the queues are ridiculous but there's no one here today, it's our chance!"

"There's no one here because it's freezing and it looks like they're closed."

"Don't be silly, I bet I can convince the kid behind the counter to let us go out in one. It's just that oversized pond, no waves, no wind, it'll be great. I'm even trusting you with the steering."

"That's only because you're pissed and can barely see in front of you."

"Perhaps, or perhaps it's because I love you and I trust you. I'm kidding! I'm not drunk, I swear, I'll do a sobriety test right here, right now, if it means I get to go on a swan."

She was lying, I knew she was lying but looking at her put-on sad eyes I relented and waited for her to work her magic on the unsuspecting teenager working in the arcade. She immerged a few minutes later with two life jackets and a set of keys.

"We're ready to go!" she shouted, jingling the keys and jogging towards me, "They're all locked up together so we need to set one free and we're good to go. I promised we wouldn't be any longer than an hour."

"An hour? Are you mad? You're allowed ten minutes at the most."

"Fine, but I bet when we get out on the water you'll be delighted and not want to come back."

I highly doubt that.

I stood by the edge of the water while she started to wrestle with the giant plastic swans to free them from their chains.

"I think I'll call him, Winston. Be free, Winston, we have come to liberate you," she shouted, "Come on, princess, get your arse into this thing and we'll get out into the open water."

The open water was a large pond at the side of the arcade. Not big enough to make me fear for my safety should we crash and topple over, but large enough for me to make sure my life vest was on securely.

I stepped, carefully, onto the swan as it bobbed on the water and started to shake with my weight.

"Is this thing going to capsize?" I called, becoming more unsure of this idea by the second.

"It's completely fine, I promise. Now, it's time for Captain Elle to board."

She stepped off the makeshift jetty and into the seat beside me.

"Are you ready for this?" she asked.

"Absolutely not."

"Then off we go."

She started to peddle as hard and fast as she could which didn't last very long. The sheer effort she was putting in should have set us off at full speed but with only one of us actually peddling we chugged along slowly.

"Christ, I'm sweating already," she said, puffing and rolling up her sleeves, "This is a fucking workout."

I concentrated on steering, which wasn't that difficult considering there was no one else on the water to bang into and we were moving at the speed of a very old snail.

"Can't you go any faster?" I asked.

"Would you like to have a go? I'm busted here!"

I laughed to myself as she continued to peddle as fast as she could. Something told me that we wouldn't be spending anywhere close to an hour on the water so I made the most of the scenery and tried to ignore Elle, who was getting more out of breath and starting to curse even more than usual.

"Do you want to head back to the car?" I asked.

"No, just let me rest for a bit and we can float around on the water. I really should take up spinning or something."

We bobbed along in the water, not saying much but still being content in each other's company until I felt the water at my toes.

"Elle?"

"Hmmm?"

"We are starting to take water aboard, captain."

"Fuck! Really?"

"Just a little, it's on my side."

158

"Pull your feet out of it."

"How flexible do you think I am at eight-and-a-half-months pregnant, in a tiny seat meant for normal-sized people?"

"I just meant lift them a bit so you don't get a cold."

As I moved my feet, the weight in my body shifted and all of a sudden I felt a large gush of water leave my body.

Oh fuck

"Holy crap, Amy, you're really taking in a lot of water on your side. I'll get us back to dry land in a jiffy, just hang on."

"That's not coming from outside the boat," I said, "My waters have just gone."

"Are you sure you haven't just wet yourself again?"

I really regret telling her that story.

"Yes, I'm sure. This was definitely my waters. The contractions haven't started so don't panic, let's just get home."

She peddled furiously as I took deep breaths in the hope that I wouldn't spiral into a complete state of panic adrift on a giant, plastic swan. We were close to the jetty when Elle decided to jump off and pull the swan by the neck to get it stable enough for me to climb out. Unfortunately, in her enthusiasm to get to dry land she misjudged the distance and fell short of the wood and straight into the water.

"Elle!" I screamed, "Are you ok?"

The water was up to her thighs and she looked to be in shock, but she instantly shook herself and waded towards the bank, dragging the swan behind her. She pulled herself up onto the jetty and gave me her hand to help me out.

"You're freezing," I said.

"N... n... no shit," her teeth chattered as she spoke, "Let's get you to the hospital."

I still hadn't felt any contractions so I convinced her to let me drive home instead of getting someone here to collect us.

"I don't want to make a fuss," I stressed, "The waters have just gone, we have plenty of time to get down the road and it's not like you can drive."

She was wrapped in my coat and still shivering beside the car.

"I'm not asking permission, either get in and we'll drive back together or I'll go by myself."

She didn't hesitate to get into the car but I felt like it was more to do with the heat that this option offered as opposed to actually wanting to be in a car when the driver was in labour.

I asked her to put on the radio and find some good songs we could sing along to and distract me from what was really going on. Elle's voice was terrible, but it was helping to get me through the drive without worrying that I was going to end up delivering this baby in the back of the car.

"You see if this is another false alarm, I'm going to get that baby out of you myself," she said, in between songs, "It's like he really doesn't want to go on the operating table. It must not be dramatic enough for him."

"He doesn't have a choice, there's too much scar tissue from the previous two to try and get this one out of me the good old-fashioned way."

"Yuck," she replied, "Don't fancy being you."

"You're not helping, Elle," I said.

"Sorry, yes, I forgot that I was meant to be distracting you, wasn't I? Does this mean you won't get the nice gas and air thing to relax you? I love that stuff."

"No, I won't."

I love that stuff too.

"So if you're in labour now, what are you going to do if he wants to come out au naturale?"

"It's taking all of my energy to not think about this child wanting to do that. He could potentially rupture my uterus, and my best friend is not doing a very good job of distracting me from that particular fear."

"You were a lot less panicked about it when you were delivering a poo, you just pushed."

"Is that us never talking about it ever again?"

A new song came on the radio and she went back to wailing along with the music while making up her own lyrics as I gripped the steering wheel and concentrated on the road ahead. My priority was getting to the hospital and getting checked over, I would think about contacting Ben after that. I knew for certain I was in labour and this definitely wasn't a false alarm but I also thought I was in labour when I was on the bathroom floor in the café so I decided to err on the side of caution.

We hit traffic when we got near the hospital, which drove Elle to shoving herself towards me and blasting the horn at everyone around us. She wound down the window and stuck her head outside in order to shout abuse at the driver in front of us for taking a fraction of second too long when the lights changed.

"Can you stop that?" I said, pulling at the end of her top to get her back in from the window, "Nothing that you are doing right now is helping. Just come into the maternity ward with me then when they say I'm actually in labour, go out and call Ben. That's all you've left to do, understand?"

As usual there was no parking anywhere near the hospital so I abandoned it in the first semi-safe place I could find and resolved that getting a ticket was worth it if I didn't have to trek any further to the main entrance. I could feel things happening in my stomach but tried my best to keep concentrating on the next few steps ahead of me. If my mind started to wander to any further than that I knew panic would take over. Elle continued to walk ahead of me as some sort of incentive to get me to keep up but I couldn't walk any faster, even if I tried. Eventually she gave up and hooked my arm instead. She matched her pace with mine and started mimicking some sort of heavy breathing in an attempt to be helpful.

"I have to stop that, it's making me light-headed," she said, after a few minutes, "We're here, you've made it and the baby hasn't dropped out. My job is done."

"Go phone Ben," I ordered.

"I thought you wanted me to wait and see if it was the real deal?"

"It is, now go."

A midwife had spotted us walking in and was by my side within seconds, asking me questions and getting me hooked up to machines to check everything. I had already apologised in advance in case it was another false alarm but she laughed and said: "Third time's a charm."

She continued to mark charts and look at monitors but she began to sport a furrowed brow.

"Just give me a second," she said, before leaving the room and nearly banging into Elle.

"I can't get through to Benny, but I've sent about twenty text messages and told River to stalk him until he answers," she explained.

"I think there's something wrong with the baby," I replied.

"Did they say something?"

"No, the midwife looked a bit worried and then left the room."

"Calm your tits, princess, let's just wait and see what she says when she came back."

After, what felt like an eternity, the midwife finally came back to the room with a doctor in tow. She looked too young to be a doctor but I wasn't about to start off our relationship with insulting the woman so I kept my mouth shut, let her do her job and hoped that Elle would do the same.

I was a bit disappointed it wasn't my lovely, cute doctor but I figured it was more important to deliver safely then lust after a man that wasn't my husband when the baby was here.

Good plan.

"Mrs Cole there's a bit of a concern with the baby's heart rate and we think it would be best if we get you down to theatre right away," she said, "There's no immediate danger but I think this is the best course of action."

I could feel the colour drain from my face and I couldn't verbalise any type of answer so I nodded my head and looked at Elle. She too, looked whiter at hearing the news but held onto my hand tightly and tried her best to give me a reassuring smile.

"Ok then, off we go," announced the doctor and within minutes I was being pushed down towards the delivery suite, in my bed, with Elle by my side still grasping my hand.

Ben is going to miss the birth all because I didn't phone him in time. How could I have been so stupid?

"Elle, will you stay with me? I can't do this on my own and if Ben doesn't make it I need someone," I asked.

"Of course, I won't leave your side for one second."

The bed was parked outside the doors of the department and I tried to get my breathing under control. I was a mess of emotions: terrified, elated, excited, nervous and really, really tired. Elle was humming some tune that I didn't recognise but I closed my eyes to listen to the melody and tried not to feel completely overwhelmed about what was about to happen.

It's time to pull yourself together, Amy, if Ben isn't here it's not the end of the world – he'll get here eventually and for now you've the next best thing. You can do this, Amy, let's go and meet your baby.

Chapter 21

"Why do all babies look like my great uncle Albert?" asked Elle.

I was still numb from the waist down and rather foggy but lucid enough to realise that Elle was insulting my child.

"Don't look at me like that," she said, "He was a looker in his time, you should take it as a compliment."

She was beside the bed pacing with the sleeping bundle and I felt nothing but love and relief that I had done it. I know the hard part came after labour but knowing that I had successfully brought this child into the world was a sense of achievement matched by nothing else that I would ever experience.

At that moment, Ben came bounding through the curtains and found me lying on the bed with a very contented look on my face.

"I'm sorry," he said, "I'm so, so sorry."

"Hush, it's ok, I'm fine, we're fine, everything is fine."

"Where is he?"

Elle coughed and Ben realised that she was holding the baby, smiling.

"Benny, come and meet Elle Junior," she said, handing over the tiny bundle of perfection.

"We are not calling my daughter that."

"It's... it's a girl?" he said, smiling broadly, "You were so certain it was a boy."

"Shocking that Amy was wrong about something, I know," replied Elle, "but she's definitely a girl. Right, you two, I'll let you all get acquainted while I go save River from being bullied by all of our children.

"I'll call you later, princess. I'm really fucking proud of you."

She gave me a wink and disappeared through the curtains to leave Ben and I to breathe in the new-born scent and form our first memories of this child of ours.

"I can't believe she's a girl," he said for the tenth time.

"Are you disappointed?"

"What? Are you kidding me? How could anyone be remotely disappointed in this baby? I can already tell she's going to be something special. We should just cut our losses on those other two yobs and just concentrate on making this one perfect."

"Agreed."

We enjoyed those few hours on our own with her, before the parents descended and our boys. Ben's parents were first to arrive and were both shocked at the reveal that she was a she, but by now it seemed ridiculous to think that she could have been anyone else.

I wasn't sure if it was the drugs or the euphoria of having her in my arms but as I looked down on her mess of dark hair I whispered her name and I finally felt that this wasn't a dream. This moment was here at long last and I got to meet the final piece of the puzzle of my heart.

"Ben?" I asked.

"Yes, Sweety?" he replied, barely looking up from his phone.

"This is your daughter, Ciara."

He sat down the phone and came up to sit beside me on the bed. He petted her head with one finger and whispered: "It's a pleasure to meet you, Ciara, that's a beautiful name for a beautiful girl."

He picked her up out of my arms and started to walk around with her, whispering secrets and promises that only she was allowed to know. I gave in to the exhaustion and let my eyes close. I had done my part, for now.

She was safe.

Chapter 22

"Is she dead?" I heard a familiar voice shout.

"Why would she be dead? What a stupid thing to say, she's obviously sleeping, now stop shouting and don't wake her," said another familiar voice, equally as loud.

I blinked into the fluorescent lights above my head and waited for my eyes to adjust into waking. My mother and father were both perched on either side of my bed, grinning unnaturally.

"Hi, guys," I grumbled.

"I told him not to wake you," said Mum, "he has no concept of how loud he is. This is a maternity ward, James, not a bloody pub."

Dad rolled his eyes and came up to give me as kiss on the forehead.

"You did a very good job, love," he said.

"She didn't do anything," replied Mum, "all she had to do was lie back and let them pump drugs into her while they scooped the baby out. It's not like it was in my day."

"Again, Mum, 'your day' was the 1980's, not medieval times and I'm not getting into an argument over this."

"Who's arguing? I'm only saying — "

"Well don't say anything. Just hold your granddaughter and make smiley faces at her."

She closed her mouth and turned her attention to the crib sitting beside my bed.

"Are we the first here?" she asked.

Here we go.

"Elle was at the birth and Ben's parents were here a little while ago," I replied.

"There you have it, do you see how far down the list we are, James? Practically treated like acquaintances."

I didn't have the strength to argue with her, nor did I care about her dig; today was a happy day.

"What do you think of the name?" I asked, knowing that she would have something negative to say. She hated both my children's names for the first few months of their lives. At the time she would just refer to them as 'big one' and 'small one'.

"I think it's very nice," she said.

*It's a miracle, Eloise Galbraith actually approves of your name choice for your own child without an argument.
Perhaps she's mellowing out, now that she's a grandmother of three?*

"I was surprised you came up with it; I thought it was going to be something ridiculous like 'Chandelier'."

Ah, there she is. I knew it was too good to be true. She would never miss out an opportunity to say something passive aggressive.

"When is your face going back to normal?" she continued, "I can't see much of a difference but your father says he can see an improvement."

I glared at Ben in order for him to intervene and for once, he actually managed to understand my hint.

"Amy, you should get some rest before the boys come up to meet their little sister," he said, "I'll walk you both out."

I knew I shouldn't let her bother me, but it would be nice if she could just realise how a normal conversation worked. It doesn't have to be a battle, we could just…talk.

Another time I would need to figure out a plan of action in order to try and forge a more mellow relationship with my mother but I had more important things to do at this moment. Today was for forging a relationship with my own daughter and I wanted to make sure she never felt the way my mother made me feel for one second.

I loved my mother, I truly did; I just didn't particularly like her most of the time and I'd made my peace with that.

I was excited to see my boys and find out how they would react to meeting Ciara for the first time. I was nervous for her (which was ridiculous, I know) but I felt it all the same.

Elle took them up that evening so they could be formally introduced to the newest member of the family and I knew something was up with Arthur at once.

He couldn't feel like he has middle child syndrome already, could he? He's intuitive and all but this is ridiculous.

He came and sat beside me on the bed, snuggling underneath my arm and was very quiet.

Ben was helping Adam to hold Ciara as Elle discreetly took candid photos of us all. I couldn't wait to see them. I vowed to print the pictures out and not scrutinise my face and weight. This moment was perfect and I wanted to remember it, always.

"What's up, buttercup?" I asked Arthur.

"Nothing."

"There must be something going on? You're never this quiet. Has something happened in school? Is Stanley giving you any trouble?"

"No, he's ok now. We're friends, I think."

And all it took was the threat of a make-believe drug cartel.

"Please tell me what's going on? I can't help if we don't. What do you think of Ciara?"

He shrugged and didn't offer an answer.

"You know, just because there's another member of the family doesn't mean that we love you any less? You are the most special Arthur in the whole world."

"You could love me a little less, if you wanted, it's really embarrassing when you make me kiss you 'goodbye'."

"Nope, I'm going to keep doing that until you're one hundred."

"You'll be long dead by then, you're already so old."
Thanks, kid.

"What's the problem then?" I pressed.

"She doesn't match."

"What do you mean? Because she's a girl? Girls are great! Mummy is a girl and I'm pretty spectacular."

"No, her name. It's 'C' and we are 'A' so she doesn't match."

"Is that all?" I said, laughing, "How about you think of a special secret name for her that only you and Adam can call her with an 'A'?"

"Can we?" he asked, instantly brightened by the idea.

"I promise."

This mother-of-three thing is easy enough; I don't know what I was so panicked about it.

"Adam," called Arthur, "Mum says we can call the baby 'ass-hat' if we want."

"Wait, I said what now?"

I knew it was too good to last

The boys stayed for a while longer but when Ciara started to stir and wanting fed, Elle took it as her cue to get home with them.

"They can have a sleepover with me, Benny you can make the most of the quiet house tonight before reality hits tomorrow," said Elle.

The evening was drawing in and I ordered Ben to go home and rest while I caught up with sleep in between feeds. He was delighted at the thought of having a quiet house to go home to and I was exactly where I wanted to be – for now. I knew I would start cracking up and wanting to get out of here when the drugs properly wore off.

***

It wasn't a restful night. Ciara was up every half hour and the pain of the operation was starting to sting. I began to long for the comfort of home and the familiar feel of Ben sleeping beside me.

By the time it was time to leave I couldn't wait to feel the fresh air on my face and smiled through the pain of each bump of the car journey home. I hadn't lost my mind, it just meant I didn't have to try and eat the stuff passing as food in the hospital.

When we came through the door, we were greeted with Elle, River and the children brandishing balloons and confetti to welcome us all home. I was shocked that she hadn't included fairy lights in her decorations and I tried to look happy at the sight of confetti everywhere.

I'm going to be sweeping that up for weeks.

"Welcome home, Ciara!" they all shouted in unison.

Ben sat the car-seat in the hallway and led me into the living room so I could lie on the sofa with my feet up. I enjoyed the buzz of everyone around me, chatting happily and I enjoyed the fact that I didn't have to do a damn thing to entertain them either. They were all too busy staring at the baby and passing her around. I took the opportunity to be a rubbish party guest and fell asleep. I didn't care if it made me terribly dull, and I knew they wouldn't care either. I would be surprised if they noticed, unless the baby started to cry and wanted fed.

If this had been my first born, I would have been scolding them all for passing her around and 'spoiling' her by holding her for too long; but since I no longer followed any type of parenting book and realised that the notion of 'spoiling' your child with affection and love is utter bullshit I happily sat back and watched how each of their faces changed and lit up as they took her in their arms.

Have you ever watched people when they're holding a baby? There's something so indescribably beautiful about how their face changes. They make it their mission to try and get the child to smile or somehow acknowledge that they have been seen by them – despite a new-born's inability to do so – but they keep trying. It's really very lovely. My family seem to lose all sense of decorum (not that they had much to begin with) and really go all-out in their attempt to be her favourite. Eventually she gets fed up of looking at the beige blobs and demands to be fed so that's the cue for the milk maid to be summoned.

I sat back on the sofa feeding my tiny daughter and listened to the different conversations going on in the room. Apart from the sleep deprivation, the pain from the operation and general fogginess of giving birth I felt happier than I had in a long time.

I wanted to keep this little moment in my heart for the rest of time, because I knew life couldn't get better than it was right now. Everyone I loved was in one room and I was so grateful for every second of life that I had lived since the day I was dragged from the water.

My rock bottom was just the launch pad from which I made the life I'd always wanted.

Six months later

Chapter 23

Christ, I'm tired

The bubble of happiness had well and truly popped. My house was a mess, I don't remember the last time I had more than four hours sleep and I think I may murder my husband if he comes within strangling distance of me, today.

All that doesn't matter though, because today I was officially going back to work.

Ben and I finally agreed on a child-minder that we both liked, Abby, and I was counting down the hours until I was able to drink a hot drink while it was still hot. I can even have an adult conversation with someone – well, as much as Elle is able to pretend she's an actual adult.

I'm so excited.

I had grandiose plans about the family's new morning regime, which involved yoga for me, organic breakfasts and getting everyone ready and out the door without a screaming match. I knew none of this was actually going to happen because I was never going to willingly get myself out of bed and exercise without some sort of monetary incentive. I lay in bed, staring at the ceiling and checking the time every few minutes.

You could get up and have everything ready for the kids? Or you could try to close your eyes for a few more minutes before Ciara wakes up and wants to hit you in the face with her chubby fists? Sleep it is.

After mere seconds of shutting my eyes I was rudely wakened by my two eldest children who were demanding breakfast. I had, of course, forgotten to set an alarm and I now had thirty minutes to get us all ready and out the door.

Perfect.

It wasn't the Zen-like return to work I had planned or envisioned, but with anything I attempted it usually happened this way. Mercifully, Ciara had decided not to be a complete dictator and was actually not struggling against the porridge or the idea of getting dressed. Like my other children, she preferred her 'fun' dad but I held onto the hope that there was some unspoken female loyalty in there somewhere. The child-minder's house was on the way to the office so we waved 'good-bye' to the men folk and I ran towards freedom. Well, not-so-much running, more like brisk walking. I had been neglecting my pelvic floor exercises and I wasn't feeling confident about anything beyond walking speed at this stage.

Ciara had already spent some settling-in mornings with Abby so gave little-to-no fucks that her mother was walking out the door and leaving her behind.

Traitorous wretch; would it kill her to cry just a little?

I waved to Barbara as I walked through the café and up the stairs. Our relationship was still in the teething phase but I did like her. She would bring me extra fresh cream with my buns when I called in, so she obviously knew the way to my heart. Michael said she was invaluable to the place and was a firm customer favourite so I knew she was an asset. I could hear Elle and Sylvia chatting animatedly as I walked through the door and I was faced with countless balloons filling up our entire ceiling.

"Welcome back!" cried Elle, with an unnaturally high voice.

"Stop sucking all the helium," shouted Sylvia, with a matching sound.

They both fell about laughing and I realised that Elle had found a kindred spirit in my absence. My chest stung a little with petty jealousy but I smiled at the effort they'd gone to.

"This is amazing, thank you both," I said.

"Get yourself set up and we will get you caught up with what you've missed," replied Elle, "not that you've missed much, you haven't stopped your daily 'check-in's' since Ciara was ten days old."

"I was just making sure everything was ok, not because I thought you couldn't handle things."

She eyed me suspiciously, but settled on giving me a hug.

"It's good to see your mug back here, it's been missed and that Sylvia one is useless."

"Hey! Less of it," shouted Sylvia, as she dragged the helium canister into the corner.

"I'm kidding," said Elle, "You've been a star and now we get to be one big happy family."

"For a week," I reminded her.

"Yes, a week. Now, let's get down to business I have a lot to do and pack before I head off to the wilds of Canada."

This would be her second trip with River over the last six months and it still worried me that she would never come back. They had agreed that moving there permanently would be unfair to the girls and Keith but they still made the journey every three months to spend a few weeks over there in order to make sure things were ticking along. Elle spent her time exploring while River did work and I was always so jealous of her pictures. We were planning on all of us heading out there to stay in a beautiful cabin, this summer. I couldn't wait – but I wasn't looking forward to a long plane journey with three children.

When she came and told me she wasn't moving I cried so much I couldn't breathe. Elle was shocked that I would ever show that much emotion and I blamed it on postnatal hormones – an excuse I was planning to use until I was fifty. I knew the thought of her leaving was hideous to me but I wasn't expecting the sheer relief, of finding out that I wasn't going to be losing her full-time, to be quite so powerful. She'd taken to calling me 'marshmallow' since; I didn't mind it too much but hated when she shortened it to 'Marsha'.

I sat back and watched the world's oddest presentation by them both. Sylvia had obviously taught Elle how to use *Power Point* so I was treated to a very lengthy slideshow about her new diet and how it helped her fibre intake and subsequent bowel movements.

"I hate to interrupt," I said, "but can we just keep it to the business stuff and maybe I can watch the rest at a different time?"

They looked at each other as if they weren't prepared to go off script, but after some messing about on the computer I was finally given some insight into how things were going. I noted that on top of all the slides she had the words: '*Badass Business Inc.*' typed out and I couldn't help but smile.

Is that name growing on me or is this sleep deprivation? Say nothing...

By lunchtime I was up to full speed and I was happy to hear that Sylvia had stepped away from her online, fetish performances.

"I mean, it was good money and all, but it was just getting too weird for me," she explained, "I'm very much coming from a place where sexual exploration is normal but there was this one guy who really wanted me to make scrambled egg and shove — "

"Let me stop you there," I interrupted, noting the table of mothers and small children sitting beside us, as we ate our lunch downstairs.

I wasn't sure how I was going to get along with her while Elle was out of the country but I promised to give it a shot; besides if she was truly awful then the business would have been in chaos and Elle probably would have murdered her by now. I just had to embrace a little bit of change.

Easier said than done.

"Barbie," called Elle, "Pull up a chair and eat with us, it's your lunch break too."

She willingly obliged and happily brought her food out from behind the counter. As the four of us gathered around the table it felt like old friends in the canteen at school, laughing and talking nonsense about boys.

"Fuck me, why does the conversation always have to gravitate back to men?" asked Elle, "We are brilliant, independent women who have more than four brain cells between us, so why can't we think of other conversation points?"

"We could talk about my yeast infection, if you like?" asked Sylvia.

"Nope," I answered, firmly.

"I decree, from this day on, we are to meet at this table for lunch and not mention anything to do with the male of the species or our children for the whole meal – we are women, not just wives and mothers. So you'd better start thinking of discussion topics for tomorrow or I'll crack up."

"Ah, yes, there's nothing like organised conversation to really show the patriarchy we are spontaneous individuals capable of original thought," laughed Barbara.

I like her.

I enjoyed the food as well as the ability to enjoy tea at the right temperature. Having conversations with people who could talk back was an added bonus. I loved it all, but by the time it came to leave to pick up the kids I was half running out the door to have Ciara back in my arms. I missed her smell and her sucker punches, I knew it wouldn't be long before all three would be demanding my attention at the same time and I would be irritated beyond measure but that was all part and parcel of motherhood and I wouldn't change it.

Ciara adored her brothers; her eyes lit up when they were in the room and they doted on her until she started to pull their hair when they got close enough. When that happened, they opted to keep a safe distance from her until she calmed down. Watching the three of them together, especially those times when they didn't notice I was there, was magic.

I made that.

In those seconds of peace I would love Ben even more for helping to create these three little beings; but that warm, fuzzy feeling would usually end by the time he opened his mouth and said something to annoy me.

He was currently on a health kick and it was driving me crazy. He kept prancing about in active wear and fiddling with his watch that tracked his movements. Sometimes, while we were in mid conversation he would start randomly doing jumping jacks to 'get his heart rate going'.

Do you know how hard it is to have a serious conversation with a man who is doing star jumps while you're talking about family finances, and not want to throw a spoon at him?

The answer is: very.

Tonight he had his running club to go to and he was usually unbearable when he got home. He'd only been going for six weeks and at first he was really enthusiastic about it and would come back on a runner's high (or whatever he called it) but these last couple of weeks he would return lethargic and standoffish. Anytime I asked him what was wrong he avoided the question and I didn't push him on it for fear it would result in a pointless argument or he would drop to the floor and do crunches.

Of course when I told Elle this she was first to jump to: 'he's having an affair'; but that as a possibility didn't even occur to me.

After the kids were in bed, and he had left to go meet his group, I picked up the phone to call her so I could kill some time and avoid tidying the sitting room.

"What's up, Marsha?" she said.

"Nothing really, Ben's away to his running club."

"He's still going to that? I was chatting to Sylvia about it and she said those clubs are notorious pick-up points for extra, extra-curricular activities."

"Oh, great, so now you're gossiping to Sylvia about my marriage?"

"Hardly gossip, I was trying to see if she knew any scandal about them so I could be a better friend to you."

I'm not buying this for a second.

"He's not having an affair," I said, resolute in my trust for him.

"You're probably right, but there's definitely something going on and if he's not going to tell you himself then we'll just have to find out on our own."

"How do you propose we do that?"

"Easy! We follow him."

"Because all strong marriages involve following each other?"

"Do you want to find out what's going on or not? The kids are with their dad, River can sit in your house with your lot and we can get to the bottom of this. Are you in?"

I knew he wasn't cheating on me, I just knew it; but I couldn't shake the feeling that there was something going on that he wasn't telling me and it was driving me mad. What little sleep I was getting was being plagued by stressful dreams, and when I woke up I felt like there was a stranger sleeping beside me.

"I'm in."

Chapter 24

Elle and River arrived within thirty minutes and I had spent the time getting changed into black clothing.

"Isn't that the same outfit you were wearing when we followed Keith?" she asked.

"Yes, it's basically my sleuthing gear."

"Badass," said River, nodding in approval.

Elle and River said their 'goodbyes' – which still involved a nauseating amount of kissing – and we jumped into the car to head towards the industrial estate where Ben had said they met up every week.

"They'll be long gone by the time we get there and I've no clue what route they take," I said, "This is going to be completely pointless and if he finds out I've been following him he'll crack up."

"Look, it's an amateur running group, they can't have got far and we'll keep our distance or just hang out near to where he parked and wait for him to get back."

"What will that prove?"

"That he's doing the whole run and not canoodling someone."

"He's not having an affair," I repeated.

"Then you've nothing to worry about."

We drove quickly towards our destination and the closer we got, the less confident I felt with this plan. My surety that I knew Ben wouldn't be lying to me about what he was doing began to waver.

Stop this, you know him. He wouldn't do this, he wouldn't be that stupid. He's probably just cross that he's not beating his run time or something ridiculous.

When we pulled up to the meeting point there were little-to-no cars about, but I could see Ben's in the distance.

"Now what do we do?" I asked.

"I'm going to run into that gym place and see if they have any idea where the group runs and then we can head off in that direction."

I was surprised that she'd come up with a decent plan, so I waited impatiently for her return as I tried not to spiral down the rabbit hole of suspicion. She emerged a few minutes later and jogged back to the car. She was out of breath by the time she sat down in her seat so I had to wait an agonising few seconds before she could tell me what she'd found out.

"Ok, don't freak out," she began

All good sentences start this way.

"There's no running club."

"What? That's impossible; they must have got it wrong."

"He was adamant," she continued, "he told me there was one a year ago but that programme is over now and there hasn't been anything like that since."

I'm going to kill him.

"Then where the fuck is he?" I shouted.

"That's that 'freak out' thing that I was worried about," she replied, "Just let me think for a few minutes and then we will figure something out."

My head was spinning, I couldn't get my brain around the possibility that Ben could be cheating on me. My resolve in his innocence was crumbling at every second and I didn't know how to pull myself back from the edge.

"Maybe he's just running by himself? The group finished, he didn't want to stop running and lose fitness before the next group starts up so he's training by himself?" she said.

"There hasn't been a group for a year and he has only been running for the last six weeks; that theory makes no sense."

I decided to get a closer look at the car to see if there were any more clues as to what Ben was up to.

I peered in through the passenger-side window and spotted his coat and water bottle but was no clearer to finding out what was going on. I looked around at the business park and couldn't find anywhere that was open so I started to go back towards Elle, in her car.

"What's the verdict?" she asked.

"No clue, I guess we just sit here and wait."

She put on the radio and we listened to the music in silence, both lost in our own thoughts. She was probably mentally packing for Canada whilst I was trying to figure out the logistics of being a single mother. My feet were starting to get pins and needles, so I decided to get out and stretch my legs for a while but Elle pulled me back into my seat before I made it out the door.

"Get down!" she ordered, "He's coming."

I saw a man and a woman walking in our direction, chatting happily, each of them holding something in their hands. Ben seemed relaxed and pleasant to be around – not the Ben I was used to after 'running'. Perhaps he was grumpy at home because he was leaving her. My heart stung with the betrayal, the burning became so unbearable I thought I was going to be sick.

"It might not be what it looks like, don't jump to conclusions," said Elle.

"You're the one that convinced me that something was going on in the first place and now you're telling me not to jump to conclusions?"

"I only suggested following him because I thought it would be something ridiculous that he was up to, not because I thought he was doing the dirt. Just wait, confront him at home."

She switched on the engine but before she took off I threw open the door and jumped out of the car.

"Amy!" she called after me, "Don't do anything stupid."

Stupid is my middle name.

"Benjamin Cole!" I screamed.

He nearly jumped out of his skin as he spotted his fuming wife striding towards him.

"Amy? What are you — "

My fist connected with his face, limply, before he could finish the sentence. The shock of it must have knocked him backwards, because it certainly wasn't down to my pathetic attempt at a punch.

"What the hell was that for?" he asked, rubbing his cheek.

His fancy woman put herself between the two of us to prevent me from striking another blow. My hand was killing me; I'd never thrown a punch in my life and it was obvious that it was something I should never have attempted. Elle came up behind me and put her arm around my shoulder.

"Elle?" asked Ben, "Can you tell me what you are doing here? Or should I brace myself for your next attack?"

"I'm not ruling it out, Benny," she replied, "Didn't take you for a blonde man, did you have to be such a cliché?"

I was upset, but I wasn't sure if it was because I had caught my husband with another woman or because of the pain in my hand. I didn't know what to think or what to do. I was in complete shock at everything. Lashing out and hitting him wasn't something I would have ever believed I was capable of and yet, here we were.

"Ben, are you ok?" asked the blonde.

"Yeah, Michelle, I'm ok. This is my wife and her friend."

"Pleasure," she replied with a deadpan expression, "Do you want me to stay?"

"No, you can head on. I need to chat with Amy."

She waved from her car and sped off, leaving the three of us staring at each other in some sort of anticlimactic Mexican standoff.

"Would you like to explain why you've just tried to punch me in the face?" he asked.

"Tried? Do you want me to do it again and show you?" I replied

Now I'm threatening him? What is going on with me?

"All I know is that my husband has been disappearing to go to a running club that doesn't exist and for the last few weeks has been coming back to his family, like a bear with a headache, and refusing to talk to me about what is going on; now I find him here with another woman."

"Sounds like a reason to punch someone to me," said Elle.

Ben stared at us, completely bewildered at what he was hearing.

"Are you being serious? So you jump straight to affair?"

"What was I supposed to think? What the hell is going on?" I demanded.

"I was at my drama group," he said.

Say, what now?

"The drama group that I've told you about for the last six weeks; oh, and that was the producer you assaulted me in front of."

"You haven't once mentioned anything about a drama group, Ben; I think I would know if my husband had a new love of drama that I knew nothing about."

I searched my brain to see if I had completely overlooked anything but I was confident that my ass-of-a-husband was trying to gaslight me and weasel his way out of this situation.

"This is completely ridiculous, just tell the truth," I continued.

"I am, I have been this whole time, basically you have spent the last month not actually listening to what I've been saying and then decided to show up here and hit me in the face."

Elle was uncharacteristically quiet and I could feel her start to move backwards in the direction of her car.

"Stay where you are, Elle, we are in this together," I hissed.

"Amy, the name of the play is 'The Running Man' could that explain things in your head a bit more?" he said.

Fuck. Those words did, in fact, sound familiar.

"I'll take your blushing as a 'yes'," he continued, "I'm getting in my car now and I'm going to the shop to get a bag of peas for my face. I'll see you at home; I don't feel like being around you right now."

Elle and I watched him walk towards the car, both of us feeling bruised after our fall from the high horse, pretty badly. She drove me home and I saw that Ben's car wasn't outside.

"You really had no idea?" she asked.

"Of course not! Do you really think I would have hit him in the face if I knew he was at a drama group? He's never remotely shown an interest in acting and now I'm meant to know that he was a thespian this whole time?"

"I don't know how you're going to fix this one, Amy; his little face was so crushed."

I hated thinking about his expression. She was right, he looked so hurt – not physically, I think we could both agree that my attempt at a punch was pretty pathetic – but his eyes looked like he had been betrayed. Every time that vision appeared in front of me, it made my stomach feel queasy.

We went into see River who was pacing the floor with a sleeping Ciara.

"She woke up as soon as you left," he explained, "but she wasn't looking a feed, she just wants me to walk around."

I smiled and took her from him; the warmth of her body was like a soothing balm to my shame.

"You look spectacularly sexy, caring for that baby, Mr Wild," said Elle, "I think you're going to have to give me one of those."

"Now that's an offer I can't say 'no' to," he replied as he pulled her in for a kiss.

Gross.

"Can the happy couple please get the hell out of my house and be smug somewhere else, you both repulse me."

They stopped kissing and Elle explained: "Amy punched Ben in the face and ruined his chance at stardom all because she hasn't been listening to a word he's been saying for the last six weeks."

"Out!" I shouted.

They retreated from the house and I was left in the quiet of the house by myself. I was reluctant to put Ciara back to bed; I figured that if Ben came home and saw me with her he could be reminded that I was the mother of his children and he couldn't stay mad at me forever. What's the point in having children if you can't use them as emotional pawns?

I stayed up for as long as I could, waiting for him to come home, but I was running the risk of falling asleep on the sofa with the baby in my arms if I waited any longer. I gave up my watch and took us both upstairs, in the hope that he would be home before I closed my eyes.

Chapter 25

I woke up the next morning to find that his side of the bed was empty nor was he on the sofa. I checked my phone and there was one message sent, after midnight, from him which read:

> **Ben: Staying at a friend's to cool off. I'll see you tomorrow.**

My mind started to spin a million miles per hour. What friend? Cool off? He just decided to take a night off from his family and leave me here to deal with the kids and panic about the state of our marriage while he calmed down?

Are you kidding me?

As soon as I read that text message, I had relocated my spine and was working myself back up onto my saddle, to look down on his poor behaviour once more.

The kids were treated to a breakfast served by a raging, silent mother who couldn't help but bang cereal boxes, cupboards and utensils the whole time.

"Where's Daddy?" asked Arthur.

Something we'd both like to know.

"He's gone to work early, he had a meeting," I lied.

"He was meant to tell me if he got the part in the play that he wanted," he replied.

Brilliant, just brilliant; the kids knew and I was completely oblivious. Crap, crap, crap!

"I hope he did, that Gerry guy, who he was up against, sounds like a real div," added Adam.

"You both knew about the play?" I asked.

They both laughed at the seemingly ridiculous question and I used the opportunity to get back down off my horse and sit in the mud. I felt awful.

"Of course," said Arthur, "He's been practising really hard and doing all his exercises for salmonella."

"For stamina," corrected Adam.

My rage subsided the more they spoke. Had I really been so checked out and self-involved that I completely missed this? It was obvious that I had, but I still didn't know how I could have possibly got things this wrong for this long. A lot had gone on over the last few months but I always assumed I had my head on straight with our home life. What is it about life that it can trick you into believing that you're pottering along nicely and then suddenly you end up arse-over-tits and living with a stranger?

I need to fix this but I also need to kill him for staying out all night. Fine balance.

I got the kids off to school and left Ciara at the child minder's, while I stopped with Barbara to get some peppermint tea to soothe my stomach. The anxiety of the situation was making me want to get sick every few minutes and I hated feeling this way in public.

"Is everything ok?" she asked.

"Problems at home," was the only explanation I offered for my pale face and shaking hands.

She gave my hand a little squeeze as she handed over the cup.

"Breathe," she soothed, with a smile.

I managed to reciprocate the gesture before heading upstairs to find Sylvia already in the office, standing on top of the desk jumping with scissors in her hand.

"What on earth are you doing? If you're trying to orchestrate a work-place accident in hopes of a claim then you're in for a big disappointment – unless you want a pay-out of staples and half-chewed pen lids?"

"What?" she asked, looking genuinely perplexed, "I'm just trying to burst all these balloons but we don't have a ladder, I figured I can reach them if I jump."

She started her insane idea again until I demanded she get down and revoked all scissor privileges until after she watched several health and safety videos on the internet.

She was onto her fourth video when Elle finally appeared – over an hour late for work.

"Well? How did it go last night? Any more fisticuffs?" she asked.

"He didn't come home. He stayed at a friend's and went to work from there."

"He what? Are you serious?"

"Deadly."

She blew out a whistle through her teeth and shook her head in disbelief. Her reaction did little to calm my anxiety about the situation and I lay my head on the desk in defeat.

She kneeled beside my chair and rubbed my back.

"This is a fight, a bad fight, but a fight nonetheless. Don't start catastrophizing this, you will work it out," she said.

I had already walked my way through the worst-case scenario all morning. Life as a single mother terrified me but I secretly hoped that it would play out like the movies. Ben would be the bad guy while I had a tough time but pulled myself together, got a makeover and fell in love with a prince.

That could happen, right?

"Why don't you phone him and meet for lunch? It saves you waiting all day and fighting him in your head the whole time. Just don't punch him this time."

"You punched him?" asked Sylvia, "That's pretty rough."

"Get back to the videos you scissor-wielding menace," I snapped back.

Her head disappeared behind the monitor again and I returned my head to the desk. I really didn't want to see him yet; I wasn't even sure what I would say to him. I wasn't sure how annoyed I could be at him staying out all night when it was my behaviour that drove him to it. I hated this moral grey area, I much preferred it when I could just be in the right and everything was his fault.

The morning passed slowly and I stuck to completing odd-jobs that needed done but I had been avoiding. I needed to keep busy, but by doing something that required very little thought process. By the time it was our daily lunch gathering I had made myself well and truly miserable with pointless overthinking. I played with my salad and listened to the other three women talk about whatever they wanted.

Elle cleared her throat to get everyone's attention and I looked up for the first time to see what she wanted.

"I know we decreed that this was to be a sacred 'no-men discussion' time but one of our attendees could really use our help," she said.

She told them what happened last night, and I tried my best not to interrupt as she explained the whole situation.

"Is that all?" asked Sylvia, "That's barely an argument. I once threw paint over my boyfriend's car because he was flirting with some waitress when we were out for dinner. Turns out she was his cousin, so it was all pretty innocent and I had to pay to fix the car but he never flirted with anyone again."

Wow.

"It seems like a pretty serious argument but he definitely shouldn't have stayed out all night. That was a bit of a dick move," said Barbara, in an attempt to bring sanity back to the table, "If I was you, I'd apologise sincerely for last night but don't let him off the hook for his behaviour."

It seemed like the most obvious and logical move but I worried that I would screw it up. I knew I was so angry about his sleepover that I would probably offer the most sarcastic apology in history which would, in turn, result in an argument.

"You're right," I admitted, "I know you're right. I just have to bite the bullet and get this over with."

"That's the spirit," laughed Elle.

I got out my phone and text Ben telling him to be at home by six because we needed to talk about things and he replied with: 'ok'. I never knew that a word as innocuous as that could cause such rage in a person, but it did. I spent the rest of the day in emotional turmoil. I kept flitting from anger to embarrassment, righteous indignation to shame within minutes of each other. It was exhausting.

I could hear the jingle of his keys in the door and I resisted the urge to greet him at the door. Instead, I sat at the head of the kitchen table and waited for him to come find me. He went into the living room to see the kids and my stomach ached when I heard them laugh with happiness at seeing him.

He eventually joined me in the kitchen and he looked awful. I was relieved to see that my pitiful attempt at a punch had not resulted in any marks on his face but he looked pale and tired.

"How are you?" I asked.

"Shit."

He sat down at the opposite end of the table and stared at his hands, refusing to look me in the eyes.

"How could you think I would cheat on you, Amy? After all this time you still don't know me?"

"It was a misunderstanding."

"Yes, a misunderstanding which resulted in me getting assaulted," he spat.

"I'm sorry," I shouted, "I'm sorry for everything, ok?"

Yes, because shouting an apology is always the best way. For goodness sake, pull yourself together!

I cleared my throat and started again.

"I'm sorry," I repeated, "I'm sorry that I didn't listen to you properly about the drama group and I'm sorry that I acted the way I did last night. I'm disgusted at myself for hitting you."

I let the words hang in the air and resisted the urge not to add: 'but you should have come home and not stayed out all night like a selfish arse.' I hoped that if I offered a sincere apology then he would offer his own without me pointing this out.

"I'm sorry for not coming home," he said, quietly.

Thatta boy, Ben

"I stayed at Simon's, from work, and barely slept a wink. He kept giving me really large whiskeys – they were disgusting.

"I was so angry last night but I should have come home and been with you all. Can we just gloss over the rest? I'm so bloody hungover and tired. All I really want is a lie down and to forget last night ever happened."

I've said it before: the man doesn't hold a grudge.

I have never moved so quickly around the table than I did in that moment. As we hugged I could smell the stink of stale whiskey off his hair so he was ordered to go upstairs and shower and sleep for an hour before dinner.

"What if we go out?" he asked, "I bet Mrs White would sit with the kids, she hasn't had a middle-of-the-night knock at the door and babysitting request in months."

I smiled and agreed to ask her. I wanted some time to ourselves so we could actually talk to each other, away from the house. I wanted to hear about the drama group and the part he wanted without the kids running in or Ciara crying for whatever reason she plucked out of the sky, in that particular moment.

Within the hour we were dressed and heading out the door to a local pub for some food, wine and quality time as a couple. I couldn't remember the last time we'd made the effort to do this and I already felt like a weight had been lifted off my shoulders.

Ben looked handsome, despite his hangover, and I was grateful that this was how the evening was panning out and not a horrible screaming match.

I knew this whole situation could have gone on for much longer but, thankfully, he always craved an easy resolution so our world could get right back on its axis.

Our family was our world and although we were still adjusting to the addition of Ciara we knew we were stronger together. At the start of our marriage we only ever had to worry about each other but with the kids it felt like every little decision could result in a colossal knock-on effect that could mentally scar them for the rest of their lives. It's hard work, even the easy stuff, but I knew if Ben and I could find our way back to each other then we could weather the storm. I didn't know who I was without him and I didn't want to find out.

We reached the bar and walked hand-in-hand through the door. We were surprised to see a crowd of people gathered there already and I worried we had walked into an event. Ben handed me the car keys and went to the bathroom while I waited to be seated.

A man dressed in black tie appeared beside me and asked for our names.

"I'm sorry, we haven't booked," I explained, "I didn't realise this bar was quite so exclusive."

"No need to apologise, this is a private event for 'SWAM' members, are you a member?"

I looked at the servers behind him, handing out the free champagne and fancy-looking nibbles and I figured that we both deserved a night of sophistication after a horrible argument.

"Yes, yes we are."

Our host nodded and took our names.

"If you'd like to give me your jacket, you can place your keys in the fishbowl on the counter over there," he explained.

"My keys?" I asked.

"It's tacky, I know, but we thought it would be a retro nod to the raffle days. It's completely voluntary, of course."

I like raffles.

"Sure, why not? I never win raffles; this could be my lucky night."

He smiled and took my jacket while I placed the car keys into the bowl and grabbed two glasses of champagne from a passing server. Ben eventually found me trying to catch the eye of the waiter with the puff pastries.

"What's going on?" he asked.

"We're gate-crashing a party," I said, smiling, "I can be the fun one too, Mr Cole."

"You're always fun."

He gave me a quick kiss on the cheek and took his glass of champagne from me.

"I'm starving," I said, scanning the room for the nibbles, "We'll stay here for a little bit but then we really need to find some proper food."

"Deal. What is the party for?"

"Not sure, some swimming group, I said we were members and we were entered in a raffle."

"Cool! What's the prize?"

"He didn't say, but this whole party looks fancy so it's bound to be something cool."

We both stalked separate servers and unashamedly loaded up our napkins to bring back to each other. We were stuffing our faces with various nibbles when a couple came over to introduce themselves.

Their names were Carla and Damien McEvoy and they were both really friendly. For instance: they kept laughing at everything we were saying and I knew for a fact neither of us were particularly funny.

"We haven't seen you at one of these before," said Carla.

"We're new to the scene," I said.

That's right, Amy, keep it vague and let them do the talking

"It's always nice to see some fresh faces, otherwise it's like we're just meeting the same people over and over. Where's the fun in that?" she smiled.

"Yes, well I always find that variety is the spice of life."

She clinked my glass and nodded approvingly.

"Have you been members long?" I asked.

"A few years, I dipped my toe in the water when I was single but since we married I really jumped in with the lifestyle. We both love it and it keeps us young."

"Well it's important to enjoy things as a couple," I added.

Ben had returned from another one of his hunts and brought back more champagne. I was glad I didn't have to keep the gig up by myself because I really had no idea what else I could offer to the conversation. Other than the breast stroke, I knew very little else about swimming.

"I like the breast stroke," I said.

Both Carla and Damien spluttered in their glass and I realised I must have said something wrong.

"You are just a firecracker aren't you?" said Damien, "That's ok, we are too. We prefer just to get talking about things instead of this small talk nonsense."

"I'm the same!" I replied, enthusiastically, "I hate small talk, it's so fake and if we can't be honest with our fellow members then what's the point in 'SWAM' anyway?"

"Exactly," he smiled.

I am killing it. These people think I'm a hoot; Ben really needs to up his game.

"I have to go to the bathroom, I hope you two can keep my husband out of trouble," I said, waving over my shoulder.

The place was becoming less crowded as people were separating and finding seats together in smaller groups. Everyone was smiling and seemed to be having a great time. I was really surprised that the swimming community of the town was so friendly. Now that Ben had his drama group, perhaps I should look into joining these guys. They were really welcoming and I had already made a couple of friends.

I was fixing my make-up, in the bathroom, when Carla came in to keep me company.

"Are you having fun?" she asked.

Elizabeth McGivern

"Yes, thank you, you guys are so friendly. I was just thinking about — "

My sentence was interrupted by Carla's mouth on mine. I pulled away instantly, shocked at what had just happened and feeling completely confused.

Chapter 26

"I'm sorry," she said, "I'm never this impulsive I just thought you gave me a look to follow you to the bathroom and so I went for it."

"Wow, ok, erm, Carla this is really flattering but I'm just out for a nice evening with my husband," I replied, "I'm sorry if I gave you the impression that it was more than that."

She started to cry, so I awkwardly put my arm around her shoulder to try and comfort her.

"I'm sorry," she said in between sobs, "I know I'm old and out of your league."

"What? No! You're beautiful, I'm just not into women in that way and I'm happily married."

"Then why on earth are you at a swingers meet-up? Are you a voyeur and you let your husband do the swap? We can do that too if you like?"

"I'm at a what, now?"

We looked at each other with matching confusion until she finally said: "Amy, you do know this is a swinger's meet up don't you?"

"No, no I did not."

"You said you were 'SWAM' members?"

"I thought it was a swimming thing."

"It stands for: Swingers With Authentic Marriages. We have these events so we can get to know others who swing in a safe environment."

I kept looking at her with my mouth open; I wasn't sure what I could possibly say to make this situation any less awkward so I remained quiet.

"That's nice," I said, eventually.

She started to cry again and I knew I couldn't be a total monster by leaving her in the bathroom upset. I continued to pet her hair and tell her she was pretty until she managed to calm down enough to fix her mascara and return to the party.

"I'd better get Ben and get the hell out of here," I said.

"You're welcome to stay, we aren't sexual predators," she laughed.

"I know, but this champagne is going straight to my head and we should get some proper dinner."

I didn't want to stay in this party for another second and I knew Ben was going to flip out when I told him.

Maybe I could just fake a stomach ache and not tell him the truth?

When we returned to our husbands they were standing silently beside each other. One look at Ben's face told me, he had already found out what kind of party this was.

"Amy? A word, please," he said.

He pulled my arm behind the pillar and looked completely panicked.

"This is a fucking swingers party," he whispered, "We have got to get out of here, where's the keys?"

The keys.

"They're in the raffle bowl," I explained.

"Raffle bowl? Amy, that's not a raffle bowl that's where couples leave their keys if they want to swap partners for the night."

"How do you know that?"

"Everyone bloody knows that, it's a famous thing!"

"I didn't know that," I said, plainly.

"I'll tell you what: you get the keys back and we can have a long talk about why you shouldn't give your keys away to strangers when you're out for dinner."

I rolled my eyes and went to find the bowl but it was gone. Ben was still standing behind the pillar looking worried while I went on the hunt for the keys. Suddenly a voice was heard over the microphone and we all turned to find the man with the clipboard standing on a stage holding the bowl.

"Good evening, everyone," he said, "I hope you've all been enjoying the night, so far, and have made some real connections with your fellow 'SWAM' members."

People started to applaud as I pushed my way through the crowd to try and get as close as I could to the stage. He continued with his speech, talking about how grateful he was that the community of 'SWAM' had taken off over the last five years.

"Tonight is a wonderful testament to the fabulous people who are committed to authentic marriages and adding some spice into their life, this is a non-judgemental place so I hope you all feel like you can really connect with other like-minded people.

"We thought we would have a little retro nod to those who really started these parties with a little key-in-the-bowl action and bravo to all of you opted to take part."

There was more applause and it drowned out my attempts to get his attention. He eventually caught my eye when I started to manically wave in his direction.

"We have one eager participant here who wants to get things rolling so let's all give her a warm round of applause and welcome her to the stage."

Oh Christ.

I found myself standing on the stage with this man holding a fish bowl full of potential sex partners and a smiling crowd beneath me.

How did I get here?

I tried to whisper to him that I just wanted my keys back but he couldn't hear me and just kept cracking jokes to the audience while I tried to fish around for my own keys.

I pulled at the familiar key ring and freed them into the safety of my hands.

"Hold them high and let's see if the owner will claim them," he said, while the crowd all looked round in anticipation.

"They're actually mine," I explained into the microphone, "We decided this whole bowl thing wasn't for us. We already made a real connection to the couple we were talking to."

I looked out at the crowd and saw Ben mouthing at me to 'stop talking' so I got off the stage as quickly as I could and ran towards him to get our coats. We had just made it to the door when Carla and Damien stood in our way.

"That was a really sweet thing to say," said Carla, "So, your place or ours?"

Chapter 27

Ben and I stood outside the bar, pretending to make a call, while our 'friends' tried to hail a taxi to their house.

"Amy, we are not going home with these people; do you understand?" he said, fervently.

"She was just so sad in the bathroom, so I thought I could make her feel better and bolster her self-esteem. Self-esteem is very important to women."

"Then tell her she looks nice in her dress, don't go home with her! I can't believe I'm even having this conversation."

"I'm not planning on doing anything with her, I just thought we could hang out to make sure she knows it's not a personal thing, we just aren't swingers."

A taxi had pulled up and the two of them were getting into the car.

"Come on you two, the night is getting away from us," shouted Damien.

"Be there in a minute!" I shouted back.

"What the hell is going to happen in a minute, Amy? I am not getting into that car because you don't want to hurt her feelings!"

"Just give me a second and I can think of a logical reason why we can't go, which will get us out of this situation without crushing this woman."

We were both silent as he stared at me and I tried to think of the impossible.

"Ok, the way I see it there's only one way out of this," I said.

"And that is?"

"We run and hide behind that car until they leave."

"Amy, that is the stupidest idea I've heard of."

I shrugged, took off my heels and started sprinting as fast as I could in the opposite direction of the taxi, closely followed by Ben.

We both hunched behind a car and remained there, waiting for the all-clear. We spotted Damien in the distance, who seemed to be looking for us but he gave up after a few minutes and went back around the corner. We decided to stay where we were for several more minutes, just to make sure they weren't driving by in the taxi, to see if they could spot us.

When we felt it was safe, we got back to the car and sat for a while, not talking or moving, just digesting the evening's events.

"Will we just go get a burger and go home?" he asked.

"Yes, please."

We were both lost in our own thoughts during the drive and we sat in silence in a car park eating our burgers. Suddenly, Ben started to laugh.

"What would you have done if I had have been up for the idea of wife swapping with those people?"

I thought about it for a second, looking at my husband who was so proud of his seemingly hilarious hypothetical and said: "Well, you would have been in for a treat, she's a great kisser."

I took another bite of my burger and looked out the window while Ben stared at me in disbelief.

Chapter 28

"When I come back from Canada should I expect to find you shacked up with a new husband or a wife?" asked Elle.

"Nah, I'll stick with Ben – for now."

"Glad to hear it," she laughed.

It was her last day in the office before her and River set off for their latest trip across the pond. It was only going to be a week but I wasn't looking forward to spending that amount of time, alone, with Sylvia. I never quite believed that there would be a more disruptive person to work with than Elle but Sylvia was really living up to that summation.

Her work ethic was better, her pitches and ideas were great and I really needed the help so I decided to use this week without Elle to try and get her out of the bad habits that she had got away with under Elle's supervision.

I had planned to make Ben's favourite dinner, this evening, so we could sit down and chat about the play properly. We were both in a good mood and getting back in sync with each other, which always made life more pleasant for everyone. If things kept going this way we may even break the post-pregnancy sex drought.

It had been a long six months for us both but he hadn't pressurised me and I wasn't particularly interested in anything sex-related, mostly because that would mean less time for sleeping. After our experience at the swinger party the conversation of sex had obviously come up. I explained that I hadn't purposely been avoiding the topic; it was just not a high priority for me at the time.

He tried his best not to look disappointed but in the spirit of reconciliation I decided to make the effort and tonight was going to be the night. We had transformed the spare room into the nursery, so Ciara was out of the way, and we had a semblance of privacy in between her wanting fed. I knew there was some sort of lingerie lying in a drawer somewhere and I had planned to put the moves on Ben so he wouldn't have to worry about rejection.

Before my pregnancy, everything had been great in that department and although our sex life hadn't deteriorated back to where it was a few years ago, I still felt a bit rusty.

Maybe I should look at porn to see if I could pick up a few new moves?

I quickly decided against that plan. I figured that looking at porn to learn about sex was about as realistic as watching a documentary on hospitals to learn how to be a surgeon.

Elle had already left for the day – claiming she was going to meet a client, when in actual fact I knew she was going shopping for her trip – so the only sounding board I had for new ideas was Sylvia.

"Sylvia?" I asked, nervously.

"Yes, boss?"

"I was wondering if we could talk as friends for a minute and not as employer to employee?"

"Sure thing, boss."

Great start.

"I was thinking of spicing things up with Ben and I was wondering if you know of any fun games or something we could try, that's not too explicit or out of my comfort zone."

"Have you tried water sports?" she asked.

My cheeks blushed with shame at the memory.

"Yes, we have but it's not something we want to repeat. I was thinking of something a bit tamer?"

"You're a dark horse, Amy; didn't peg you for the type that enjoys that, I'm impressed."

I smiled and stayed quiet, hoping she would hurry up and mention something else. I scolded myself for not just looking up things on the computer instead of putting myself through this excruciating conversation.

She started to draw something on her notepad and after twenty seconds she showed me a crude drawing of two stick figures in an impossible position.

"What on earth is that?" I asked.

"It's called a 'waterfall'," she said, without offering further explanation."

"You should try that tonight and he'll love it."

"It looks complicated."

"If he's got a half-decent core, it'll be fine."

She threw over the notepad and I spent the next few minutes studying the drawing.

How on earth does 'it' bend that way?

I waited until she left for the bathroom before crumpling it up and putting it in the bin. There was no way I was risking having to wake up Mrs White to try and explain why I had to take Ben to the hospital with a broken penis.

I vowed to keep things modest and just let the evening go smoothly, with no big scheme that could backfire in my face. If the past had proven anything, it was that any plan I tried to do would inevitably fail. I had an hour before the kids needed picked up so I grabbed my bag and decided to pop into town for a bra that wasn't beige or covered in baby spew. The thought of trying to squeeze myself into the black thing I'd bought with Elle all those years ago, put the fear of God in me so I reasoned it was safer to wear something simple.

At this time of day the traffic was light and the parking was easy so I had plenty of time to find something. I locked the car and had started to run towards the entrance of the shopping centre when I heard my name being called.

"Amy? Amy Cole?" shouted the familiar voice of my old work colleague and frenemy: Rita.

Not today, please not today.

"How are you?" she asked.

I turned to look at her and found that she was cradling a small, neat bump.

"Hi Rita," I said, with genuine surprise, "Congratulations."

"Oh, this? Yes, I know I'm massive, right?"

She wasn't.

"I bet you're thinking: 'who ate Rita?'"

I wasn't.

"I can't wait to get this baby out of me and hit the gym so I can fit into normal clothes again! You must be the same, how long have you to go?"

"Excuse me?"

"When are you due? I've three weeks left."

"I had my baby six months ago."

There was a painful silence after I answered and I could see her trying to scramble her thoughts together in order to think of something to say.

"I applaud you for not rushing back to the pre-baby weight and clothes," she said, eventually, "Brava, Amy, you're a pioneer."

Really? That's what she went with?

"It's been nice Rita, but I really need to go. I have a few messages to do before I pick up the kids."

I turned on my heels to leave when she called out: "No!"

I stopped in my tracks and turned to her once more.

"I just wanted to ask about labour," she said, "None of my gal pals have been through this and the internet keeps telling me horrible things so I just wanted to get the low-down from an experienced mother. I'm a bit... scared."

I couldn't believe my ears. Rita was actually asking a genuine question and showing actual emotion. It was almost as if she was human. I offered to get a quick cup of tea with her and she could ask me all the questions she wanted. I knew she didn't deserve my kindness or my help but I wasn't about to let pettiness stop me from helping a woman in need. Even if she did think I still looked pregnant.

She asked countless questions, most of which she could have asked her midwife but she claimed she couldn't because she didn't want to seem 'crass', and by the end she seemed to be a little more calm about what to expect. I told her to call by *Joseph's* any time she wanted to chat or to meet other mothers, but I knew she never would. I predicted that her child would only be attending exclusive day-care facilities for the one percent. I'm not sure that actually existed, but if it did then Rita would find a way to get her child in.

As I got up to leave, I felt good that I was able to be the bigger person and help ease her worries for a little while. I had no time left to shop so I headed back to the car and tried to remember if I had anything in my underwear drawer that could work.

After Rita's comment about my weight, I had started to go off the whole idea of being naked in front of Ben, but I vowed to power through my self-conscious doubts and sleep with him.

The afternoon dragged and I was no closer to finding anything suitable by the time I heard Ben come in from work. I hadn't a clue how I was going to seduce him but I kept reminding myself that pouring hot wax on him was not the solution.

Should I just tell him we are having sex? Ugh, why am I sweating so much?

I could barely eat dinner because of my nerves and by the time the kids were in bed I was barely speaking. It didn't go unnoticed by Ben who decided to turn off the television to try and get me to open up.

"What's going on, Amy? You've barely said a word all evening. Are you worried about something?" he asked.

"It's nothing," I lied, "I'm thinking about what work I have to get done while Elle's gone."

"Are you sure?"

"Yes, sorry, I'll zone back in for the rest of the evening. Now, tell me all about this play."

I sat and really listened to Ben talk about the drama group for the first time. A woman from work had told him about it and he had always missed acting on stage since he left school. He thought if it didn't take up too much time then he would give it a go. The play was about a marathon runner in some bizarre post-apocalyptic universe, and he really wanted to be the lead so he had to get his stamina up by exercising while reading lines. He had been worried that someone else would get the lead but the night I accosted him at the car, he had just found out that he got the part. The enthusiasm in his voice was wonderful. I hadn't seen that spark in his eyes about a project for years. The joy in his voice made me smile and I just knew that if I didn't kiss him then and there the moment would pass and we would spend another night sleeping beside each other like roommates.

He was shocked by my impromptu affection but he didn't resist the kiss or pull away to ask what was going on. All my body hang ups disappeared. This was the easiest and most natural thing in the world and in that moment I realised just how much I had missed being with him.

We didn't speak or ask questions or try any fancy new positions; I didn't worry that my stomach had more stretch marks from my last pregnancy, or flinch with embarrassment when his hand brushed across my scar. It was easy and perfect; it was... us.

Chapter 29

"You know if you didn't want to talk about the play you could have just said so instead of jumping on me like a sex-crazed maniac?" he teased.

We were curled up on the sofa and I had been enjoying the post-coital silence but he could never resist the chance to get a joke in. I poked his belly and got up to find snacks in the kitchen. I grabbed the throw from the sofa and wrapped it around me to hide my modesty from the dog, who was annoyed at being left out of the room. He decided to take the opportunity to attack the end of the blanket as I walked down the hallway. He had grown on me – a little – but I still refused to accept that we had a dog. I told myself that he was simply a houseguest and would eventually be moving on somewhere new. The kids and Ben loved him so I was always outnumbered when I suggested that we find a nice farm for him to move to.

I was reaching for crisps when Colin managed to do another tug of the blanket and pulled the whole thing off, leaving me completely naked in the kitchen. When I turned to get it from his mouth, he made a break for the door and left me trying to cover myself up with a tea-towel.

"Ben!" I called, "Ben, can you bring me out my clothes?"

There was no reply and I knew he had managed to fall asleep within the two minutes I had left the room.

How does he do that?

I looked around the room for something bigger to cover up with but I was dismayed to discover that I, for once, had actually taken the laundry upstairs. I decided that between the window at the front door and the window in the living room, it made more sense for me to make a run for the upstairs and hope that no one came to the door while I was mid-sprint. I took a deep breath and decided to run, but in my rush, I ran into the door hitting my foot which made me shout in agony. Colin appeared to see what the noise was and then proceeded to jump up to try and steal my tiny tea-towel. I struggled down the hallway with him, until I realised that I was mooning anyone walking past the house. I dropped the towel and decided to make a break for it. As I turned to run towards the steps I was faced with a woman and a small girl about to ring our doorbell.

I screamed and sprinted up the stairs as fast as I could, leaving a groggy Ben to pull on his clothes and answer the door.

I hid in our bedroom waiting to hear who the people were and hoped that they weren't going to report me as some sort of neighbourhood flasher.

I couldn't make out what they were saying but called Ben upstairs after I heard the door close.

He was surprised to find me naked in the doorway.

"What are you doing?" he asked.

"That doesn't matter, who was at the door?"

"New neighbours, they were just coming to say 'hello'. Did you know Mrs White was leaving town? She wants to move closer to her daughter. Seems a bit sudden, she didn't mention anything, did she?"

"No, maybe she got sick of her neighbours using her as a free babysitting service," I said.

"That's that gravy-train gone then. Why are you naked?"

"The dog stole my blanket, twice, and then I flashed our new neighbours."

"Of course you did. I look forward to having awkward encounters with them for the next twenty years then," he laughed.

"How long can I expect you to tease me about this?"

"For the next twenty years."

I smiled at the thought of us in twenty years and I hoped that we would still be teasing each other and laughing at our private jokes, whilst embarrassing our adult children. I didn't worry about time marching on anymore, at one stage I would have panicked about every passing minute and the inevitably of death but the more time I spent learning how to be present with everyone I cared about, the more I enjoyed life as it happened.

I used to drown in daydreams of the past and waste days ruminating on times gone by but since we lost Joseph I was more and more determined to be here and be present in every moment – the mundane and the wonderful ones. After all, you never knew when you were doing something for the last time. Soon, Ciara wouldn't wake for me in the middle of the night so no matter how tired I was, I still got up and managed a smile for her. One day the boys wouldn't want my attention, they would crave the approval of their peers over me, so no matter how many times they drew the same spaceship to show me I would still tell them it was the best thing I'd ever seen.

I know there would be days when I wished for it all to hurry up a bit, so I could sit back and relax, but today was not that day and I hoped it wouldn't be tomorrow either. I hoped I would have patience and enthusiasm or at least enough caffeine in my life to fake it. I hoped that Elle and I would have another twenty years of adventures ahead of us and that we would grow old disgracefully. I hoped that I would never stop looking at Ben the way I had tonight and we would always make each other laugh.

But mostly I hoped that the dog would run away. That would be the greatest gift that life could give me.

***

My hope of training Sylvia to be less 'Elle' and a bit more 'me' failed miserably. I couldn't fault her work, but I really wished I was assertive enough to demand that she would wear shoes and stop whistling when she was writing press releases.

Despite all my progress in personal development I still couldn't stand up to people, for fear they wouldn't like me. I figured I could just put in earphones when she whistled and I couldn't really demand she put on shoes when Elle refused to do the same.

I just have to accept that I work in a free-spirited work environment. Or accept that I'm a wimp.

Elle returned from Canada, tired from travelling but enthusiastic and refreshed from her trip. The more she spoke about her time there, the more I worried that they would change their mind and permanently move, but I reasoned that as long as the kids were young she would want to stay put.

Thank you, baggage.

We were sitting down to our lunch when I looked towards the door and saw Joseph's wife, Isabella, walk in. I stood up instantly to greet her and she smiled kindly.

"Please, ladies, I didn't mean to disturb you," she said, "I was only calling in to see Michael."

Elle called for him and he appeared within seconds, concern etched across his face.

"Why does everyone always look so worried when I walk in anywhere as a surprise?" she laughed. "Perhaps I just wanted to have a coffee?"

"Do you want a coffee?" asked Elle.

"No, I want a job, actually."

Elle and I looked at each other; neither of us sure how to let her down gently.

"We don't really have any openings at the minute," said Elle, "I think you're great but with Sylvia, we don't really need any more help."

Isabella started laughing and shook her head.

"As much as I think it would be an interesting experience to work with you both, I was thinking more along the lines of working in the café," she explained, "With Joseph gone, I don't get to hear about all the goings on here anymore and I could use the company."

My heart ached for her and if Michael didn't give her a job this instant then I was going to have to make one up for her, with us, and hope that she wanted to be paid with the large amount of jellybeans we had accumulated in our drawer upstairs.

"Of course, Isabella, this is your place you can do whatever you like," he said, earnestly.

"It's not; I'm not here to take this away from you. As far as I'm concerned, this is your café now; I would just like a couple of hours to keep me busy."

He looked happy about her request and led her into the kitchen to talk privately.

"Do you think I'll be fired?" asked Barbara.

"Nah, I doubt she's here to do much more than keep herself occupied and this place would fall apart without you," said Elle, confidently.

Her reply worked and Barbara looked more at ease knowing that she was still needed. The bell of the door jingled again and in the doorway stood a vaguely familiar woman with a very dishevelled appearance. Her hair looked like it had been backcombed, there were food stains all over her blouse and her top was buttoned up wrong. Her eyes were scanning the room until they landed on mine.

"Amy!" she called with relief.

I walked towards her to get a closer look at this woman. She clearly seemed to know me but I didn't have a clue who she was. It wasn't until I was centimetres in front of her that I realised, to my utter shock, it was Rita. Long gone was her petit bump and immaculately groomed appearance, she looked as if she had spent the better part of a week being dragged backwards, through a hedge.

"Rita?" I asked, not quite believing my eyes, "Are you ok?"

"Do I look ok?" she cried, bursting into tears and throwing herself into my arms. I looked over my shoulder, completely panicked by this outpouring of emotion and flapped my hand to get Elle to come over and save me. She appeared beside me and unhooked Rita's arms from around my shoulders. Elle continued to hold her hands and led her over to the sofa for a sit down while Barbara went behind the counter to get her some tea.

Sylvia joined us all on the sofas and we sat quietly waiting for Rita to stop crying and speak. After several minutes she wasn't any closer to calming down and had taken to using the end of her sleeve as a tissue.

"Rita?" I asked, tentatively, "Is there someone I can phone?"

"Like who? My no-good boyfriend who does nothing all day but play video games while I try to work fifty-hour weeks to keep a roof over our heads? Or my parents, who are retired and don't think a grandchild 'will work in their lifestyle'? Or maybe you can phone my bitch of a sister, who has the figure of a supermodel and the perfect life? Which one of those do you think will be here to help me?"

None of us answered, we just sat there and let her cry some more, until she eventually ran out of steam.

"I'm sorry," she said, "I am just having such a terrible time of things right now and you said I could come here for a chat."

This is what you get for being nice to people.

"Work has sent me off on maternity leave early because I fell asleep at my desk a few times," she continued, "It's not my fault I can't get comfortable at night!

"My stupid boyfriend claims he's developing some revolutionary app, but all I can see him do is laze around all day, playing computer games with his friends and posting vague, inspirational crap on his website.

"My family don't have a sympathetic bone in their bodies and they're totally obsessed with my perfect sister, so they never even want to hear about anything in the real world and everyday I'm getting bigger and bigger and there's nothing I can do about it."

She started to cry again, even harder this time, while we all looked at each other awkwardly.

"I hear you, sister," said Sylvia, "and if you think it's going to get better when the baby arrives, it isn't. He's going to get worse, your arse is going to keep spreading and your family will be nowhere to be seen."

Her sobs got louder and Elle threw a menu at Sylvia to get her to stop talking.

"What?" she protested, "I'm just trying to tell the truth? It's best she knows these things now."

I rolled my eyes and told her to go back upstairs to man the phones while Elle and I had a private word with Rita, in case there was a slim chance of making her feel better.

"It's tough," I said, "Pregnancy is really tough, but you will get through this."

"Of course you bloody will," Elle added, "You're a strong woman and you can handle anything, with or without your useless boyfriend and horrible family.

"This is just a blip. Seasons change, shit happens and people dust themselves off after they fall. You've just had a little trip and you're doubting your bad-assness but it will come back to you after a long nap."

"I would really like a nap," she said, through tears.

"Well you're in the right place. We are going to make you the best little nap space right upstairs, you're going to sleep this off and when you wake up you can get back to kicking arse," replied Elle.

"You really think it will help?" she asked.

"I know it will."

Elle disappeared up the stairs with all the cushions from the sofas around the café and reappeared ten minutes later. I had failed at making small talk with Rita so we had been sitting in an uncomfortable silence ever since Elle had left.

"Come with me, poppet," she said, "We're going to get you nice and comfy."

Rita and I both followed her up the stairs to a supply cupboard, next door to our office. Elle had obviously pulled out the brushes and mop bucket that usually lived there and managed to throw up fairy lights inside the room. There were cushions thrown on the floor and several sleeping bags covering up the lino. There was a faint smell of lavender coming from somewhere and whale song coming from Elle's phone on the shelf above us.

"It's super comfy," said Elle, "There's even a blow-up mattress underneath all those sleeping bags."

We both assisted her with taking her shoes off and helped her sit down on the mattress. Elle had arranged the cushions so she was half sitting up and tucked her in with a soft, cotton throw.

"I'm going to close the door a little to keep the light out – but not the whole way in case you get claustrophobic. Just bang the wall if you need anything," said Elle as we backed off, quietly, to let Rita rest.

I didn't say a word until the office door was closed but as soon as it was I bombarded her with questions about how on earth she managed to pull that transformation off in ten minutes.

"You're an interior design speed demon," I marvelled.

"Not really," she replied, coyly, "That cupboard has been like that for a while."

"What? How have I not known this?"

"Sylvia came up with the idea while you were on maternity leave," she explained, "It's a little time-out room if we get too overwhelmed, or start pissing each other off."

"It works," said Sylvia.

"I don't know if you noticed this, but Sylvia and I have quite a similar temperament and sometimes we would clash if we spent too much time together," continued Elle, "So anytime we felt that things were going that way we would do a little meditation in there to help calm things down."

You've got to be kidding me.

"And you didn't think of telling me this because?" I asked.

"I thought if you knew about it, you'd want to spend your whole life in there," she laughed.

She has a point.

"Now the secret is out, you can use it any time you like," she continued.

I couldn't believe she'd managed to keep it a secret for that long and I was annoyed that she hadn't told me, but I was more excited about being able to use it. I daydreamed about being able to read in there for fifteen minutes when Elle was trying (and failing) to do cartwheels in the office, in order to 'get her creative juices flowing' or when Sylvia started oversharing.

This could be the answer to all my work problems.

We let Rita sleep for an hour before waking her up. She looked so cosy in the nook, but school run time was approaching and we didn't want her to wake up and find us gone.

"That was amazing," she said, stretching her arms and legs as far as she could, like a cat, "I can't thank you enough."

We both helped her up to a standing position and she genuinely did look a bit better. Her cheeks were rosy from the heat of the room and the strain under her eyes had relaxed.

"What are you going to do now?" I asked.

"I'm going home to talk with Denver and make him pull his weight, then I'm going to have a bath and burn these clothes."

What kind of a name is Denver?

"He'll have to shape up or ship out," she continued, "I have a baby to raise."

She straightened up and gave us all air kisses before she strode down the stairs like a woman on a mission.

"Even when she looks like a hot mess she still seems like she's got her life more together than I do," I remarked.

"I wouldn't envy that façade too much," replied Elle, "I predict that woman will either murder her boyfriend this evening or she will start renting that cupboard on a more regular basis."

Chapter 30

Ben's rehearsals were in full swing and he was gone most evenings in the run up to the opening performance. I didn't mind having time without him and I even managed to separate myself from my phone long enough to start reading again.

I loved the escapism of it all, but it took me much longer to get through books these days as I never made it the whole way into a chapter without falling asleep. This had nothing to do with the quality of the book and more to do with my inability to stop myself from nodding off.

Ben would usually find me asleep on the sofa with a book over my face, when he came in from practise. He was always so sweaty when he got back, but he looked happy so I didn't object when he kissed me.

I wondered if I should try and convince Elle to take up a hobby after the play's run was over but there was nothing that I fancied doing. I couldn't hold a note or paint, the thought of exercise filled me with dread and my memory was getting worse, so trying to learn a new language would be less than impossible.

I considered pottery or archery and thought they would both be too dangerous in my hands and I didn't feel the urge to take up self-defence classes – even if I did have a weak punch.

I gave up my search of self-improvement and comforted myself in the knowledge that because I couldn't find anything suitable it meant I was probably perfect to begin with.

I laughed at my delusion and followed Ben upstairs so we could go to bed together. I always slept better when we went to bed at the same time and I liked to finish the day listening to the gossip from behind the scenes of the play.

It came as no surprise that the group was full of drama queens and there was always some sort of back-stabbing going on in each person's attempt to get the limelight.

"It's like a soap opera," I said, "I love it."

"I think you're going to be disappointed by the actual performance after hearing all the things from the practises."

"Probably," I teased, "but I'll still get to see you on stage for the first time. Will you be nervous?"

"Ha! Professionals such as me do not get nervous about trivial performances."

I arched my eyebrow, waiting for the truth and he finally nodded a confession.

"It's just the thought of everyone staring at me, it's really off-putting," he admitted, "It would be easier if they all had their back to the stage."

"Perhaps you should have looked into radio plays to begin with? Might be a bit easier than convincing the audience to turn around every time you have a line…"

"I'll be alright on the night; the lights blind me that much I can barely see anyone."

He gave me a soft kiss, before rolling over for sleep and was snoring within seconds. I still had no idea how he was able to do that. It was impossible for me just to switch off and fall into unconsciousness. I had to wind down for about twenty minutes before I could even get sleepy – and I had to hope that some random thought wouldn't come into my head, which would make it even harder for me. I had lost many an hour of sleep wondering about random topics such as: who decided an 'apple' should be called an 'apple' or figuring out what I should have said to my first boyfriend when he broke my heart. It was ridiculous.

When we first started dating, I used to tell Ben that the sound of his snoring was soothing, now I kicked him in the shins 'by accident' when it gets too loud – which is most nights.

I lay there, staring at the ceiling, and wondered about trivial things that needed done around the house. I made lists about repairs that needed completed in various rooms and thought up new campaign slogans for our clients. I thought about Elle and River and if they would have more children or if Sylvia would stay with us or go back to the webcam game.

I kept thinking and overthinking, dissecting every facet of my life until I finally drifted off and had a fitful sleep.

I was plagued with a vivid, recurring dream that had been haunting me for several weeks. It always started the same way: I was at the beach staring at the water and watching the children play when suddenly we were faced with a tsunami coming towards us. Everyone ran away from the wall of water but I didn't, I just stood there, oblivious to the danger and waited for it to hit. It woke me every time and I couldn't figure out if I was waking up out of fear or out of habit.

I knew I would spend the first half of my morning trying to pinpoint the deep psychological meaning behind it, when in reality it was probably down to the fact that I watched too many disaster movies.

Despite my logical reasoning, it had still unnerved me and the feeling hadn't left by the time I had reached the café and saw Isabella sitting on Joseph's stool, sipping an espresso and reading the newspaper just as he would have done.

I instantly burst into tears, breaking her concentration and making her walk towards me to pull me into a hug. The moment only lasted a few seconds and when it was over she returned to her seat without saying anything while I dried my eyes and walked up the stairs. I was thankful that neither of my co-workers had arrived yet so I could take a few minutes to collect myself.

I felt worry creep into my body. This had been a few occasions where I was caught off guard with emotion and I wasn't sure where it was coming from. Of course with the influx of hormones in pregnancy I was used to letting strange things causing tears but Ciara was nearly seven months old, surely I couldn't still blame that?

I knew I was worried because the feeling was familiar, too familiar. Other symptoms started to add up too, like: increased appetite, quick to anger, trouble in my sleep pattern and the dream. It was all pointing to one thing: depression.

Elle came through the door, carrying several large boxes, halting my terrifying train of thought with her banging and cursing.

"Why did we have to pick an office with so many fucking stairs?" she asked.

"Because we can't afford anywhere else" I replied.

"Ah, yes, that's the reason."

"What's in the boxes?" I asked, knowing I would regret the question.

"I was roped into doing the decorations for the girls' school play, so I have to make a hot air balloon with a wicker basket or something like that."

"That seems a bit unreasonable."

"Doesn't it? Fucking posh bastards, trying to guilt me into helping out."

She started taking apart the boxes and pulling out several random objects – none of which could be used to construct a hot air balloon.

"What are you planning to do with those?" I asked, as she studied half a hose and a horse shoe.

"I've not a fucking clue."

She started to laugh at her predicament but when she turned to see if I found it just as funny, she realised I wasn't even smiling.

"What's wrong with you?" she asked.

I wasn't sure if I should tell her what I was worried about, in case she thought I was being dramatic, but there was no point in lying to her.

"I'm a bit worried about something," I said, simply.

"Spill."

I started to tell her about how I was feeling. I told her about the recurring nightmare and once I started I couldn't stop. I started to list all the other instances I could think of that would point to my diagnosis and by the end I was sure she was going to rush me to the doctors and convince them to pour a bottle of antidepressants down my throat.

I sat and waited for her to say something but she stayed still, as if she was digesting all the information put in front of her.

"I don't think you're depressed, Amy," she said.

"You don't?"

"No, I don't. Look, I'm not saying you're not going through some stuff – hell, we all are – but I think you're being hyper-aware of every emotion you're feeling because you're afraid of being where you were again."

"Wouldn't you be?"

"Of course, and if you honestly think you are going down that path then I will go to the doctors with you and hold your hand to make sure you get the help you need but I think all of this is grief."

I hadn't considered this a possibility. I assumed I had done my grieving for Joseph. I still thought about him every day, but I was up and out of bed and getting on with life. Elle had to be wrong.

"Just because you're up and about, doing all the things you normally do doesn't mean you've worked through the loss. He changed both our lives and there's not a timescale on getting over someone you love," she continued, "I love you, Amy, but you're not great at being able to verbalise how you're feeling until it all bubbles up over the surface and explodes in some way."

"Like hitting Ben?" I asked.

"I don't think we can blame Joseph on you being a shit listener," she laughed. "This could be grief, it could be depression, it could be sleep deprivation caused by my adorable godchild or it could be all of the above. What I do know for certain is that you're not going to get the answers sitting here and talking to me about it. Make the appointment, ask your questions and get treatment if you need it."

"What if it is depression and I end up back at the bottom?"

"Then I'll be standing right beside you giving you a leg up and making sure you're not there for a second more."

I smiled and she gave me a wink, then went back to searching through boxes for craft supplies. She was no closer to finding anything when Sylvia finally decided to show up for work.

"Where the hell have you been?" shouted Elle, without taking her head out of the box to check who had even come into the room.

"Lads, you're not going to believe this but I've only gone and won the bloody lottery," she announced, "I'm minted!"

Chapter 31

We both gaped, open-mouthed, at her announcement.

"I have been staring at the ticket all night and then went to the shop this morning to confirm," she explained, "I'm rich!"

She started to scream, while jumping up and down. The news didn't seem to be sinking in with either of us and it was noticed by Sylvia.

"Guys, don't worry," she continued, "I'm not going to go mad, quit my job and forget you both. I'm still going to be a regular working girl."

"So you're not quitting?" asked Elle.

"No, that's not my style. I couldn't be one of those stuck-up people who shop all day, I love it here."

I really didn't know how to react. On the one hand, she was needed here and I had grown used to her haphazard nature and on the other I wouldn't have to put up with her whistling.

"Come on," she shouted, "Can you be happy for me?"

"We are delighted for you. It's just a shock," I admitted.

"Well, you can let it all sink in while we are out celebrating tonight – my treat! I'll go tell Barbara to get her glad-rags on and we can all go crazy."

"It's a school night," I said, weakly.

Elle and Sylvia both glared at me and I decided to shut my mouth instead of trying to convince them to wait until the weekend.

Sylvia disappeared downstairs to find Barbara while Elle started to pack up all the junk that was lying around the floor.

"Have you given up?" I asked.

"Fuck that, our friend is a millionaire, I'm just going to get her to buy me a hot air balloon."

***

One thing about heading out on a school night was: there were no queues for anywhere. It also meant that we were the only people in the bar too. I could tell the barman was disappointed at having to stay on, because four women decided to be spontaneous and celebrate a cash windfall. I felt bad for him so told him that he should just be extra nice to Sylvia because she was feeling generous tonight and it could result in a big tip for him. It seemed to work, or at least it resulted in him throwing in a smile now and again.

We convinced him to put the music on and turn on the disco lights so we could throw our handbags on the floor, dance around them like young things and sing our hearts out. I laughed a lot and felt more like myself than I had done in a long time; but still there was something holding me back. In the back of my mind I could still feel the familiar drag of the dark cloud I feared. It was as if there was something in my peripheral vision that I could never quite see clearly, but it was always there, always watching.

I left them dancing and went to the bathroom to get some quiet but it didn't take long for Elle to follow me in.

"Are you having fun, princess?" she asked.

"Yes, I am. I'm enjoying it even more because there are no other people here and we aren't being squashed like cattle."

"This could be our social life from now on, you know? Any time we are out with Sylvia, we can make sure we're always in the VIP section of bars."

I laughed instantly and reminded Elle that there were no places in town that actually had a 'VIP' section and we were far too old to be an entourage.

"Both fair points," she conceded, "We had better make the most of this one night then."

I followed her back to the dance floor just in time to bust a move to a song that reminded me of my university days. A time when I thought I was already an adult and had the world at my fingertips. I hadn't even met Ben yet but I was certain that something amazing was just around the corner for me. I loved the naïve optimism of youth but it's not like I became jaded with things as time marched on. Sure, I'd had my knocks and perhaps I was starting to slip under the control of depression once more, but this time I was ready for it. I had a support network surrounding me that wouldn't let me disappear into myself and I was more aware of the lies it used to tell me.

I was no longer on antidepressants. I had managed to wean myself off them during my therapy spell and it was such a proud achievement for me. I guess that's why I was reluctant to return to the doctor, for fear of going back on them and feeling like I had failed at being 'normal'. I feared going backwards in my recovery and I knew it was going to be a fear that I would regularly face during the tough times for the rest of my life. No matter how hard I worked or no matter what progress I made, I would always feel like it could all be taken away from me at any time.

The difference this time was: I was not going to let fear control me. I had the power to control where this spiral was going. I had learned enough about myself through therapy and through life as a whole, to realise that going to see the doctor and maybe going back on medication was not a setback or a failure, it was the smart decision. Maybe Elle was right and this was grief, maybe this would all pass but what was the point in taking that gamble? What harm would seeing someone do?

It was up to me to change things and I knew, deep down, I had the strength to do it. This was not four years ago, I was not the same woman – not even close.

You've got this.

I let the music wash over me with happy memories. I felt that same optimism I felt all those years ago and in that moment I once again felt that something amazing was just around the corner.

Eventually the barman had enough of our private party and wanted to go home. He flashed the lights for last orders and announced that we needed to settle the bill.

"Don't worry, ladies, I've got this," shouted a very drunk Sylvia, "I know how to treat my buddies."

We all laughed and staggered a bit. We had taken our shoes off so we could really get dancing and now, with the alcohol taking hold, we were all unsure on our feet.

"That's £137.60," he said, holding out his hand with the obligatory smile.

"Shit? That's all my winnings and then some. Sorry, guys, you're going to need to contribute," she admitted.

We all looked at each other and then Sylvia, completely confused as to what she was saying.

"How much did you actually win?" asked Barbara.

"One hundred big ones!" she shouted, "I know I said money wouldn't change me but I really do feel like a fancy fucker."

It was hard to imagine her as 'fancy' as she swayed and hiccupped in front of us.

Sylvia had previously instructed us not to bring our purses or it would 'insult her generosity' so now we all did a mad scramble at the bottom of our handbags to try and scrape together some money. We managed to club together £7.83 and handed it over to our stony-faced server.

"I promise I will be here first thing in the morning to settle the remainder of the bill," I said, "I'll even give my home address to send the owner round to my house if I don't make good on my word."

"Get it here by lunchtime or I'll get fired," he replied.

"I swear."

We all left the bar, mortified at our situation and stood outside trying to find a taxi. It had already started to rain and it was freezing.

"I don't mean to be a downer but we've just handed over all our money to the barman so even if we do get a taxi how are we meant to pay for it?" asked Barbara.

"I doubt any of our other halves will be awake and we are chancing that they'll have cash on them," said Elle.

"This really is such a glamorous night, I'm glad I got to experience how the one percent live," I laughed.

Soon we were all laughing. I didn't care if we were cold or wet, I didn't care that our millionaire friend had only actually won £100; it was still a pretty great night. Just as we were about to start our long walk home the bartender appeared outside to close the shutters.

"Are you ladies ok?" he asked.

"We gave you our taxi money," laughed Barbara.

"You wouldn't have much luck getting one now anyway, most of them clock off early on school nights. I've my van around the back if you want a lift? I'm Tony, by the way."

"YES!" we all shouted in unison.

Within minutes we were huddled in the back of Tony's large work van, that had no actual seats, but two small wooden shelves on either side that were low enough to the ground that we could all perch on. We just had to hope that there were no emergency stops or we would all end up face-first on the ground.

Barbara was sitting up in the front, giving our driver directions when suddenly I felt Elle nudging my ribs, urgently.

"What's wrong?" I asked.

"Are we completely stupid? We don't know this guy and we've all just willingly jumped into the back of an unmarked van with him. He could be taking us anywhere and we are just waiting here like sitting ducks."

She's right. Isn't this how horror movies start?

"What are we going to do?" I asked, feeling more panicked by the second.

"We've got to find some weapons," she explained.

In my drunken stupor I accepted that this was the only logical answer to our predicament. I'll text Barbara and tell her to give him directions to the football field close to my house, that way we can run and hide in the bushes.

"Why?" I asked.

"Obviously because then he won't be able to follow us home and murder us in our sleep."

"Obviously," I agreed.

"What if he has a gun?" asked Sylvia, mirroring the urgency in Elle's voice.

"We'll all get our weapons and then we'll rush him as soon as he opens the door. That way we can catch him off-guard and leg it into the bushes."

I was thankful that my best friend was such a survival expert in this hopeless situation so after she sent the text message, we all got to work crawling around the dark floor in search of something we could use as a potential shiv.

The van began to slow down and Barbara shouted back to us: "Why do you want us to stop at the field?"

The three of us all looked at each other trying to think of a reasonable explanation as to why we needed to stop at this peculiar location.

"I can drop you at your door, it's no problem," shouted Tony.

Yeah, I bet you can you serial killer, nut-job.

"No thanks, Tony, we can all get out here," replied Elle.

We felt the van slow to a stop and we all stood as tall as we could (which, in a van, was still a crouching position), brandishing our weapons. I had found an empty milk crate, Elle was trying to make a tape measure seem menacing while Sylvia had decided on using her shoe as a potential club.

My heart was beating out of my chest and when the van door slid open we all started running and screaming at Tony,

231

knocking him to the ground. We grabbed Barbara by her wrist and got her to run with us into the field to find some sort of bushes to hide behind.

"What the hell are you thinking?" asked Barbara.

"Saving your life, Barbie!" replied Elle, "You're welcome."

"You could have really hurt that guy, we need to go back and see if he's ok," she said.

"Are you crazy? He could have been a murderer!" I stressed.

"Guys, he was giving us a lift home after we short-changed him on our bill. He was a nice man that you all just knocked over and left in a heap."

When she put it like that it did sort of make sense that he was just doing a nice thing for four women, stranded in the rain.

"I'm not taking that chance, I'm sure Ted Bundy seemed like a 'nice guy' too," announced Elle, "Look, all we have to do is keep alongside these tree things and cut across the road to get to my house. We can all just hide out there until he goes."

"What if he's injured?" I asked.

"Don't you go believing that 'nice guy' routine, Amy, we have to get somewhere safe."

The alcohol was starting to wear off and I was definitely feeling the cold. We were all in ridiculous footwear for trekking through the undergrowth and we could barely see two feet in front of us. We eventually decided that we were far enough away from the van that it was safe for us to turn on the torches of our phones, to help lead us through the wilderness.

I don't know how long we had spent crawling around in the mud but it felt like hours. Eventually we got to a road and Elle pulled us all out through the bush, one by one. As I stood up and brushed myself off I looked to the left and realised we were back where we started, next to the van and with Tony, who was calmly smoking a cigarette.

"You ladies ok?" he asked.

Crap.

"Yeah, we just thought we would erm take in the scenery," I stuttered.

As soon as Elle realised where we were she jumped in front of me and pointed an accusing finger at Tony and said: "Look, mate, are you going to murder us and use our skin like a coat?"

"Nope, I can't say the thought had crossed my mind, but I was starting to worry that you might be out to get me. You are the ones that just attacked me, remember?

"Do you want a lift or not? I'm tired, I'm cold and I really want to go home. As funny as it was, watching you lot roll around in mud for the last ten minutes, I just want to go to bed – I've the early shift tomorrow."

He threw his cigarette away and climbed back into the driver's seat. We looked at Elle and waited for her to decide if we should get back into the kill van or not.

"Fuck this, I'm cold," she announced and climbed into the back of the van once again.

I was last to get left at my door and I spent the large part of the journey apologising for the bill and for thinking he was a murderer. He didn't say much but continued to put the volume of the music up to drown out my drunken ramblings. I promised to be prompt with the rest of the money and would give him a big tip for all the inconvenience.

"It's not necessary but maybe the next time you're out celebrating you can head to *Roma's* and party the night away," he asked.

"Why? Do you work there sometimes too?"

"Nope."

He revved the engine and sped off down the road, leaving me in a cloud of exhaust fumes.

I was delighted to be reunited with my bed and didn't bother to get changed. I took my shoes off and collapsed onto the duvet, waking Ben in the process.

"Jesus, Amy, you smell like you've rolled in manure," he coughed.

"There's a very real possibility that I may have."

He switched on the light and I got a glimpse of my reflection in the mirror across from the bed. I had scrapes on my knees and my hair was standing on end with several twigs and leaves strewn through it. Clumps of mud had gathered on my feet and elbows, and the sheet was dark brown from where I had laid down on it.

"What in the hell happened to you?" he asked.

"Just an average night out really. Danced, drank, stiffed the bartender for the bill, got caught in a downpour, thought we were being kidnapped, attacked a Good Samaritan, crawled around in some mud like an army cadet and eventually got home in one, very smelly, piece.

"Fancy sex?" I asked with a hiccup.

"I'm going pass on that, but I am going to help you into the shower," he replied.

"I love you Ben, you won't ever try to murder me and use my skin as a coat, would you?"

"No, Amy, I would use it as a blazer – I'm classy like that."

Chapter 32

After our late night excursion in a field, all of us were walking around gingerly, the following morning. My knees and elbows were cut to pieces and I forced Elle to come with me to pay the outstanding bill, in order to apologise for her part in attacking Tony.

"If anything it gave him a good story to tell his mates," she said.

"I don't care who he tells, as long as it isn't the police."

Barbara had treated us all to a hangover-busting smoothie of her own creation. It was brown and lumpy and we all resisted the urge to ask what was in it, instead we accepted it gladly in the hope that it would make us feel human again.

The chill-out nook was being used for twenty minute intervals by all of us, for powernaps, and it was the least productive work day in the business by half. I spent a large proportion of the day looking up fast-acting hangover remedies ahead of Ben's performance in his play, this evening. He had been up from the crack of dawn, rehearsing his lines around the house, and had taken the day off work to meet the group to do a dress rehearsal this afternoon.

"I cannot sit through an amateur dramatic performance feeling like I'm going to be sick at any minute," I wailed, "Why did I drink so much?"

"I don't think you drank too much, you're just a lightweight. I feel fine now that I had that powernap," announced Sylvia.

I glared in her direction, mentally blaming her for my predicament, despite the fact no one was forcibly pouring the alcohol down my throat.

"We could go for the cure before the curtain goes up?" suggested Elle.

I didn't have the energy to even verbalise what a stupid idea that was so instead I lay on the floor and waited for death.

By the time I was on school run I was starting to feel a bit more human, but my knees were stinging like crazy and it didn't help that they were rubbing off my jeans. I couldn't even wear a skirt to relieve the friction in case anyone spotted my injuries and asked what I'd been up to.

Fight through the pain to avoid future embarrassment, Cole. This will teach you to try and be young. Stick to falling asleep on the sofa, with a book or a true crime documentary. Actually, scratch that, no more true crime or you will keep accusing innocent people of being murderers. Ugh, I need sleep.

The one productive thing that I did manage to complete was to secure a last-minute appointment with the GP, to talk about going back on antidepressants. It wasn't my smartest idea to go and talk about me being potentially depressed when I looked like a hungover mess but I didn't want to put it off for longer than necessary in case I lost my nerve.

I left the kids with Elle, before I went to face my fears and start my fight against depression once more.

***

I hated doctor's waiting rooms, mostly because they were full of sick people and rubbish magazines. It was a pretty depressing place to be at any given time, but especially when you were already feeling depressed.

I spent the time in the waiting room looking at the curled up edge of a poster hanging on the noticeboard which was full of information about flu shots. I made a mental note to remind my parents to get theirs and to brace myself for the abuse I would get back from Mum who – despite being in her seventies – refused to believe her 'real' age was above fifty.

I was eventually called and found myself sitting opposite a stern-looking man, who didn't bother to look up from his screen as he busily typed in notes from the last patient. I was immediately put on edge and was considering faking a sore throat to get thrown out of here for wasting his time.

When he finally looked up from his computer, his eyes fixed on my face and he smiled, broadly.

"Sorry about that," he said, "Bloody useless with computers, so it takes all my concentration to type anything."

I felt more relaxed and decided that I was going to be honest and face the problem head-on for once in my adult life. His name was Dr Fielding and was new to the surgery. He was pleasant and made time to get to know me a little, even though I knew he wasn't really meant to with so many patients waiting outside. It was because of those extra minutes, when he spoke to me like a person and not a file, that I was able to open up about my history and what I was worried about now.

He listened intently and shuffled through my file in order to see what medication I had been on in the past. When I eventually stopped talking he remained quiet for a painfully long time, as I waited to find out what he thought could be done.

"I think you're a very brave woman," he said, "I think being open and proactive about these sorts of things is always the way forward. Most would put their head in the sand and hope that it would just disappear on its own."

I blushed, guiltily, at my coping mechanism of the past but I kept eye contact with him.

"You've been through a lot over the last four years and you've also overcome a lot. I see you've been through cognitive behavioural therapy and also had a baby recently? That, alone, would put some strain on your mental health –

especially if it wasn't the easiest time. Hyperemesis and Bell's palsy? Well, at least you recovered from that nicely.

"And you mentioned you'd had a recent bereavement? All in all, Amy, you've been through the mills and you're still operating at full capacity. If that's not something to be proud of then, I don't know what is."

Hearing it all out in the open was a shock for me, it was as if someone was retelling a highlights reel of my physical and mental wellbeing over the last few years. When I listened to it objectively, I finally realised that I was a lot more capable than I was giving myself credit for. Yes, I wasn't feeling great all the time but who the hell does?

"If you want to go back down the road of medication then we can explore that possibility and perhaps introduce a very low dosage back into your life," he continued, "but my professional opinion is: you don't need any. It's been a tough time for you but it won't last forever and from the outside looking in, you're handling it better than most."

I smiled and revelled in the relief his words brought me. I could have tried to talk myself out of the idea that I wasn't actually depressed for months, until I made myself crazy, but hearing it from someone objective was all the kick I needed to believe in myself again.

I left the surgery with a spring in my step and stopped for doughnuts on the way to Elle's house so we could celebrate my diagnosis of: I'm human.

Her eyes lit up when she spotted the box in my hands and took them from me at once.

"Don't you want to hear what the doctor said?" I asked.

"I assume it was good news and you're not crazy or you wouldn't have brought doughnuts," she replied.

"I could have brought them to soften the blow of my bad news."

"Who would bring doughnuts to do that? No, you would buy scones if it were bad news."

"Noted," I laughed.

Over tea and doughnuts I told her about my appointment and she looked very pleased that she was right about the depression.

"I told you so," she said with a smug smile on her face.

"You didn't really; all you said was that 'it was probably grief.'"

"Well the doctor agreed with me and in my books that means I was right and I could probably be a doctor. Fuck, imagine that?"

"That's a truly terrifying thought."

She shot me a scathing look but after running the idea over in her head again she agreed with my reaction and went back to stuffing her face with another doughnut.

"You know I bought some for the kids too?" I said, as she was reaching for another.

"Well that's just irresponsible parenting, Amy, I'm saving our children from a lifetime of obesity and the possibility of type-2 diabetes."

I decided to join her and had another doughnut in the hope that it would get rid of the last of my hangover before the play.

"Is River coming with us?" I asked.

"Yeah, he said he wouldn't miss it. I wish I could."

"Hey! That's not very supportive, just think of all the nonsense Ben has done for you over the years, and you never know it could be incredible."

"I highly doubt that, but you're right about Benny, he's been a good sport so I might as well be there to clap at the end of this car-crash."

The kids and I headed home to get ready for the play and found that Ben had already left. He had scrawled a quick note saying he had to go back in early to run lines with someone's understudy who had been called up unexpectedly. One of the main cast members had apparently eaten some dodgy chicken and was unable to perform.

My parents were coming over to sit with Ciara while the boys and I had a night at the theatre. It all sounded very posh but unfortunately the 'theatre' was actually the local community centre. It was always freezing and filled with those really uncomfortable, metal chairs.

The doorbell went and I was shocked that my parents were actually early for a change. I was even more shocked to find that it wasn't my parents on the other side of the door but Ben's mother and father.

"Surprise!" shouted Althea, "We are here to see our superstar son on stage."

She was already through the door and had pushed past me before my brain had registered what was happening.

They have bags, why do they have bags?

"Aimsy, darling, why are you standing there with your mouth open?" she asked.

"You have bags," I replied, not moving from the door.

"Don't worry, dear, we aren't going to be staying on your sofa we have booked a room in the B&B in the next street over," she explained.

I breathed a sigh of relief knowing that no matter how bad the evening was going to get, I would not have to spend more time than necessary with my mother-in-law.

My parents arrived shortly after and the four of them all made a fuss of Ciara while I tried to tame my sons' hair into some semblance of tidiness, but I eventually gave up. I settled for clean faces and matching shoes before we waved 'good-bye' to my parents and headed down to the community centre. I wanted to get there early, in order to get decent seats so we'd be able to see Ben and not get stuck behind a pillar.

We were almost the first to arrive and walked in on them finishing off a rehearsal. We caught Ben's eye and we all started waving enthusiastically. He jumped down from the stage and came over to hug us all.

"Mum, Dad, I can't believe you're here," he said with genuine surprise.

"We couldn't miss our son's theatrical debut, could we?" said Althea, gushing with pride.

Ben looked embarrassed by her words and pulled me to one side, looking more nervous than I had ever seen him before.

"Are you ok?" I asked, "You look a bit green."

"A bit of pre-show jitters, it's nothing. This is going to be a disaster," he whispered, "The understudy didn't really think that he'd ever be called so didn't bother to learn all his lines. He's backstage writing phrases on his arm."

"That's not so bad, it'll be alright when he gets up there," I lied.

He didn't look convinced and put a fake smile on his face any time his mother looked in our direction.

"There's more," he continued.

This doesn't sound great.

"Part of the scenery fell apart in rehearsal and hit one of the other guys on the head."

"Holy crap, is he ok?"

"He says he's fine but it knocked his hearing aid out, we haven't been able to find it and now he keeps shouting his lines."

I bit my lip in an effort not to laugh in his face, but he knew I was amused by the disasters.

"This isn't funny, Amy, the local paper is here to review it and it's going to be mess."

I felt guilty for laughing, after all, they had been working so hard on the show and it would be a shame for it all to go tits up on opening night.

"Is there anything I can do?" I asked.

"Just try not to laugh too hard when it all starts to fall apart."

"I promise," I said with a smile.

He sighed in frustration and headed backstage to get ready with the rest of the actors. Althea had managed to convince a family to move into inferior seats so we could all sit together by telling them we were the immediate family of 'the star'.

Her voice had so much authority in it they simply did as she asked and apologised to her for inconveniencing us.

How the hell does she do that?

The lights were going down and I managed to spot River and Elle sneak in at the back just as the show began.

Ben was the first on stage, jogging on the spot as he began a brooding monologue about his lost love. He was good, really good. I was instantly pulled into the story and my heart swelled with pride for my talented husband. I even overlooked the fact that he was wearing more make-up than me as he stood under the spotlight.

We settled into the next scene where he was joined by his male co-star who was introduced as 'Troy'. It wasn't hard to work out that this was the understudy because he looked like a rabbit caught in the headlights any time it was his turn to say anything. A few times he pulled up his sleeve to read things from his arm but the heat from the stage lights had smudged them. At one point he thanked Ben's character for 'saving his light during the wart'.

Ben looked at him blankly but continued to deliver his lines and ignored the fact that the discussion wasn't making any sense. By the end of the scene it really felt like the two of them were having completely different conversations.

I started to squirm in my seat with every passing line and soon they were joined on stage by the guy with a hearing impairment.

"JAMES? TROY? WHY ARE YOU STANDING HERE SO OPENLY? THE ENEMY WILL SEE YOU. QUICKLY, COME WITH ME, I CAN HIDE YOU BEFORE THE NEXT PATROL," he roared at his bemused co-stars.

The three of them hid behind a cardboard wall as several others marched by.

"KEEP YOUR VOICES DOWN OR WE WILL BE SHOT, WE MUST BE AS QUIET AS CHURCH MICE," he continued.

I dropped my head into my hand as the audience began to snigger at the hammy, overacting.

This is going to be a long night.

I looked around at the audience and most people had the same confused look on their face as I did, followed by cringing anytime the actor roared at Ben and the understudy.

Each scene became more painful than the last and the audience couldn't help but laugh when the shouter exploded on to the stage yelling: "THE SILENCE IS DEAFENING."

By the time the intermission hit we were all a little shell-shocked from what transpired. Elle was quick to find me at my seat looking completely bewildered.

"What the fuck is this play about?" she asked, "Does the guy have PTSD from warts? I can't follow what the fuck is happening."

I tried to remember what Ben had told me about the story but all I could remember was it being something about a dystopian future where arms dealers ruled over cities with an iron fist. Unfortunately, the understudy had read that line incorrectly so everyone in the audience thought that the universe was being run by armadillo overlords.

"This is fucking insane," she said, "Thanks for making me come, I'm having a ball."

She ran back to River before the second act started and I wasn't sure if she was being genuine. The boys were mesmerised by the whole thing and it was only Althea who looked as confused and exhausted as I did.

When the second act began, the understudy was under the spotlight delivering his dramatic monologue and back story. He had started off well but half-way through he was losing steam and started throwing in bits and pieces of other famous speeches from movies.

There was mention of aliens at one stage and when he couldn't think of the final line he threw up on stage. Unfortunately, Ben didn't see it in time and ended up running straight into it, while delivering his line and landed on his back. Ever the professional, he continued with the scene, despite his back dripping with vomit and he managed to finish up with minimal gagging at the smell.

When he returned to the stage he was in a new top and the understudy had been replaced with a female stagehand reading from the script.

This is anarchy .

The climax of the action was meant to take place in a graveyard at night – as we had been informed by the screaming sidekick. However, whoever was in charge of the backdrops had left the sea scene on and it had jammed. Four men were scrambling to push it up as Ben lay dying and delivering his moving, final words – none of which were heard over the banging and cursing of the people at the back of the stage.

The curtain fell and no one knew if the play was over until it reopened and the actors were lined up and bowing.

What was that?

I mentally prepared myself for trying to fake enthusiasm for what had just transpired but Ben knew me better than anyone and I had no idea how I was going to get out of this. He eventually came down to our seats from back stage but before he could get to us, Elle ran up and threw her arms around his neck.

"Benny!" she screamed, "That was the best fucking piece of theatre I've ever been to in my life."

His face lit up at the genuine praise and I could see how relieved he was to hear something positive after the disaster that had just been put on.

"Did you really think so?" he asked.

"Man, it was so good," added River, "It was so thought-provoking and abstract. It was like a rollercoaster for the soul."

He thanked them both and turned to me and said: "So? What did you think?"

I knew there was no point in trying to lie to him or pull some random theatre-critic jargon out of the air so I said the one thing that I could, which was completely honest: "I am so proud of you. You were fantastic."

I didn't need to lie about that. He gave it his all and didn't give up, even when the scene was literally falling apart around him. I couldn't have been more proud of him.

It wasn't long before he was whisked away by his mother to be showered with praise from her and his father. There was an after party for the cast and their families, but we made our excuses and headed home instead.

"I really need a shower, I still smell like vomit," confessed Ben, "He can't even blame food poisoning, he was just so nervous."

The boys spent the rest of the drive home pretending to vomit until I had to threaten them with grounding if they didn't quit it. My parents were surprised to see us home so soon and had been happily dozing on the sofa when we all came in to tell them about Ben's success on stage.

Ben's parents called in to pick up their bags and brought a bottle of bubbly with them to toast their son. The kids were ushered off to bed, while the grown-ups chatted some more about the play.

"I have a couple of questions about the show," said Althea.

Don't we all.

"Now, I understand the significance of the armadillo overlords but did they decide to do some sort of chemical warfare against the human race with the flu?"

"The flu?" replied Ben.

"Yes, that man – the one who vomited – kept talking about a germ factory," she explained.

"Oh, yeah he was meant to be saying 'Germany'," clarified Ben.

"Well now I'm completely confused, what on earth has Germany got to do with armadillos?"

The questions carried on like that until the bottle was empty and I started to tell people to get out so I could get some sleep. I figured they were going to complain about me no matter what I did, so I might as well be direct.

As Ben and I lay in bed, after everyone had left, I lay my head on his chest and listened to him talk enthusiastically about the play. He had moved past the fact that it was a total disaster and now had taken to calling it a 'learning opportunity'.

His optimism was wonderful and I decided that I would buy the local paper the next day and frame the review – whether it was bad or good – that way he would know that we were proud of him and what he did.

My plan went array when I saw the headline the next morning which read: 'The Running Man? Run for the exits'

I set the paper back down once I read the whole article, in which Ben was described as a 'stiff, yet bumbling lead'. I didn't think he'd want this particular summation of his acting abilities framed in the hallway. Instead, I went online and ordered him a plastic Oscar statue which had 'Best Leading Man' written on it.

He could put in on the mantelpiece and tell people about his hugely successful career as an actor and hope that they didn't see the performance for themselves.

A few weeks after the play debacle, he brought up the fact that the group was starting auditions for their next production within the next month or two. He admitted that after the last time he wasn't planning on treading the boards anytime soon, but suggested that I tell Elle.

"She has a flair for the dramatic and would definitely love the limelight," he said, "Maybe she'd have fun."

"She's already talking about their next trip to Canada so I don't think she'll be around for them," I explained.

"Abby is taking the week off when the kids are on half-term so I'll have Ciara and the boys all to myself. I don't know if I'm excited or terrified by this.

"I'm dreading the thought of leaving Sylvia alone in the office, if Elle is out too, but I don't think I'll get much done with all three of the kids hanging out with us."

"Have you any exciting plans?" he asked.

"Maybe one, I think it's about time I introduced Ciara to some of her peers."

"Ok? And how do you plan on doing that?"

"I'm taking her to 'Smug Club', of course."

Chapter 33

In the midst of half-term holidays, I packed up Ciara and bribed my older children with chocolate if they behaved reasonably well during an hour at 'Smug Club'. I reminded myself that it wasn't actually called that, but 'Special Mums United in Growth' was such a mouthful I didn't know how someone hadn't it shorted it to 'smug' by now.

Even though Mags wasn't chairperson of the group anymore, she was still behind the scenes, closely monitoring the play mornings and arranging the group activities. I walked through the doors and I was instantly transported back to the day I first met Elle.

Not much had changed from the room that housed the parent and toddler group, but it didn't look anywhere near as scary as it did on that day.

I caught Mags' eye and she waved enthusiastically, from across the room.

"Amy," she smiled, "It's great to see you all."

Her welcome was genuine and she invited my boys to sit in her office and play on the computer, while Ciara and I joined the floor activities with other kids her age.

She enjoyed grabbing random toys and shoving them in her mouth, while I tried not to think of the germs that would inevitably pass between kids here. I didn't bother to look around and try to make new 'mum friends'; I felt like I had already reached capacity in my life and Elle counted as at least three people because of her demanding character.

I looked towards the seat where I sat on the day she breezed into the hall and into my life. If I thought hard enough, I could even see the scene play out in front of me. As I let it unfold, like a movie I had watched a thousand times, I wanted to reach out to the poor, broken woman who sat on those seats and let her know that things would get better.

She was filled with so much hurt and self-loathing that it made my heart hurt just to think of her.

My train of thought was interrupted by a crash coming from the direction of the kitchen.

Two women had bumped into each other and one had dropped her cup. The tea spilled on the floor and she looked mortified at the accident.

Several others had gathered around to help clear up the mess and comfort her. I knew it was embarrassing to spill something in public but her reaction seemed a bit over-the-top for something so trivial. I kept staring at the commotion until Mags appeared and took the woman to one side. They sat on the chairs away from the crowd, and the woman put her head in her hands.

This isn't about tea.

After a few minutes, Mags called a hush to the group. Everyone stopped what they were doing and looked towards her direction.

"Guys, Helen has had some bad news this week," she began, "She needs to be shown that she is not in this alone, nor will she ever be."

Mags led her to the centre of the carpeted area, where they would usually sing nursery rhymes. She sat on the floor and invited Helen to do the same.

"We are never here to judge another parent, we are never here to make people feel alone or less of themselves because we do things differently. We come here every week, to be the village that it takes to raise our children.

"We are your family Helen, and we are here for you."

The group started to clap and one by one they joined Helen on the floor. I began to panic that they were going to start singing '*Kumbaya*' but they all sat with her in silence, with their heads down as if they were all saying some sort of quiet prayer. After a few minutes, the spell was broken and Helen looked immeasurably better. They all went back to what they were doing, as if the last few minutes hadn't even happened.

Just as Mags was about to go back to the kitchen I called her over to get some answers.

"Not to be rude," I began, "but what the hell was that?"

"It was a healing circle," she replied, as if that answer cleared everything up. When she realised I was no clearer to understanding she added: "After Elle came to see me, to bury the hatchet, I started to think about how things were carried out here.

"I basically realised that a more inclusive and supportive group was much better for the community than the way things had been run for years. We have so many single parents, those who live in different countries from the rest of their family or even those who just have no one to care, so I took it upon myself to make sure that this group would always be a safe space for parents.

"I never wanted to make people feel that they were alone again. When I think of the way things used to be – the way I used to be – it fills me with so much shame. Now, my only goal is to help run a place of comfort for anyone that needs it. Sometimes it's just a shoulder to cry on, but other times it's practical help like: visa advice, divorce proceedings or finding out what financial aid they're entitled to.

"It's tough but it's much more rewarding than serving tea and being a smug bitch," she laughed. "That means you can't call us 'Smug Club' anymore."

I blushed at her use of the name but was delighted that she had taken the initiative to make a stand and really help people. At *Joseph's*, we could give them respite from the real world but Mags could make a real difference to someone's situation.

I was proud of her.

After I managed to drag my children away from her computer, we took the short walk up to the café to check on Sylvia and make sure she hadn't burnt down the office. I was happy to find that she was in the middle of a business call and had secured a meeting with a bar in town.

"Where's that for?" I asked.

"That place we were in the other week," she replied, nonchalantly.

"You mean the place in which we ran up a bill we couldn't pay and accused the barman of being a serial killer?"

"That's the one. Turns out they need help with revitalising their image, they're getting a few undesirables around the place."

"No shit, Sylvia, they're talking about us."

"You think? Well, either way we're meeting them next week. By the way, your friend Rita is in the nook."

Of course she is.

I knocked on the door and she pushed it open with her foot. She was sitting, cross-legged, on a beanbag in the middle of the room, breastfeeding a tiny baby.

"Amy," she whispered, "How good of you to drop in."

She does realise this is my workplace, doesn't she?

"I decided the café was far too busy for Astrid and I to really bond during this feeding time so we came up here to relax and really embrace the moment," she continued.

"Congratulations."

"Oh, yes, it really was the most amazing experience; nothing like you had prepared me for. Mine was completely natural and I just breathed her out in her own time. It was the most peaceful and beautiful experience."

Of course it was.

"Did I tell you? Denver's app was sold for more money than we know what to do with, so it really did pay to stand by him – and I'm already in my pre-pregnancy clothes.

"Really, I've no idea why people make such a fuss over this whole child rearing thing. I've been crushing it. The house is immaculate, Astrid is already showing signs of being a gifted child, she's sleeping through the night and I look as good as I did before I got pregnant. In fact, my skin and hair is incredible."

Don't hit a breastfeeding woman, don't hit a breastfeeding woman, don't hit a breastfeeding woman.

"What age is little, Astrid?" I asked, trying not to choke on my own jealousy of her child sleeping the whole night through.

"She's seven weeks old."

You've got to be kidding me.

"Well you're free to use the nook today, but unfortunately it's being dismantled tomorrow," I lied.

"Oh, really? Is it because you're going out of business?"

"No, actually we're expanding and need the extra office space."

She looked momentarily disappointed by the news but quickly composed herself so I wouldn't think of her as anything other than perfectly composed.

"That's exciting; I knew you had it in you to achieve something, other than making giant babies. I'll be out of here as soon as she's finished. It was a nice idea to have this little hovel here but it really is a bit manky. I wouldn't want to expose Astrid to mould."

I couldn't hit a breastfeeding woman but I could tell her exactly what I thought of the condescending bull that she put me through, each and every time I saw her. I had swallowed my feelings about the toxic way she spoke to me for long enough and she had crossed a line.

"As always, Rita, its' been a pleasure but I'm going to have to insist that you get your fake ass out of my workplace and don't come lurking around here ever again, you complete and utter gobshite."

I closed the door without letting her reply and returned to my office to find Sylvia swinging Ciara around and the boys fighting over my computer.

"Boys, get away from the screen!" I shouted.

"Will your friend be much longer?" asked Sylvia.

"She's no friend of mine, make sure she's evicted within the next half hour and remind her she's barred."

"Wow, you're cut-throat."

"And while I'm at it: this is a bloody office so wear some damn shoes while you're here."

"But Elle said — "

"I don't give a damn what Elle said, I'm telling you to wear shoes."

"No problem, boss," she smiled, "You're really turning into a badass – I like this side of you."

"I can assure you, Sylvia, I've always been a badass."

I gathered up my brood of children and headed home to spend the afternoon sorting laundry and patting myself on the back for finally telling Rita where to shove it. I couldn't wait for Elle to phone so I could tell her about the changes to 'Smug Club' and finally telling Rita to sling her hook.

I was riding on a high when the doorbell went. It wasn't expecting my parents, but that never stopped them from showing up, but as I got to the hallway I spotted Joseph's wife, Isabella, standing outside.

I opened up the door and invited her inside as pleasantly as I could.

She wasn't as welcoming as Joseph, but our relationship was improving with every day – although a house call was definitely not something I would have ever expected.

"I'm sorry to drop in on you like this but I wanted to run something by you, do you have a moment?" she asked.

"Of course, please come into the kitchen and I'll put on the kettle, but don't be expecting anything nearly as nice as yours in the café."

She smiled and followed me down the hallway to the kitchen. She was a dainty woman, but I could tell by the way she carried herself that she had immeasurable strength, the kind that I could only dream of.

She was the type of person that never had to raise her voice or curse in order to be heard. She could demand the attention of a room just by walking into it, and she looked much younger than her years.

"How can I help?" I asked, earnestly.

"Before Joseph left this earth we would spend our Sunday afternoons walking around that lake you had the wedding at," she said, "We were creatures of habit, you see.

"I haven't been back since he died but it's a precious memory to me. I expected when he retired that we would spend more afternoons there, but it wasn't to be."

"Would you like me to take you there?"

"Don't interrupt, dear."

I shut my mouth and my heart skipped a beat at the scolding.

Yep, I'm still terrified by her.

"As I was saying, I have got permission to have a bench dedicated there to him and I was hoping to get some artistic input from you. I'm not great with words but Joseph used to speak highly of you. I would like Elle to paint it – the more colourful the better – and for you to write something meaningful for the plaque. If you don't mind, that is?"

I didn't reply, I wasn't sure if I should say anything and risk getting told off again.

"You can speak now, Amy," she added.

"Thanks," I replied, breathing with relief, "I would be absolutely honoured to help you with this and I can answer for Elle too, she'd love to."

"That's lovely. The dedication is in two weeks so you'd better get to work. Will that be enough time or should I ask someone else?"

"No!" I shouted, louder than necessary, "We will have it done, please, we really want to."

Isabella smiled, slipped down from her stool and headed towards the door.

"You didn't have any of your tea," I called.

"Don't be silly, Amy, my husband would roll over in his grave if he knew I was drinking that swill."

She closed the door behind her and left me completely awestruck at her visit. I hunted out my phone to tell Elle all the news and make sure she started working on ideas for the bench.

This project was going to be our most important yet and it had to be perfect.

Chapter 34

It was the day of the dedication and a beautiful Sunday afternoon. Isabella, Maria, Michael and the rest of their family had all gathered together, in order to remember the towering patriarch of the family and I was nervous as hell.

Elle and I had worked through fifty ideas and were never able to agree on a design concept. We had never argued so much about our work in the whole time we were in business together. Emotions had run high on any number of occasions but we made it here.

We both looked at the family who were all chatting together and smiling, as they looked out towards the water.

"Pretty beautiful place to get married isn't it?" remarked Elle.

"It is," I replied, staring off into the distance with everyone else, "Are you ready to do this?"

"Not at all."

"Me either, let's go."

I clapped to get the crowd's attention and invited Michael to say a few words before we unveiled the bench. I didn't envy his job, but I knew he was up to the challenge. He thanked me for the introduction and cleared his throat. I could tell he was fighting back emotion and I longed to let him know it was going to be ok.

"My boss was a jerk," he said.

A what, now?

"He was stubborn, condescending, a complete control freak and he was always complaining about everything I did in the kitchen.

"I couldn't stand the man and every day, when I got home from work, I was so thankful to be away from him.

"However, my father-in-law, who invited us to dinner every night, was my hero. He was patient, understanding, endlessly generous with his time and money and never met a person he didn't want to help. When I left his home after dinner every evening, I felt happy and I felt loved.

"That's what family is. They have the ability to drive you crazy, but you would go to the ends of the earth for them if they asked.

"Working with Joseph was a challenge, but it turned me into the man I am today and it's one I'm proud of. He pushed me to better myself, he taught me to care about what I was doing, he motivated me to the best version of myself I could be and when I was at the end of my rope with him, he would remind me that, above all, we were family and that is the whole reason we were striving to create something in that café.

"It was about more than food and hot drinks, it was about creating a legacy and thanks to him – and the work done by Amy and Elle – the café is recognised as a special place in this town for people to gather and heal themselves. They can take time out of life and soothe their soul with a hot drink and a friendly ear.

"Joseph always wanted to hear people's stories and he was endlessly fascinated with knowing about every person that walked through the door. Everyone obliged, everyone saw the kindness that radiated from him and his genuine nature. Everyone.

"If that's not a legacy to be proud of, then I don't know what is."

The crowd began to clap as they all recalled their own memories of this remarkable man. Isabella pulled back the sheet and revealed the turquoise bench, ornately decorated

257

with little reminders of who Joseph was. Coffee cups, crossword puzzles and hearts were just a few that stood out. I gave Elle a hug and told her it was beautiful. She couldn't say anything in return through the tears and I held my breath as I waited to hear Isabella's verdict on our work.

We walked over to the bench in order to take in our completed project and Elle read the plaque aloud: "Everybody has a story, make sure yours counts."

She smiled as she said it and added: "He really was a nosy bastard, wasn't he?"

We both laughed and wiped way our tears in time for Isabella to find us.

"Well, ladies, he would be proud of what you've done here today. I am pleased."

Thank Christ for that.

"We are going back to the café to have a little party, will you be joining us?" she asked.

"No, thank you, we'll leave that to the family. I think we'll just stay here for a while," I replied.

The crowd began to disperse and just as Elle and I were about to sit down on the bench to take in the view my leg was attacked by Colin, my nuisance dog.

"What in the hell?" I shouted.

We looked up to find Ben, River and all the kids a little way down the path.

"We thought you might like some company?" shouted River.

"Can you grab the dog, Amy? Sorry, he pulled really hard and the lead slipped out of my hand" called Ben.

For goodness sake.

The more I tried to run towards the dog and grab his lead, the more he ran ahead thinking it was a game. I tried calling him with my happy voice, my stern voice and my kind voice, but he was having none of it.

He was getting closer to the edge of the water and I started to panic.

Can this dog swim? Can all dogs swim?
Within seconds he had fallen into the water and was half swimming, half drowning in the water.

I could hear the children shouting for me to go into the water and get him out but I had spent enough time in that bloody lake to last me a lifetime.

"He's fine, dogs are natural swimmers," I called back.

This seemed to exacerbate their upset and I realised that I was going to have to suck it up and get into the water before the stupid dog killed himself.

I waded into the freezing cold and started striding towards the middle of the lake where he had inexplicably managed to get to in the few seconds of being in the water.

I swam further and further until I managed to grab his lead and pull him towards me. He clambered onto my shoulders, whimpering as I headed towards dry land, once more.

The smell hadn't improved over time, but I was happy to see the relieved faces of my family, waiting to greet me on the bank. They all rushed forward and swept Colin up into the huddle of bodies, to get him warm, while I struggled to grip onto the grass and pull myself out of the water.

"I think there's towels in the back of my car," suggested River, "Come on, guys, let's get him warmed up."

They all ran down the path, each of them crowding around the tiny, damp, dog in order to make sure he was ok. Only Elle remained, smiling, as she looked down at me, sprawled on the grass.

"I mean, are they fucking kidding me?" I gasped.

"It's ok; when I tell the story to other people I'll make sure you don't come across quite as pathetic as this."

She sat down on the grass beside me and helped me onto my elbows.

My breathing was starting to level out and I vowed to start to going to the gym on Monday.

"One of these days, Amy, you're going to make it through some special event as a respectable lady," said Elle, "and although today was not that day, it is the day for us to finally decide on a name for our business."

"Technically, I didn't go into the water until after the ceremony," I replied, "and we both know you were always going to wear me down with '*Badass Business Inc.*'."

"Really? That's great news, because I already ordered the headed paper and the business cards."

"Of course you did," I said, laughing.

"There's really only one thing left to decide then."

"What's that?" I asked.

"Well, as far as I'm concerned, we've conquered the business world, our personal lives are reasonably sane, we kicked cancer's butt, we took on depression and won and we have this whole parenting thing down.

"We're basically perfection personified at this stage. It's all very unsettling."

"So, what's your question?"

"My question, Amy Cole, is: now what?"

Four years earlier

Joseph

The café was quiet, it was always quiet. I didn't know what was wrong with people in this town. It felt like unless coffee came with some ridiculous name and price-tag then people weren't interested.

My wife had made this place beautiful and even that idiot, Michael, was a good cook.

I didn't know what I was doing wrong.

Maybe Isabella was right, perhaps it was time to give up on this stupid dream and go back to our roots in Colombia. She could see family and I could...I could be bored and wish I was back here.

I wasn't ready to accept defeat yet. I'm not an old man; I still had value, knowledge, drive. All I was missing was customers.

When we were trying to decide whether or not to leave Colombia, I left it up to God to give me sign and I promised to follow it, no matter what. It worked out well. We've had a happy life.

Perhaps I was stupid to leave the old café and start someplace new, but I really thought this would work. I wanted something better than the carwash, better than the greasy spoon that just got by. I wanted a place to be proud of.

"So here I am, God, asking you for help again, I need a sign.

"One last time, tell me if I'm doing the right thing by keeping this place open or if I should just cut my losses and retire like Isabella wants."

262

My prayer was interrupted with the bang of the door and a bedraggled woman tumbled through the entrance, dragging a small child behind her. I took her order, returned to my newspaper and decided to leave her to her thoughts.

The child had discovered the blocks and was playing but I was more interested in his mother. She looked troubled and as I watched her drink her coffee I could tell she was having some sort of argument with herself.

I turned back to my paper and told myself to mind my own business. As soon as I dismissed the idea of talking to her I wondered if this was the sign I had been waiting for.

"Surely, God, didn't work that quickly? But then again, what was there to lose? What harm could one conversation do?" I mumbled to myself.

I closed my paper and took a seat across from her, hoping that I didn't startle her or interrupt her thoughts.

"Hi," I said, "Do you like your coffee?"

"Erm, yes?"

"Are you not sure?"

"No, I mean yes I'm sure, I like it."

"Good, good. It's good coffee, nice food too if you're staying a while longer. My son-in-law will be in to start the lunch specials.

"You are welcome to stay as long as you like, I'd be glad of the company. Business is… slow."

She didn't answer and I was about to leave her to her drink when I decided to give it one last try and said:

"What is your name? I am Joseph; it is good to be meeting you."

She smiled at my introduction and replied: "My name is Amy and that small child who is trying to pull down your gnome display is my son, Arthur."

"Well then, Amy, tell me your story."

"My story?"

"Yes, your story. Everyone has a story and I would like to hear yours."

263

Amy Cole has it all figured out

Don't forget, you can claim a free book when you sign up to my newsletter. Full details on how to claim yours is below!

FREE DOWNLOAD

Get your free copy of
'Christmas and Other Things I Hate'
when you sign up to the author's
VIP mailing list.

★ ★ ★ ★ ★

amazon kindle   nook   kobo READ ON   iBooks

Get started here: www.mayhemandbeyond.com

Can't get enough of Amy and Elle? Why not join the Badass Bitches Reader Group on Facebook for life, laughter and chick-lit!

Other titles by Elizabeth McGivern, OUT NOW

Elizabeth McGivern

Acknowledgements

I first 'met' Amy and Elle while I was on a walk. I was watching them have a conversation – which would later be documented as their first in the café – and when I got home, I went straight to the computer and typed it out. Since then, I've watched hundreds of conversations between them. They're all in my head, of course, and I'm aware that I need to stop talking to my imaginary friends as much as I do, but these two needed their story to be told.

I will forever be grateful to those who took the both of them into their hearts and it made me incredibly happy to hear how they reminded you of yourself, or others in your life.

I'm not sure if I'm jealous that you have someone like Elle by your side, or if I should be concerned for your safety.

This series has been the most wonderful and frustrating experience of my life, but I will always be proud of putting pen to paper (so to speak) and telling this story.

I wish I could take all the credit but, as always, there has been a core group of people, who have helped keep me sane, as well as offering practical help and invaluable advice.

Lasairiona and Sarah, you both are the most supportive, badass bitches around and I am proud to have you as my friends.

Betty, you're the best editor and mother a girl could ask for. I would be lost without you.

Conor and the boys, together, you are indomitable and I'm very excited to find out what comes next.

Although this is the end of Amy's story I hope that anyone that reads these books can take away something positive from them. Whether it's realising that mental health is not a taboo subject and doesn't have to define the rest of your life, or that lube with eucalyptus should be used sparingly.

Whatever the lesson, thank you for reading and for being part of this journey.

Elizabeth McGivern

Elizabeth McGivern is a former journalist turned hostage-in-her-own-home surrounded by three men and a horrible dog named Dougal.

In an effort to keep her sanity she decided to write a parenting blog after the birth of her first son so she can pinpoint the exact moment she failed as a mother.

In an unexpected turn of events, the blog helped her to find a voice and connect with parents in similar situations; namely those who were struggling with mental health issues and parenting. It was because of this encouragement – and wanting to avoid her children as much as possible – her debut novel, *Amy Cole has lost her mind*, was born.

Elizabeth lives in Northern Ireland although wishes she could relocate to Iceland on a daily basis. To witness her regular failings as a parent you can find her on:

www.mayhemandbeyond.com
Facebook.com/elizabethmcgivernauthor
Instagram: @elizabethmcgivernauthor

THE END

Made in the USA
Monee, IL
17 February 2021